A Witch to Remember

Also available by Heather Blake:

Wishcraft Mysteries

Magic Potion Mysteries

A Witch to Remember

A WISHCRAFT MYSTERY

Heather Blake

CROOKED
LANE

NEW YORK

Published in the United States by Crooked Lane Books, an imprint of The Quick Brown Fox & Company LLC.

Crooked Lane Books and its logo are trademarks of The Quick Brown Fox & Company LLC.

Library of Congress Catalog-in-Publication data available upon request.

ISBN (mass market): 978-1-64385-350-5
ISBN (hardcover): 978-1-68331-978-8
ISBN (ePub): 978-1-68331-979-5
ISBN (ePDF): 978-1-68331-980-1

Cover illustration by Michelle Grant
Book design by Jennifer Canzone

Printed in the United States.

www.crookedlanebooks.com

Crooked Lane Books
34 West 27th St., 10th Floor
New York, NY 10001

Mass market Edition: September 2020
Hardcover Edition: April 2019

10 9 8 7 6 5 4 3 2 1

For my family, with
much love.

Chapter One

"This wedding might be the death of me, and I'm not even the one getting married. So much to get done, so little time."

Startled by the statement, I studied my sister Harper a little more closely. June sunshine highlighted the humor in her big golden-brown eyes. She was joking, which made sense since the wedding ceremony would be a small affair, fifteen to twenty people max. "We both know there's not much left to do at all, and please don't tease about the death thing."

I'd seen enough death in the past couple of years to last me a lifetime.

Maybe two lifetimes.

While some of the deaths had been natural, most of them had not.

As we wended our way along one of the paths that twisted through the vast village green on our way to Divinitea Cottage, a tearoom where my informal bridal luncheon was being held in fifteen short minutes, I didn't want to think about death. Any death . . . but especially Harper's. Not too long ago, she'd had a close call. It had been enough of a scare. I couldn't even bear the *thought* of life without her in it.

But as hard as I tried to dissuade morbid thoughts from encroaching on what was supposed to be a cheerful day, I couldn't keep from remembering all the murder cases I'd been involved in during the two years I've lived in this quaint village. The cases had scarred me. Some literally. All figuratively.

While the Enchanted Village, a touristy witch-themed neighborhood of Salem, Massachusetts, appeared at first glance to be postcard-perfect, it wasn't always. Every so often, evil visited these charming cobblestone streets. It walked past the boutiques with their colorful awnings, drank a glass of wine at the Cauldron, and watched kittens play in the window of the Furry Toadstool pet shop.

And sometimes . . . the evil came to stay, residing alongside the magic.

Both of which were well concealed.

Especially the magic. What most people didn't know was that witches inhabited this village, working and living alongside mortals who simply thought the Enchanted Village was a popular tourist area. Here, witches like my sister and me—Wishcrafters, who could grant wishes—could practice the Craft out in the open without fear of being caught.

Well, *I* could.

Harper was currently off witchcraft.

Abstaining. Again.

I was holding out hope that she'd change her mind about using her Craft abilities. Soon. Otherwise . . .

Drawing in a deep breath, I forced those particular worries from my thoughts and tried to think only of the afternoon ahead at Divinitea. Time that would be spent celebrating my upcoming wedding to Nick Sawyer, the village police chief. Waiting for Harper and me at the cottage were a few of my nearest and dearest, and

I was looking forward to enjoying an afternoon of love and friendship.

With a smirk, Harper said, "I think your sense of humor is lost somewhere under that hat, Darcy."

"This hat *proves* I have a sense of humor." Before we left my house, Harper had presented me with an ivory fascinator decorated with tall, glittery feathers, rhinestones, and a birdcage veil that was nothing short of overwhelming.

Glancing up at the hat perched on my head, she laughed. "It's a work of art."

"Oh, it's *something*, all right." I smiled at someone who openly stared at the ostentatious creation.

I hadn't been receiving too many curious glances, only because it was the third day of the Firelight Psychic Festival. Here on the green, I was literally surrounded by curiosities in the form of mediums, animal communicators, tarot readers, chakra specialists, crystal healers, palm readers, astrologers, and many more mystics. Despite most of the vendors looking like your average everyday joes and janes, there were some who took their appearance to the next level with turbans, caftans, top hats, and long coats. With the fascinator, I blended in.

Amid all the booths, tents, and demonstrations, the village buzzed with upbeat energy. Music thumped, the scent of fried dough permeated the humid air, and the thrum of voices chatting and laughing surrounded us.

"And there *is* plenty to do still—for the reception, especially." Harper wore an emerald-green maxi dress that flowed behind her as she strode along, her tiny, rounded belly leading the way. She was six months pregnant. She held up a hand and started ticking off a list. "Final fittings, final check-in with vendors, pick up your rings, follow up with the people who haven't RSVP'd, finalize the music playlist . . ." She lifted her other hand. "Package wedding favors . . ."

In two weeks, Nick's and my wedding would be held in our backyard, attended by only our closest friends and family. The reception, however, was going to be a big party right here on the village green that practically the whole village was invited to. I wasn't the least bit stressed about any of it.

I was concerned with other big life events that I didn't even want to *think* about.

I suddenly felt queasy as we walked along. Worry and anxiety weren't good companions to the thick fried-oil smell hanging in the air.

But there was time enough to stress about everything else later. Today was supposed to be a happy, joyous day.

Thankfully, Harper had everything with the wedding under tight control. I could only imagine how she was going to behave when she was an actual bride, but I'd find out soon enough. She and village lawyer Marcus Debrowski planned to marry at Christmastime. He was currently out of town, helping his mother settle into her new house in Florida, and I thought some of Harper's hyperfocus on my wedding had to do with his absence. Harper didn't think he was coming back until Tuesday—the day of her twenty-fifth birthday—but that was because she didn't know we were having a little surprise party for her Monday night, where a bonus surprise would be Marcus's early return.

I reached over and forced her closest hand down. "Everything with the wedding will be fine," I said.

"Take a deep breath before you deprive your poor baby of oxygen."

After a rocky start to the pregnancy, Harper and her baby were now as healthy as could be, thanks to a little magic and some modern-day medicine. I glanced at the amulet she wore on a long chain that bumped against the top of her belly as she walked—a protection amulet she hadn't taken off since the day she put it on back in February. It had done its job remarkably well, and I thanked my lucky stars for the magic in my— and her—life.

Tufts of her light-brown pixie-cut hair fluttered in the breeze as she said, "I know, it's just that I want everything to be perfect for you and Nick. You both deserve it."

I smiled at her. "It will be."

"But—"

"Hush. No more worrying today, okay? Today's about celebrating. There are people waiting for us at Divinitea, so let's get a move on."

I hadn't wanted a big, fussy bridal shower, much to Harper and my best friend Starla Sullivan's collective dismay. To appease them, I'd suggested a luncheon instead, and they'd jumped at the idea, even though I capped the guest list at seven. Including me.

Holding the festivities at Divinitea Cottage had been a favor to Dr. Dennis Goodwin. He wanted to ensure the tearoom, which was owned by his wife Amanda and her cousin Leyna Noble, was booked solid for its grand opening. I'd gladly agreed to Dennis's plan, since Harper and I literally owed him our lives—he was a Curecrafter, a healing witch—but he needn't have worried. Divinitea, which also specialized in tea-leaf reading, had been packed solid since its doors opened a few days ago.

"Look, it's Feifel Highbridge's tent," Harper said with an impish look in her eyes as she stepped off the path onto a thick carpet of freshly mowed grass. She patted her belly. "Should we see if he can guess what I'm having?"

Feifel "Feif" Highbridge was one of the top-billed psychics at the festival, and over the past couple of days I'd overheard people raving about his readings. But a psychic proclamation wasn't necessary when it came to the gender of Harper's baby. "We already know what you're having."

At Harper's last obstetrical appointment, a detailed ultrasound had revealed she was carrying a little boy.

A perfect little boy.

"I know, but let's ask Feif anyway." Harper grabbed hold of my arm to steer me toward a large ornate tent that looked like it belonged on the set of *Arabian Nights*. Domed, the tent was draped in yards of gossamer and satiny fabrics colored in deep reds, purples, and golds. "Let's see how good of a psychic he really is."

I dug in my heels. "Let's not. Don't you think it's rather rude of us to attempt to debunk *guests* of the village?"

"It's not personal, Darcy. It's *research*."

The arched entrance to Feif's tent had an OUT TO LUNCH sign clipped to it. "What a *shame*," I said with a shrug. "He's not here."

"Yes, I can feel your disappointment. But aren't you curious, Darcy? Can people really see the future, read people's minds, talk to the dead . . . ?" Harper gestured far and wide, sweeping all the tents and booths into her question.

"I'm not curious at all." I lifted the veil out of my eyes as a breeze kicked up.

"How can you *not* be curious?"

"It's simple," I said. "I believe in things I can't see. In things I don't quite understand. I believe in magic."

She put her hands on her hips. "That seems a little naïve to me."

"Does it? Do I need to remind you that we're"—I dropped my voice—"witches?"

Despite that particular—and undeniable—fact, Harper still didn't fully believe in the wonder of magic. The skeptic deep inside her longed for *scientific* proof that magic was real, and I had the uneasy feeling she'd never completely accept her abilities and her heritage until she found what she was looking for: one big *aha!* moment that would explain everything.

It simply was never going to happen.

Not with the Craft.

And not with these psychics, no matter how much she *researched* them.

Harper looked around and said, "What if some of these people are phonies?"

Whether Feif—or any of these mystics—had true psychic ability, I didn't know. As long as they weren't hurting anyone, I was of the thought to live and let live.

Do no harm. The tenet was the cornerstone of the Craft. Witches couldn't use the Craft to emotionally or physically hurt one another. Not without dire consequences, at least. It was my greatest wish that everyone would adopt the rule, whether they were a witch or not. But even though I could grant wishes for others, Wishcraft laws stated I could not grant my own. Otherwise the world would have been a much more peaceful place.

"What if they are phonies?" I asked. "Are you going to throw them out of the village?"

The corner of her mouth lifted in a half smile as she looked around. "I might."

I couldn't help laughing at the thought of her strong-arming anyone. At just five feet tall, she was more elf than henchwoman. Yet . . . "I don't doubt it, Harper. I don't doubt it. Now, come on. We're going to be late."

"All right, but don't you think there's enough time for a quick stop at one of these food stands?" She eyed the offerings—everything from fried Oreos to lobster rolls. "I do."

"You know Divinitea has food waiting for us—lots of it."

"But not corn dogs."

I could hardly argue. The menu offerings for today's tea included items such as salmon-and-herb sandwiches, shortbread, scones, custards, and quiches. No corn dogs.

"Do you want one?" she asked.

"No, definitely not."

"Your loss." Grinning, she veered off to stand in a long line.

Since I certainly wasn't going to deny a pregnant woman her craving, I found a shady spot next to a tree to wait.

From here, I could just see the top of Divinitea's quaint eyebrow dormers and thatched rooftop at the other end of the village square. That the tea cottage's opening had overlapped with the arrival of the Firelight festival wasn't a coincidence but had been planned carefully, as the festivalgoers were ideal long-term customers.

That Divinitea had managed to open this week at *all* was a bit of a miracle. There had been issues with obtaining the property, hoops to jump through regarding zoning, and construction troubles. The renovation issues hadn't had anything to do with the ability of the crew and everything to do with vandalism—thefts, graffiti, and property damage. It had stopped only when Amanda and Leyna commissioned a protection spell. Even though the culprit had never been caught, most every witch in the village had a suspicion of who had been behind the acts: Dorothy Hansel Dewitt.

Dorothy, newly separated from her husband, Sylar—and therefore newly jobless as well, since she'd worked for him—had fought bitterly to buy the property herself to open a gift shop to feature her handmade woodcrafts. As a Broomcrafter, a witch who could work magic with wood, she had an undeniable talent for creating masterpieces, ranging from wooden bowls to stunning besoms. She hadn't been pleased when the previous owner of the cottage rejected her offer to buy the place in favor of Amanda and Leyna's bid. Much to everyone's relief, Dorothy had not tried to set the place on fire. It was no secret that she was a firebug—especially when she was angry.

Dorothy was not a witch used to being denied something she wanted.

Something I knew quite well.

"*Psst!* You! Hey you! You there."

I glanced around and found an older woman eyeing me from a booth across the path. A large banner behind her had PSYCHIC written on it in silver curlicue letters.

I put my hands to my chest. "Me?"

The woman nodded and beckoned me closer.

"No thanks." I stayed put. "I'm not interested in a reading."

Not that I wasn't curious, but there were too many secrets tucked inside my head that I wanted to stay exactly where they were, thank you very much.

"Come here, child," she said in a stern voice.

Ordering someone around perhaps wasn't the best way to snag a customer, I reflected.

Yet . . . I oddly found myself crossing over to her, so maybe she knew precisely what she was doing. She still wasn't going to get a reading out of me, no matter what tone she used. I could, however, make idle conversation until Harper was ready to go. I didn't want to be rude.

The booth smelled of roses and was filled with displays of stones, glass balls, candles, and delicate crystal figurines of fairies, cats, and witches. Eyebrows raised, I approached with caution.

The woman thrust out a thin, arthritis-gnarled hand and said, "I'm Mathildie. You can call me Hildie. That's with an *ie*. Nice hat." There was a slight warble in her voice that came with age and a mischievous gleam in her eyes that I instantly suspected had been present her whole life long.

Hildie with an *ie* was a tiny woman with clear blue eyes flecked with gold that were sharp yet playful. Her ivory skin was deeply lined—almost cross-hatched in appearance. Black and white strands wove through glittery silver hair that was pulled back and clipped at the nape of her neck. She wore loose jeans rolled at the hem, a red tee, and black Converse sneakers. She had to be eighty if a day. I guessed closer to ninety.

I held out my hand to shake. "Thanks." I didn't bother explaining the hat. "I'm Darcy."

"I know who you are." Her warm, baby-soft palm met mine, and she quickly added her other hand to the mix, trapping my hand between both of hers.

"You do?" I tugged my hand, but she held firm.

"Darcy Ann Merriweather. Daughter of Deryn Devany Merriweather and Patrick Merriweather."

Shock rippled through me that this stranger knew of my family. After all, my mother had died when I was seven. My father had passed a couple of years ago. It wasn't as though she'd just met them as they wandered the village green. "How did you—"

"*Shhh*. I'm trying to concentrate."

"Hey, stop that!" Tingles spread from my hand up to my elbow. I tried to yank myself free, but for a petite woman, she was strong. "Let me go!"

Abruptly, she released my hand, and I stumbled backward.

"Just what I thought," she said with a firm nod and a sly smile.

"What do you think?" I watched those clear eyes carefully.

They gave away nothing.

Had she divined that I was a witch? Or picked up on any of the other secrets I was keeping? About the Renewal. About the . . . No. I wasn't going there. I'd promised myself I wouldn't even *think* about that particular secret for a few more days.

I wasn't sure what this woman knew. All *I* knew was that I didn't have any memory cleanse with me because I'd left my purse at home. I threw a glance at my house, on the other side of the green, and then at Harper, who was still in line at the corn dog stand. I was going to have to run home to get—

"Stay right there," Hildie said as she turned to rummage through a large apothecary chest that had to be a nightmare to haul from festival to festival.

I froze, wondering if Hildie could read minds as well.

What had I gotten myself into?

Setting a hand on my stomach to quell the queasiness, I took a deep breath. I could fix this. A little memory cleanse worked wonders.

Her wobbly voice carried as she said loudly, "A blind leap of faith brought you and Harper to this village. My question to you, Darcy, is this: do you have enough faith in yourself and your abilities to keep on leaping?"

Everything around me quieted while my head buzzed with the sound of the woman's voice and the knowledge that she knew *all* about my life. I had no doubt she was aware that I was a witch, and I instantly suspected she was too. It set me at ease. Somewhat. This was all so very strange.

Her question rang in my ears as I thought about everything I'd learned since arriving in this village, the people I'd met, the love I'd found for the enchanted world I lived in. The answer was easy. "Yes."

Hildie returned to me, a pensive look in her eyes. "In weakness, there is strength. Out of darkness, there comes light. From the ashes, there is rebirth."

Chill bumps raised on my arms. "I don't understand."

"Take this." She held out a closed fist, and the blue veins on the top of her hand fairly glowed through thin skin. "Keep it safe until you need it. You'll know when the time is right."

Warmth radiated into my hand as she dropped a shiny silvery-green seed, a little bigger than a watermelon seed, onto my palm. She then rested her hand on top of mine, and a sense of calm washed over me.

There was an air of benevolence about her as she steadied her gaze on mine and said solemnly, "You must trust your faith, because it will be tested. The first test is not telling *anyone* what I've given you until after you have used it. That includes your mother—or all will be undone. Understand?"

"But—" I had so many questions that I didn't know where to start. What was this seed? Who was this woman?

"Darcy?" Harper called out, interrupting my thoughts. "Are you ready?"

Keeping tight hold of the seed, I glanced over my shoulder. Harper had already eaten half the corn dog and was wiping her lips with a napkin.

"Just a second," I said, wanting to find out exactly how much Hildie knew. Did she know my mother *was* the Elder?

The Elder, the governess of the Craft, was a role that could be held only by a witch who had already passed away and become a familiar. My mother's reign had begun nearly twenty-five years ago, and her identity was top secret to all but a dozen or so witches. *I* hadn't even learned the truth until a year ago. The rest of the confidants were mostly family members, trusted friends, and the Coven of Seven, her council of advisers.

To my knowledge, Hildie was none of those. The truth of the Elder's identity was revealed only at her discretion. If other witches spoke of it without permission, there were steep consequences. If Hildie knew the Elder was my mother, Deryn, then she knew because my mother had told her.

I turned back to question Hildie further, but she was gone. The booth stood empty.

Of everything.

Only the banner remained, flapping gently in the salty sea breeze.

Absently I heard sirens in the distance as I looked all around, wondering if I was going crazy. But no . . . my palm was warm. I opened my hand and saw the seed sitting there, plain as day.

"Did"—I coughed—"did you see the woman I was talking to?"

Harper's eyebrows dipped. "I didn't see you talking to anyone."

How was that possible? Hildie had been *right here.* The apothecary chest, the bits and baubles . . . My heart pounded. What was going on?

Harper sniffed loudly and looked around. "Do you smell that?"

As soon as she said the words, I caught the scent of something burning and scanned the horizon. Black smoke spiraled above a building in the distance.

A building with a thatched roof and eyebrow dormers.

"Is that . . . ?" Harper asked, horror in her eyes.

It *was.*

Dealing with whatever it was that had just happened between Hildie and me was going to have to wait. I grabbed Harper's hand and started running.

Divinitea was on fire.

Chapter Two

By the time we reached the tea cottage on the other side of the green, the police were cordoning off the crowd with yellow tape as firefighters blasted the stone building with water from the hydrant on the corner. Acrid black and gray smoke darkened the skies and stung my nose and eyes.

"Darcy! Harper!" Mimi Sawyer yelled, waving her hands above her head. "Over here."

Nick's daughter Mimi was fourteen going on forty, and in two short weeks she'd officially be part of my family—which was only a technicality in my eyes. When I'd first become acquainted with Mimi, I'd thought of her as a little sister, but for a long while now I'd considered Mimi my daughter. I almost burst into tears when I saw she was safe. Thank goodness.

Harper threw elbows to clear a path as we wound our way through the crowd. She was small and mighty, but I thought it was the sight of her belly that had people giving her a wide berth.

Recently drenched, Mimi, Aunt Ve, Starla, and good friend Glinda Hansel Chadwick stood under a tall oak tree, watching the firefighters work. There were three trucks in front of the building, lights flashing. Two ambulances were nearby, and a half dozen police cars dotted the street from one end to the other. I didn't see any flames coming out of the cottage, so I hoped the worst of it was under control.

"Where's Cherise?" I asked, fighting a wave of panic when I realized she wasn't with the others. I glanced back at the smoldering Divinitea. Curecrafter Cherise Goodwin, Dennis's mother, was like an aunt to me.

Aunt Ve said, "Not to worry, Darcy dear. Cherise called earlier. She's delayed in traffic on her way back to the village from a shopping excursion in the city— she wasn't with us when the fire broke out."

I let out a relieved breath and nodded. Everyone who'd been invited to my bridal luncheon was safe and sound.

"What happened?" Harper asked. "How did the fire start?"

Clumps of the thatched roofing disappeared before our eyes, caving in under the weight and force of the water. It was surreal to watch what was happening to Divinitea while listening to peppy music and smelling fried dough. It was out of sync, this tragedy mixing with the jovial atmosphere of the festival.

"We're not sure." Ve wrung her hands. Inky mascara tracks streaked her plump cheeks and strands of her coppery hair were plastered to her forehead. She wore a soaked knee-length blue shift dress embellished with colorful beads that was probably beautiful when dry but was currently puckering and sagging in all the wrong places. "We were drinking tea and laughing it up, and the next thing we knew, the fire alarms were blaring and the sprinkler system went off, soaking us all."

I counted my lucky stars. I was so grateful they'd all made it out unharmed. Aunt Ve was my mother's older sister, and she had become like a second mother to me since I'd moved to the village. I couldn't imagine life without her in it. She'd taken me in without batting an eye, taught me of my heritage, showed me how to manage As You Wish—the personal concierge company I now owned—and loved me unconditionally.

"Did everyone else make it out okay?" I asked.

"Everyone's accounted for except Leyna." A fancy camera hung from a strap around Starla Sullivan's neck. Her golden hair lay flat to her scalp as her bright sky-blue eyes sized up the scene. Her cotton sundress was almost dry as she lifted the camera to snap a few shots.

"Unaccounted for?" I said. "You mean, she's still inside?" I threw a look at the building and swallowed back another wave of panic.

"No one knows for certain," Ve said, her worried gaze focused on the pluming smoke. "But we assume so."

"From what we know talking among ourselves—and what we've overheard here in the crowd—Leyna was last seen around twelve fortyish," Glinda said. Her crystal-clear ice-blue eyes were studying the surroundings as if she was mentally assessing whether this fire had been an accident. "She had been scheduled to meet with a client at twelve forty-five in the reading room and didn't show up. The alarms went off at twelve fifty or thereabouts."

Only Glinda could get absolutely drenched and still look flawless. Her white-blonde hair had been finger-combed off her face, and it didn't look as though any of her makeup had so much as smudged. I wanted to believe she'd used some sort of spell to look that good, but she was just naturally beautiful.

That Glinda was evaluating the scene wasn't surprising to me in the least. She'd once been a village police officer, but now she ran her own private investigation agency. Assessing situations was second nature for her.

But I suspected Glinda's interest in this fire wasn't solely because she was a highly trained investigator. As Dorothy Hansel Dewitt's daughter, Glinda had to know this fire didn't look good for her mother.

Black smoke billowed from the remains of Divinitea's roof, and unnatural-sounding pops crackled ominously from within the building. I spotted Amanda Goodwin, Cherise's daughter-in-law, speaking to one of the firefighters, and the naked worry on her face made my chest ache. It was her cousin, after all, who was missing.

Leyna Noble was an Emoticrafter, a witch who could feel what others were feeling, physically and mentally. A true empath. Unlike most Emoticrafters, who tended to be loners to protect themselves from emotional overload, Leyna had chosen to capitalize on her gift, using it in tandem with tasseomancy, tea-leaf reading, which allowed her to use her Craft in plain sight without suspicion. Paired together, her abilities were a force to reckon with, assuring accurate readings and client satisfaction. For the past ten years Leyna had traveled with the Firelight festival as one of their top mystics, before recently growing tired of the nomadic life.

Which was proving to be quite a fateful decision.

Mimi said, "I think I was one of the last people to see her. Right around twelve forty, I spotted her fast-walking through the dining room, heading for the hallway." Dark, damp ringlets framed Mimi's face.

"She didn't seem all that happy. Like she was forcing smiles for the customers."

I barely knew Leyna, but from what I did know of her, she wasn't the friendliest person around. Most Emoticrafters, because they could actually *feel* the emotions and ailments of others, were socially awkward, and Leyna was no different. It was why pairing with the outgoing Amanda, a Vitacrafter, who could easily judge people's moods—but not *feel* them—to open Divinitea had been an excellent idea. With Amanda's innate people skills and Leyna's fortune-telling abilities, the cottage was bound to be a huge success.

Until this.

I fought a sense of helplessness as I looked at the smoke, which seemed to be dying down. What had happened? Where was Leyna?

Ve said, "I'm surprised I didn't run into Leyna in the hallway. The time she went missing was right around the time I was in the restroom at the end of the hallway near her reading room and the office. But I didn't see her at all today."

I knew from a tour of Divinitea earlier in the week that Leyna's reading room was a small, private space at the end of a long hallway. Its location, far away from the dining area, enabled Leyna to focus solely on the energy of her client.

"Was the smoke coming from the kitchen?" Harper asked.

"Hard to tell where it originated," Glinda said.

"I smelled the smoke only a minute or two before the alarms and sprinklers went off. That's when we all made a run for it," Mimi said. "It was complete chaos for a few minutes."

By the sounds of it, Harper and I might have been inside Divinitea when all hell broke loose had it not been for her corn dog craving. I wasn't sure whether I was grateful or not that we'd missed out on all the action.

Starla's chin jutted toward the smoldering cottage. "I'm going to circle around, get some shots from different vantage points. I'll be right back."

As a professional photographer, she was always angling for great pictures—first for her village business, Hocus-Pocus photography; second as a freelancer for the *Toil and Trouble*, the local newspaper; and third, and most recently, as a travel blogger. She'd been roaming the world these last few months, taking a bit of a sabbatical from her work—and her life—in this village. She'd been a best friend since almost day one of my arrival in the village, and I'd missed her terribly these last few months. She'd come back for my wedding but would be leaving again in a few weeks for a trip to the Great Barrier Reef to scuba dive with manta rays. And I'd go back to missing her until she returned once again.

As I watched her take a few more photos, I'd have bet a frozen peppermint patty I would see some of these photographs in the newspaper tomorrow morning. Just as I'd have bet she'd tucked that fancy camera under her dress to keep it dry when the sprinklers went off, her priorities being what they were.

Mimi pointed at the police tape. "I'm going to get closer to Amanda, see if I can hear anything good."

Before I could protest, she darted forward into the crowd.

"She's a girl after my own heart," Harper said, quickly rushing after Mimi.

"Well. I suppose *someone* should keep an eye on them." Ve blinked innocently before she followed their lead.

I stayed put, wanting to talk with Glinda. "It could be nothing more than a grease fire that got out of hand," I said to her, letting the words dangle.

"Maybe, but I doubt it. And so do you," Glinda said. "We both know this has all the earmarks of Dorothy, doesn't it?"

Except when speaking directly to Dorothy, Glinda rarely referred to her as "Mom" or "Mother"—or any other kind of loving endearment.

Dorothy and endearments did not go hand in hand.

Especially not from Glinda, who'd grown up under Dorothy's narcissistic oppression. They were barely on speaking terms these days, after a huge fight following Glinda's wedding this past February. "It definitely has the earmarks," I said, wondering if the protection spell Amanda and Leyna had commissioned on the cottage expired recently. Otherwise, I couldn't see how Dorothy could have done this. The spell should have kept her at least ten feet from the property.

"Yet," Glinda said, "I can't help feeling that this fire seems kind of out of character for her. Dorothy usually isn't so obvious."

I didn't point out that there had been plenty of times when Dorothy had displayed her vicious side, loud and proud, from very public verbal fights to trying to push me off a ladder right here on the village green just a few months ago. And every witch in the village knew Dorothy had tried to torch my aunt Ve's house and also our family friend Godfrey Baleaux's house, even though those particular acts had occurred under the cover of darkness.

"It's reckless, even," Glinda said. "Everyone around here knows how she feels about Divinitea, Leyna, and Amanda."

"And fire," I added.

"And fire," she echoed, nodding. "She's going to be the prime suspect if this wasn't an accident."

"Do you know where Dorothy is this afternoon?" I asked. "Or *was*? Say, around the time the fire broke out?"

As concern clouded her eyes, Glinda shook her head. "I actually haven't seen her in a few days. Which is a relief, if I'm being honest. The last time I saw her was when I received a call from Sylar this past weekend to talk Dorothy down from a tree behind Third Eye."

"She climbed up a tree? Really?"

"It was a sight, let me tell you. She was perched up there like she wasn't planning to come down anytime soon. She's lucky she didn't fall and break her fool head."

Cheerful music floated through the air, and I really wished someone would shut it off for a while. The fried-oil smell had been overtaken by smokiness, and I wasn't sure which was worse. "Why was she up there in the first place? Had she been spying on Sylar?" I asked, glancing over at Third Eye. It was busy for a Saturday afternoon.

Sylar Dewitt was Dorothy's soon-to-be ex-husband. That marriage had lasted longer than anyone in the village betting pool had guessed—a little more than fifteen months. As a mortal, Sylar had no idea Dorothy was a witch, but I would hazard the guess that he was now very well aware that she was all kinds of crazy. He owned Third Eye Optical, where Dorothy had been employed right up until the divorce paperwork had been filed three months ago.

Glinda said, "Probably, but she claims she can't remember why she went up the tree."

"Was she feeding you a line, or could she really not remember?"

Glinda took a deep breath. "I don't know. Dorothy had drunk her lunch at the Sorcerer's Stove that day. She's been doing that a lot lately. Months. I can't tell you how many times the bartender at the Stove has called me or Vince to pick her up. Mostly Vince—he's more tolerant of Dorothy's behavior than I am."

Vince was Glinda's half brother, a Broomcrafter like his sister and mother, Dorothy. And he was a dabbler in the dark arts, much to most everyone's dismay. Though he was an all-around pain in the neck, I cared for him more than I should. He was the pesky brother I'd never had.

I asked, "Is Dorothy drinking because of the divorce?"

"I'm not sure. She seems . . . off. She's acting more bizarrely than usual."

That was saying something.

While I hadn't seen Dorothy in quite a while, which didn't have anything to do with happenstance and everything to do with me going to great lengths to avoid her, I'd heard of her unusual behavior of late. She's been moody, unpredictable, and extra volatile.

Dorothy and I were practically the personifications of good and evil. But I had to wonder if her recent behavior had anything to do with the upcoming Eldership renewal, the ceremony where the Elder's reign would be reinstated for another twenty-five years. Technically, it was called the Renewal or Renaissance ceremony, because either the Elder would be *renewed* or a new governess would be inaugurated—a *renaissance*.

There hadn't been a renaissance in decades—not since my mother took over as Elder. But Dorothy had been plotting for *years* for another. Specifically, she wanted to alter the rules of the Craft to have Glinda sworn in as the next Elder.

What Dorothy didn't know was that Glinda was not on her side—she was acting as a secret agent for the Craft, keeping an eye on Dorothy to make sure she played fair in the tug-of-war for the Eldership. Fortunately, Glinda believed the Eldership should remain with my family. Whether that happened or not was coming to a head soon. Really soon. Three days soon.

My stomach rolled again, and I forced away the upsetting thoughts about the Renewal and instead refocused on the fire, thinking again about the protection spell on the cottage. Was it possible Dorothy had found a way to bypass the spell?

Then I caught myself.

I wasn't on a case.

Publicly, I owned As You Wish, a personal concierge service that offered a vast array of services. I'd been hired in the past to dress as the tooth fairy, find a wombat for a little boy's party, clean out a hoarder's house, plan an octogenarian's birthday party, use my artistic abilities to paint murals, and manage a road and trail race. Sometimes I used my magic for those tasks—how often people said "I wish that" when they spoke to me was astounding—but most often it was old-fashioned hard work and creativity that saw the jobs through.

Privately, under the direction of the Elder, I worked as a Craft investigator. When there were crimes in the village that involved witches, it was my duty to investigate. Not only to make sure Crafting hadn't been used in the crime, but also to protect the Craft from outsiders. I often paired up with Nick on those cases, with him working the mortal side of the case and me working the magical. We made a great team, if I said so myself.

As of right now, this fire wasn't classified as anything other than an unfortunate accident.

Yet . . . I couldn't help feeling there was more to it than met the eye.

Especially since there was still no sign of Leyna Noble.

Why was it that everyone else had been able to make it out of the building—but she hadn't? Why hadn't she made it to her appointment at 12:45 when the alarms hadn't gone off until 12:50? What had happened during that time frame? Because right now it seemed like she'd walked down that hallway at 12:40 . . . and vanished into thin air.

I scanned the crowd, looking for Nick. The last I'd seen of him, he'd been in his woodshop in the garage behind our house, protective ear- and eyewear on as he worked on his latest project. A set of cornhole boards. Although it was his day off, as chief of police, he'd be notified of the fire. Which meant he'd be here soon. I sent him a quick text to let him know we were all okay. If our roles were reversed, I'd have been worried sick, and I wanted to spare him that anxiety.

"Has anyone called Dennis?" I asked.

"Ve did. He's on his way," Glinda said.

The breeze picked up, blowing the smoke away from us as I nodded. "Good."

Harper, Mimi, and Ve returned from their eaves-dropping foray, surrounded by an air of disappointment. "We couldn't hear a thing," Ve said. "Have mercy, putting out a fire is loud. Who knew?"

Harper nudged me with her elbow. "Look who's here and is also soaking wet."

I followed her glance. Feif Highbridge stood not too far away, drenched to the skin. His black dress shirt and black dress pants were dripping wet. Droplets fell off sleeves and hems soundlessly onto the grass. He was staring at the cottage, his thick dark eyebrows drawn low in concern.

"You'd think as a top psychic, he could have predicted this happening," Harper said, her eyebrow raised cynically.

"Are you talking about Feif?" Mimi asked as Starla also circled back to us.

"Harper's on a quest to prove he's a fraud," I said.

"I'm on a quest to prove he's *legit*," Harper corrected. "And if that proves he's a fraud, then so be it. How do you know Feif, Mimi?"

"Everyone knows Feif," she said, glancing his way as her cheeks reddened. "But he's not clairvoyant, so he couldn't have known about this fire happening. I'm sure he would have stopped it from happening if he could."

Mimi had been doing her homework on the man. It didn't surprise me. She was a lot like Harper—she loved to learn. And right now, she was learning all she could about psychic abilities. The fact that Feif was easy on the eyes was probably an added bonus in her book.

"*Hmph*," Harper said. "Unless he *set* it. I don't trust him."

I rolled my eyes.

"Well, *I* don't know Feif," Starla said, "but I wouldn't mind an introduction." She wiggled her eyebrows. "He's a looker, isn't he?"

No doubt about it, he was. It was interesting that his tent looked as if it were straight out of *Arabian Nights*, because so did he. With his swarthy complexion, brown eyes, black hair, and lean, lithe body, he'd have fit right in with a sword in hand and a harem swooning behind him.

"Does it not bother you that he could be a complete charlatan?" Harper asked Starla.

"No. I can overlook a lot for a pretty face."

Mimi smiled. "Me too."

"He's too old for you," Harper said to her.

Mimi said, "I know, but I'm not blind."

Since I knew they were mostly joking—I hoped—I wasn't too concerned about them volunteering to join his fictional harem.

Ve said, "He's certainly not too old for me . . . but does anyone know why Amanda threw him out of Divinitea earlier?"

"Amanda threw him out?" I asked, taking another look at him. "When?"

"Right after we arrived. About twelve thirty-five or so," Glinda said. "It was quite the scene as she escorted him to the front door and gave him a good push onto the sidewalk. I don't know why she did, though."

Everyone else shook their heads as well.

Interesting.

My gaze swiveled back to Amanda. She was standing next to the fire captain, her hands pressed together beneath her chin. The crowd around us had tripled in size, even though it looked like the fire was now under control. My jaw dropped when I spotted a couple in the crowd who, by the soaked look of them, had also been in the restaurant when the fire broke out.

The man glanced around, caught my eye, and then said something to his date. She nodded, and then they slipped away.

I glanced at Glinda and motioned her off to the side, away from eavesdroppers. "Vince was inside Divinitea when the fire broke out?"

"He was?" She glanced around. "I didn't see him in there, but my back was to the room."

"He and Stef Millet just left. Both were sopping wet."

I had bumped into Vince yesterday at the Witch's Brew, and he hadn't said anything about planning to be at Divinitea while my bridal luncheon was going on, even when I was talking about it. He'd also said nothing about dating Stef again. They'd had a brief romance a few months ago, and it had ended amicably. I liked Stef, a widow who worked as an event and catering planner at the Sorcerer's Stove, but he'd been seeing local real estate agent Noelle Quinlan exclusively. Or so I'd thought.

It made me suspect there was more going on with him than met the eye, too.

"Strange," Glinda said, her gaze searching the crowd, trying to pick him out, but he was long gone.

Had he been inside the cottage at Dorothy's bidding, to spy on Harper? I wouldn't have put it past her to use him to do her dirty work. He, after all, was her favorite child at the moment, seeing as how she was still mad about Glinda's marriage to a witch she didn't approve of, and her other daughter, Zoey, was in prison. Being Dorothy's favorite, however, wasn't saying much. I was convinced she lacked all maternal genes.

Harper had been under Dorothy's surveillance pretty much since we'd moved to the village. All because my little sister, as the youngest female witch in our family, was in line to become the next Elder. Dorothy wanted to stop that from happening so that Glinda, as the youngest witch in the Hansel family, could take over the role. Zoey, technically the youngest, had been excluded because she was mortal—she had been adopted at birth by Dorothy and her second husband.

I wanted to believe the Eldership wouldn't leave my family.

But it might.

The decision rested with Harper.

Not that she knew it.

I took a deep breath. Sometimes I hated the secrets that went hand in hand with the magic in this enchanted world in which I lived.

I also wanted to believe that Vince wouldn't stoop to Dorothy's level, but he was a wild card. There was no telling what side he was on in the battle for the Eldership. Or in life. Good or evil? Lately, I'd thought he was leaning toward the good side, but one never knew with him.

My palm suddenly heated up, and I loosened my grip on the seed I still held.

Faith, Hildie with an *ie* had said.

I had to have faith.

"Look," Glinda said, pointing toward the cottage. "Something's happening."

I glanced up to see paramedics rush toward the entrance of Divinitea. A moment later, a firefighter came through the doorway, carrying a limp body in his arms.

Leyna Noble.

Sooty grime covered her fair skin and darkened her long, blonde hair. She was as soaked as the others but didn't appear to be burned as she was laid on the ground.

A gasp went through the crowd as CPR was quickly started. A woman with red hair rushed forward, screaming and crying, trying to get through the barriers. Police officers held her back.

I didn't recognize the woman, but I surely recognized grief when I saw it.

Mimi came over and held my hand, and I gripped her palm tightly as we watched in utter horror as the paramedics used defibrillator paddles on Leyna. Her thin body pulsed with electricity, but no matter how many times she was jolted, she remained lifeless. After a long while, the paddles were put away, and gray ash settled on the white sheet that was placed over her body.

Leyna Noble was dead.

Chapter Three

Forty-five minutes later, the fire was out and Divinitea as a whole had been surprisingly spared from the worst of the flames, which had attacked only the attic and roof. Fire investigators were already inside the building, trying to determine how the fire had begun.

The roof had been utterly destroyed and the whole building was waterlogged and smoke-damaged. It was nothing a little magic couldn't fix fairly quickly, if Amanda wanted to reopen soon.

That was a big if. After all, it was Leyna and her abilities that had spurred the opening of the tearoom in the first place.

"Poor, poor Leyna," Ve said as she lifted her hair, twisted it, and secured it with a long, thin clip.

It was the fifth time she'd done so, by my count.

I didn't know if the repetition was from anxiety or because she was trying to look nice for the firefighters. If it was the latter, it was probably best she didn't know about the mascara tracks.

"Did you know Leyna well?" I asked.

"Mostly in passing. She's been gone from the village a long time."

"Other than Amanda, does she have family here?"

"Not much," Ve said. "Most of Leyna's immediate family has spread out over the years. I think only a couple of cousins remain here in the village. The Nobles are not a close family."

"No?"

"As you know, it's difficult for Emoticrafters to get close to anyone. Knowing and feeling what others are thinking and feeling is a heavy burden. That's true even with family."

I could only imagine.

Technicians from the medical examiner's office had arrived and disappeared behind a generic white tent that had been set up in front of the cottage to keep Leyna's sheet-covered body hidden from public view.

There was still a crowd gathered, but it had thinned considerably as people came, saw their gruesome fill, and then left again. News crews had arrived as well and milled about asking questions of onlookers, seeking salacious sound bites. I'd managed to stay out of their way as I sat on the grass under the tall oak tree, waiting for Nick to make his rounds and give me an update. He'd shown up not long after Leyna had been declared dead.

Dennis Goodwin had also appeared, quickly whisking Amanda off to his parents' house, which was sandwiched between my house and Aunt Ve's. A reluctant Harper had agreed to go home after the smoke smell started making her nauseous, but only after I pinkie-promised to call her straightaway if any new information surfaced. Info like why Leyna hadn't been able to escape the office where her body had been found behind the desk.

By all accounts, the door had been open, and there were two functioning windows in the room. It didn't make sense, and I hoped Nick would have some answers for us soon.

Mimi had voluntarily gone with Harper, and I instantly suspected that it was because she wanted to ensure Harper truly went home and didn't circle back here despite the queasiness to see what she could see, hear what she could hear.

Mimi knew Harper and her innate nosiness well.

At fourteen, Mimi had already adopted my mother-hen ways, and was remarkably adept at enforcing them. She was going to be an amazing big sister one day.

Glinda had gone off in search of Dorothy; Starla was at the Gingerbread Shack, the local bakery owned by her twin brother Evan; and Aunt Ve and I sat side by side in the shade of the tree's vast canopy, watching and waiting.

I'd taken off the fascinator and tucked the tiny green seed Hildie had given me into the band, adjusting the satin just so to make sure the seed wouldn't fall out. I set the hat carefully on the ground in front of me, keeping an eye on that small lump in the fabric. I needed to find a safer home for the seed sooner rather than later. But for now, its satin hiding spot would have to do.

Ve bumped me with her shoulder and motioned with her chin. "Look who's out and about."

I glanced upward and spotted a large red bird coasting through the air above Divinitea. Archie. The vibrant scarlet macaw familiar was the Elder's right-hand bird, and I had no doubt he was taking in every detail to report back to my mother.

My mother, the Elder.

That fact still amazed me when I stopped to think about it.

My mother and I had been in a horrific car accident when I was seven years old. It had been raining heavily, one of those pop-up early summer storms southern Ohio was known for. The roads were slick, and Mom had lost control of the car. She'd been pregnant with Harper at the time, and Harper, born after an emergency C-section, had survived the crash. I had, too. My mother had not.

For most of my life, I'd believed my mother dead and buried. But that was because, at the behest of my father, I'd lived a mortal life for twenty-nine years. Harper and I hadn't known we were witches until after he died, when Ve visited us in Ohio and told us of our true heritage. Shortly afterward, we'd moved here to the Enchanted Village.

That had been almost exactly two years ago.

But what really happened to my mother the day of the crash was that she'd become a familiar, her spirit taking on the form of a mourning dove. She'd returned to the Enchanted Village, where she immediately took over the role of the Elder, which until that time had been held by *her* mother. The Eldership had been in our family for generations, a maternal monarchy, passed down to the youngest female witch in the family upon her *death*, as the Elder was always a familiar.

While still living, on the day she turned twenty-five years old, the youngest woman in the family was asked to make a vow that upon her death she would accept the role of Elder and all that came with it. Until that momentous day came along, the heir had no idea what was going to be asked of her. It was a precaution in place to ensure that the decision of the heir apparent was made pure of heart.

For our family, the youngest witch was Harper. And her twenty-fifth birthday was in three days' time, on Tuesday. Which also happened to be the day of the actual renewal ceremony as well, since Harper's birthday fell on Midsummer's Eve this year, an unprecedented occurrence.

On sundown that night, Harper would be asked to take the Eldership's promissory vow.

Her decision would then determine what happened at the renewal ceremony.

Would there be a renewal? Or would there be a renaissance, with Glinda then becoming Elder?

I allowed myself to think about one other possibility of what could happen at that ceremony, then immediately shoved the thought out of my head. I couldn't go there. Wouldn't. My heart couldn't handle it right now.

Time would tell.

I had to be patient.

Secrets.

Though, if I had to take a guess on Harper's decision, I would predict that she would *not* take the oath. She didn't fully have the Craft in her heart and openly refused to practice it. If she denied the role, it would be the first time in Craft history a witch had done so.

Unprecedented.

The word echoed through my head. For a while, I'd been terrified my mother would simply disappear if she was ousted, but she'd finally assured me that my fears were unfounded. The worst that would happen to her was that she'd keep her familiar form but lose all powers associated with the Eldership, which were usually retained by Elder emeriti during *normal* renaissances.

Knowing Mom would still be able to live as a familiar should have been reassuring. But as the smell of smoke and burned wood permeated the air, I couldn't shake a sudden sense of foreboding.

From the ashes . . .

I shivered and chill bumps raised on my arms.

Ve patted my hand. "You're worrying again."

"I feel like . . ." I shook my head. I couldn't put into words what had come over me. The sense that something terrible was going to happen, and that this fire was just the beginning.

My stomach ached with dread as I watched Archie swoop low for a closer look at the charred building. "I'm actually surprised she's not here." I didn't need to specify who I meant. Ve knew. "With Dorothy's possible—probable—connection to this fire."

I'd already searched high and low for any sign of my mother's presence. Although as Elder she could take on any form, even her human one, she often traveled around the village as a mourning dove. It allowed her freedom to move about the community without anyone being the wiser to her true identity.

"As you know, she's in meetings all day with various Coven of Seven members," Ve said. "I doubt she could get away. There are important matters at hand."

The identities of the Coven members were as top secret as the Elder's, though I suspected I knew a few of them. Ve, for one. Godfrey Baleaux, another. I suspected Dorothy was also a Coven member, and I wondered how that was playing out with her plan to remove my mother as head of the Craft.

Not peacefully, I presumed.

Leaves rustled in the breeze as I shifted on the grass, crossing my legs at the ankles. I knew Ve couldn't tell me much about what was going on with the Coven. That said, I couldn't help testing the waters. "I imagine

Coven members are bracing for the worst, with the Renewal fast approaching."

Ve wouldn't look my way. "All avenues must be explored in case Harper rejects the Eldership."

As veiled as they were, her words gave me hope. "Then Dorothy's call to insert Glinda as the new Elder isn't set in stone?"

Ve unclipped her hair, retwisted it, and clipped it again. "Dorothy's claim that her family is the rightful heir to the Eldership has not been ignored."

I kept my voice low, always wary of eavesdroppers when we spoke of the Craft. "Has any proof been found to support her claims?"

Dorothy had always believed my family stole the Eldership from hers. It was the source of the deeply rooted contention between our families.

"I've said too much already." Ve pretended to zip her lips. "You've heard none of this from me, Darcy. Got it?"

"Got it," I answered reluctantly.

But still. Ve had given me hope, and some of my anxiety ebbed.

All avenues.

The Coven, at least some of the members, were looking for ways to thwart Dorothy's plan.

Did that include a way to keep my mother installed as Elder? I certainly hoped so. She was a kind, fair, and intelligent leader. She *deserved* to stay.

Ve sighed, long and hard. "I thought for sure Harper's child was a girl . . . a gift from the fates to stop Dorothy's plan in its tracks."

We'd all thought so, if truth be told. The news that Harper was carrying a boy had come as quite a shock to many.

If Harper's child had been a girl, *she* would have been the youngest witch in the family, even though she wasn't due to be born until after the Renewal. At the upcoming ceremony, the Eldership's reign would have been renewed for another twenty-five years. And when that unborn child turned twenty-five years old, she would be the one faced with taking the promissory vow.

But it was not meant to be.

And while I, too, had held such high hopes that Harper was carrying a little girl, my heart was already overfilled with love for her little boy. I could barely wait until he was born, to stare into his beautiful eyes and hold his tiny hand. He was going to bring nothing but joy to our family.

He already had.

Unfortunately, Dorothy had pretty much danced a jig around the village when she learned the results of Harper's ultrasound. The news that Harper was pregnant with a boy made the success of Dorothy's coup attempt more likely.

Oddly, however, in the month since Dorothy had learned the news, her bliss had all but vanished. I glanced at Ve. "Does it make sense to you that Dorothy's gone off the rails lately? Apparently, she's been drinking a lot."

Sunlight filtered through the branches and glinted off the golden flecks in Ve's blue eyes as she said, "Dorothy could be cracking under the pressure. Setting this fire isn't the sign of a sane mind."

Dorothy was already cracked, if you'd asked me. She'd left sane behind a long time ago. "She is so close to getting everything she ever wanted when it comes to the Craft. Why would she risk setting this fire? It doesn't make sense."

Ve shrugged. "Dorothy rarely makes sense. It's no secret how livid she's been with Amanda and Leyna. Nothing motivates Dorothy more than rage, and we all know she holds a grudge. If Dorothy set this fire, it's likely she believes she won't be caught. She's never been punished for setting fires before now. Why would she think that would change?"

For one thing, because before now no one had died in one of Dorothy's anger-fueled blazes.

Movement near the white tent caught my attention, and I sat straighter as I spotted Nick step outside with one of his detectives. They spoke for a moment, then broke apart, the detective heading toward his car and Nick toward us.

His dark, wavy hair was cut shorter than normal in what he called his "summer cut." The length accented his high cheekbones, long nose, and strong jaw, which was covered in stubble. He wasn't dressed in his usual uniform of khakis and a polo shirt, but rather black jeans and a t-shirt that showed off his muscular arms. His badge hung around his neck, and his gun was at his waist.

He walked with confidence as his gaze swept the area. He stopped to talk with one of the officers manning the police tape.

Ve said, "If I was but ten years younger, I'd try to steal him from you. Have mercy. Maybe five years, even."

I smiled and said, "I don't blame you one little bit."

The thing of it was, what made Nick most attractive to me wasn't even on the outside. It was his big heart and selfless nature, which sounds all kinds of hokey but was the honest truth. The outside was just icing on the cake.

Delicious icing.

"I still might try," Ve said, with a sly smile and a wink to let me know she was teasing.

"What would Andreus say about that?"

Ve and Andreus Woodshall, the director of the Roving Stones, a traveling rock-and-mineral show, had been dating for more than a year now. Both were notorious commitment-phobes, so that they'd lasted this long had amazed everyone. We all surmised that the reason behind their success was because they spent so much time apart. His schedule had him out of the village three-quarters of the year. For them, absence truly did make the heart grow fonder.

She laughed. "He's probably ready for a break from me anyway."

Andreus had arrived back in the village the day before. Nick and I had plans to have dinner with the two of them tonight. "Has he said so?"

"Well, no."

"Are you ready for a break from him?"

"No," she said. "Not yet."

"Are you blushing, Aunt Ve?"

"Oh, stop." She gave me a gentle shove. "Don't make more out of it than it is."

I started humming the wedding march.

Ve had been married four times, and I was starting to think Andreus might become husband number five if he wasn't careful.

"Stop that humming this instant," Ve insisted. "Here comes Nick."

All humor vanished as Nick approached. The grim look on his face had me immediately on edge. Frown lines creased his forehead, and his lips were pressed together tightly. His neck muscles were tight and his hands were clenched.

"What's happened?" Ve asked straightaway. "Was it arson?"

Nick sat next to me, and I caught the scent of sawdust—he probably hadn't had time to shower before rushing here from his workshop.

"Yes," he said. "The fire was started in the office closet and climbed a wall into the attic space, where it caught some of the thatching and took off, because there weren't sprinklers in those areas." He set his forearms on bent knees. "But it wasn't just arson."

"What was it?" I asked, a pit forming in my stomach.

His brown eyes, so dark they were almost black, locked on mine as he said, "It was murder."

Chapter Four

"This is a nightmare," Amanda Goodwin said, pacing the length of Terry and Cherise Goodwin's living room.

Murder.

Leyna Noble had been strangled.

Since Leyna was a witch, I, as the sole Craft investigator, was on the job. Nick, as chief of police, and I had a case to investigate, a crime to solve. Beyond that, I wanted to know who had committed this terrible crime. The Goodwins were practically family. I hated seeing Amanda suffering so.

"Amanda, please sit down." Curecrafter Dr. Dennis Goodwin, known fondly by Harper and me as Dr. Dreadful, gestured to the empty chair next to his.

He wore a black tee, black designer jeans, and shiny dress shoes. His dark hair had been cut recently, short on the sides, longer on top. He often came off as a complete jerk, but I knew there was a big heart under all the arrogance.

"Please," he added.

"I can't sit still." Amanda wore a long flowy skirt that brushed the tops of her sandaled feet and a boatneck T-shirt, both of which were covered in dark, ashy grime. Her blonde hair was pulled back in a low knot at the nape of her neck. Loose strands curled around her face. "My mind is going a million miles a minute, and if I don't move around, I'm afraid it's going to explode." She pointed a finger at her husband. "And don't you dare tell me that's physically impossible. This is not the time, Dennis."

He snapped his mouth shut, then said, "Dorothy needs to be locked up. She should have been locked up months ago, when the intimidation began." His hard gaze settled on Nick.

Nick didn't bat an eye at the veiled accusation. "You know as well as I do that there wasn't enough evidence to charge Dorothy."

There was never enough evidence. Dorothy possessed an astonishing ability to get away with her misdeeds. It might actually have been her greatest talent.

But was she truly guilty of today's crimes?

The fire, sure. I could see that easily.

But I struggled with the idea that she had planned to kill Leyna. Yes, Dorothy hated her, but premediated murder? It was a stretch. But then, I realized, it was possible she hadn't *planned* the death at all. If Leyna had walked in on Dorothy lighting up the place, I could imagine Dorothy going after her to keep her quiet.

If.

There were some aspects of investigation that we couldn't control, like autopsies. It would be days before Leyna's preliminary report came in. We wouldn't know until then whether she had been killed before or after the fire had been set.

The early hours and days of investigating often frustrated me. I wanted answers right away to all these questions.

But first things first.

The sooner Nick and I could figure out the motive behind Leyna's murder, the better.

Motive always led to the killer.

Cherise Goodwin bustled about the kitchen. "We don't know Dorothy was involved with what happened today."

After rekindling their romance, Cherise had moved in with her ex-husband Terry a few months ago, and the changes she'd made to the house were quite evident. The shades were open instead of drawn; dark upholstery had been replaced with pale greens and blues. The carpet had been torn up and hardwood floors had been put down. A wall between the kitchen and living room had been knocked out, opening up the space. Despite the beautiful changes that had taken place, I thought Cherise might need to use a little magic to remove the campfire smell once we left.

There was no way around it—we all stunk to high heaven of smoke.

Terry Goodwin wasn't home, which was strange, as he was a bit of a homebody due to his uncanny resemblance to Elvis—a well-aged Elvis, but him nonetheless. Unless Terry wore a disguise, he couldn't leave the house without being mobbed by people entranced with his looks. People who believed he could possibly be the real Elvis, and that all those conspiracy theories about him being alive were true.

"How *couldn't* she be involved?" Dennis said. "Fire is Dorothy's hallmark."

"But murder isn't." Cherise came into the living room carrying a tray of drinks. She set the tray on the coffee table, then tucked a strand of her silver-blonde bob behind her ear. "Poor, dear Leyna. What do we know for certain, Nick?"

I noticed that Archie wasn't around either. Not here in the house, or in his elaborate ornamental cage in the side yard. Although Craft familiars weren't beholden to any witch, they often had caretakers. Terry was Archie's guardian—they'd lived together for decades. No doubt my feathered friend was reporting the day's events to his boss, the Elder.

Nick said, "The fire started in the office closet. It appears there was an accelerant used—lamp oil."

Amanda stopped pacing. "There was a big container of lamp oil in the office. We were using it to fill the hand-blown glass oil candles on the dining tables." She pressed her fingers against her temples and moaned. "Dorothy used our own oil against us?"

Dennis immediately jumped up and guided Amanda to a chair. He said, "I wish you'd let me give you a calming spell."

"Not yet," she said. "I need to concentrate."

Dennis glanced over her head and pinned me with a stare. It was as if he'd known what she was going to say—which was why he'd made the wish in the first place.

I sighed and under my breath said, "Wish I might, wish I may, grant this wish without delay." I blinked my left eye twice. My spell was cast.

Whether the wish would be granted wasn't up to me. In the past, too many witches had abused our powers, so shortly after I'd moved to the village, an amendment had been added to Wishcraft laws that prohibited the immediate granting of a wish made by a Crafter—only mortal wishes, made pure of heart, were granted immediately. All Crafter wishes went straight to the Elder in some sort of supernatural communication system to be judged on their sincerity.

I suspected Dennis's wish, though manipulative, *was* pure of heart. He had his idiosyncrasies, namely his lack of any bedside manner, but deep down he had a kind soul. I'd been the recipient of his calming spells a few times, and I highly recommended them for those who were stressed out.

I wouldn't have minded one of them now, truthfully.

The couch dipped as Cherise sat down next to me. "Had anyone seen Dorothy lurking around Divinitea today?"

"I didn't see her." Amanda continued to rub her temples, and her voice shook with rage as she added, "She shouldn't have been able to get inside. Not with the spell we had on the cottage. Where's Andreus? He has some explaining to do. Isn't he friends with Dorothy?"

Ve and Andreus had taken Amanda and Dennis's seven-year-old daughter, Laurel Grace, out for ice cream to get her out of earshot of this conversation— and out of eyeshot of me.

Thanks to an old As You Wish assignment of mine, Laurel Grace believed I was the tooth fairy, and no one wanted to shatter that illusion anytime soon.

"Andreus is Glinda's godfather," I said with a wince, knowing the information wasn't going to go over well.

"Dear lord. Her *godfather*? No wonder that spell didn't work. Why did I trust him?" Amanda glanced at Dennis. "You know, I think I will take that calming spell."

Ah, so my mother had approved the wish.

Dennis gave me a grateful nod as he rubbed his hands together, then placed his fingers at his wife's temples. He mumbled a spell, then blinked his left eye twice. "Better?"

Amanda nodded. Her shoulders instantly relaxed, and she settled back in the chair. The intense strain in her features softened, but didn't vanish completely. A hint of anxiety remained in light-brown eyebrows pulled low and lips pressed together.

I said, "Even with Andreus's link to the Hansel family, I don't think he would set you up to fail." Andreus was a complicated man, but at his core, he was a dedicated Crafter. "If he purposely gave you a fake spell, he'd be putting his Crafting powers at risk of revocation. I don't think that's something he'd toy with."

Cherise said, "I agree. He doesn't play games when it comes to the Craft. I'd trust his protections with my life."

Amanda's cheeks reddened. "Leyna and I trusted him with ours, and look where that's gotten us."

Nick was watching all of us intently. "What kind of spell did Andreus give you for Divinitea, Amanda? Was it for fire specifically?"

"No, it was all-purpose protection against Dorothy, though fire was included in that. When Leyna and I went to Andreus for help when the vandalism didn't seem like it was going to stop, he told us that to fully protect the cottage from her, we needed a custom spell, using a strand of Dorothy's hair."

Hair was commonly used in spells, but getting it from Dorothy must have taken some doing. Just the idea of getting that close to her gave me the cold shivers.

"How did you get the hair?" Nick asked.

Amanda said, "Leyna bribed one of the stylists at the Magic Wand Salon to get us a few hairs when

Dorothy went in for her monthly appointment. She actually got us more than we needed—I kept the extras in case we needed more spells." She glanced at Dennis. "We should see about protecting our house. Who knows where Dorothy will stop?"

"She stops now," Dennis said, his tone firm. "She'll be in jail by nightfall, mark my words."

Nick said, "Let's not get ahead of ourselves. As Cherise mentioned before, we don't know Dorothy was involved. We need to keep open minds. Could Andreus's spell have expired?"

If Dorothy had set this fire and killed Leyna, she had to have known she'd be a suspect. I thought it would be only a matter of time before she presented us with a faux airtight alibi. Another unprovable misdeed. We needed to stay one step ahead of her, or at the very least, not so far behind her that she scurried out of our sights.

"It wasn't supposed to expire," Amanda said. "It was an infinity spell."

Nick took that in, then said, "Okay, any way it could have been nullified?"

I said, "There's the Recantation Spell." It could reverse a spell if cast within an hour of the original spell. "Did anyone know you were going to see Andreus?"

Amanda shook her head. "Just Leyna and me. It was the way Andreus wanted it. I didn't even tell Dennis until after the fact."

"Then it isn't likely the Recantation Spell was used." Cherise poured herself a glass of iced tea and squeezed a lemon over the glass. "The only other means to cancel a spell is if the person who cast the spell dies. But we know Andreus is very much alive."

Since I stubbornly refused to think that Andreus would enable Dorothy's evilness, I tried to think of any other way this tragedy could have happened. I threw out the only idea I could come up with. "It is possible Dorothy wasn't the one who lit the fire," I said, knowing it wasn't going to be a popular theory with Amanda and Dennis. "It would explain why the protection spell didn't work."

Dennis's jaw jutted. "Who else had motive? When Amanda and Leyna bought the cottage, Dorothy said they'd soon regret the decision, so it doesn't take much of a leap to conclude that *she* is the person behind what happened today."

"It is true that Dorothy has had it out for Leyna and Amanda since day one," Cherise said as she squeezed another lemon.

Amanda sighed heavily. "We can't let her get away with this."

"Open minds," I said, echoing Nick.

"Waste. Of. Time." Dennis shook his head. "Leyna deserves swift justice."

I'd last seen Leyna yesterday at the Witch's Brew, and honestly, I'd done my very best to avoid speaking with her even though she stood in front of me in line.

Dealing with an empath when you're keeping so many secrets is dangerous business.

But as hard as I'd tried to keep to myself—checking my phone, tying my shoes (twice)—she'd talked a mile a minute about the bridal luncheon and how pleased she and Amanda were to be part of it. I'd been taken aback by her friendliness, as she didn't usually say more than hello before retreating into a protective shell. I'd admired the amethyst hairpin that secured the messy bun on top of her head—a style she rarely varied—and she'd thanked me, telling me it had been a gift from a good friend.

Despite hogging the conversation, she'd seemed distracted while she talked, her blue-gray eyes darting here, there, and everywhere. Her head turned toward the door every time someone entered the café. I'd been grateful for her preoccupation as I mentally chanted my grocery list over and over, just in case she tapped into my psyche. I wasn't sure empaths could truly be blocked from reading others, but I did my best to try.

If she'd picked up on any of my concerns, secrets, or general anxiety, she hadn't let on, and when I spoke with my mother later about the meeting, Mom hadn't seemed too concerned about Leyna possibly knowing what was happening with the Eldership.

Hindsight being what it was, I regretted how I'd brushed her off. If I could have gone back, I'd have taken my time to talk with her. *Hear* her. Maybe try to figure out what *she* was thinking and feeling. It had seemed like she was waiting on someone. Who?

I glanced at the fascinator on the table. My gaze went straight to the lump in the band. "We need to figure out who else might have had motive," I said, wishing Glinda would call. She'd said she'd let me know as soon as she tracked down Dorothy. Nick had officers out looking for her as well. "Did Leyna have any enemies?"

Amanda closed her eyes. "She'd only just come back to the village. She hadn't had much time to make friends, let alone time to make enemies."

Leyna hadn't been in the village long because she'd been traveling with the Firelight festival for more than a decade. Which suddenly turned my thoughts to Feif

Highbridge and what Ve had said earlier about him. Leyna might not have new enemies, but did she have *old* ones? "How come you threw Feif Highbridge out of Divinitea this afternoon?"

Amanda's eyes flew open. "*Feif.* I'd all but forgotten about him because of the fire."

"Feif?" Nick asked.

"He's a psychic with the Firelight festival," I explained. "And he caused some sort of incident today at Divinitea."

"I never did like that guy," Dennis mumbled.

"What kind of incident?" Nick asked, scooting to the edge of the cushion.

Amanda said, "I escorted him off the premises."

"Why?" Nick asked.

"Leyna asked me to," she said, shrugging. "I don't know what prompted the dismissal. She didn't volunteer any information, and we were so busy that I didn't have time to press the matter."

"What was the relationship between the two of them?" I asked.

"I don't know. Leyna never liked to talk about anything personal. She tended to stick to topics like weather and current events. It was a bit of a surprise when Feif showed up today, insistent on speaking with her. It was the first time I'd seen her angry. She was fuming that he was there."

"Did she speak with him?" I asked.

"Yes. I heard a heated discussion and went to investigate. Leyna and Feif were arguing, something about a misunderstanding."

A *misunderstanding*. That could cover so many things that I didn't even know where to start guessing.

Amanda said, "Leyna asked me to see him out, so I did. He left without much protest."

"But he came back," I said.

She shook her head. "No, he didn't."

I nodded. "He had to have come back."

"Why do you think so, Darcy?" Nick asked.

"He was soaked. I saw him outside while we were all waiting on news about Leyna. He had to have been inside Divinitea when the sprinklers went off."

Amanda blanched, and Dennis reached over to take her hand. She said, "I had no idea. He must have come in the back door, through the kitchen."

Nick said, "I'll need the names of the kitchen staff. And also anyone else you can remember being inside Divinitea when the fire broke out."

Amanda nodded.

Nick looked my way. "How much longer is the festival in town?"

"Until Wednesday." I glanced at Amanda. "Where's Leyna been staying? I'd like to take a look around her place, if possible."

"She has an apartment here in town, above All That Glitters. I have a spare key. I'm ready to go if you are."

Nick said, "We need to let my team in there first. Then you two can go in. It'll be a few hours at least."

Amanda glanced down at herself. "That will give me time to go home, shower, and change."

We made plans to meet up later, and Nick and I were about to head out when my cell phone chimed. I glanced at the text message that had been sent and sighed.

"What is it?" Nick asked.

I stood up. "Glinda found Dorothy. We need to go."

"Where is she?" Dennis asked.

I grabbed my hat from the table. "She's passed out in the woods behind Third Eye."

Chapter Five

"Don't touch me," Dorothy said not five minutes later as she swayed hard to the right, away from Glinda.

At least that's what I thought Dorothy said. Her words had come out all slurred together, sounding more like "dounchme."

Dorothy was drunk.

Sunlight filtered through the forest canopy, dappling Glinda's skin as she dropped her hand from her mother's arm. "I looked everywhere for her, before I remembered Sylar's phone call last week about her being up in the tree behind Third Eye."

"Literally up in the tree?" Nick asked.

I was stunned by Dorothy's appearance. Since the last time I'd seen her, plump cheeks had hollowed, her curvy body had thinned, and skin that hadn't been touched by her routine Botox injections sagged. Shadows darkened her eyes, which were bloodshot and glassy.

Drinking had taken a harsh toll on her.

"Long story," Glinda said. "Anyway, I decided to check if she had returned to the scene of the crime, so to speak. I found her sleeping beneath this tree, snoring away. How many Bloody Marys did you have this morning, Mother?"

Dorothy's short white dress was covered in dirt and forest debris, as though she'd been rolling around on the ground. She reached up and picked a leaf out of her hair, frowned at it in confusion, and then let it drop. "One. Two?"

There were many leaves stuck in Dorothy's teased bottle-blonde hair, along with dirt, twigs, and a piece of moss. Usually styled in a bob, her hair currently stuck up every which way, revealing patches of a pale scalp. Her dark eyeliner had smudged, giving her raccoon-looking eyes, and her skin was a mottled red.

Glinda rolled her eyes. "More like four or five."

Birdsong rose around us as we stared at Dorothy in shocked silence, like we were viewing a carnival sideshow act that both horrified and intrigued us. From where I stood, I could just see the pitched roofline of Third Eye. Up in the branches of the trees around me, however, I'd have bet there was a great view into the shop through the high windows, not to mention Dorothy would have been able to see the back door clearly and monitor all comings and goings.

But why had she been spying? Had she truly thought she'd catch something she could use against Sylar? If he was seeing someone else, it was a moot point. He and Dorothy were legally separated.

Nick put his hands on his hips. "I can't interview her like this. She's clearly incapacitated."

Dennis said, "Or she's faking it. You should throw her into the drunk tank for the night. I bet she'll sober up real quick at that suggestion."

In this lighting, his deep-blue eyes looked almost black. He'd followed us here, saying he could provide medical help if need be.

I tried to imagine the very snobby Dorothy in a drunk tank and couldn't quite wrap my head around the hissy fit that would likely ensue.

"You should shut up," Dorothy said to Dennis, trying to point a finger his way but ended up pointing it at a walnut tree instead. Her stilettos were firmly planted in the loamy earth, and I suspected they were probably the only things keeping her upright.

Dennis said, "Oh, *that* she can say with barely any slurring at all. The speech impediment seems to come and go on its own, doesn't it? Quite a coincidence. Her alibi is going to be that she was asleep in the woods—with no one but the squirrels to corroborate. It's not like you to be so transparent, Dorothy."

She stuck her tongue out at him.

Glinda sighed.

This wasn't quite the signed, sealed, and delivered alibi I'd been expecting, as squirrel testimony was anything but airtight.

And while Dorothy was a good actress, I didn't think she was faking the drunk thing. There was that blank, glassy look in her eyes to consider, and she hadn't insulted me once. Ordinarily, she never missed an opportunity to torment me.

In fact, she didn't even seem to realize I was here.

I rather liked it that way.

Dorothy let out a loud yawn and almost fell backward. Glinda grabbed her mother's arm to prevent her from falling over. "She reeks of alcohol, Dennis, so I'm guessing she had more than just a couple of Bloody Marys this morning. Do you want to come closer to take a whiff?"

"I'm good," he said, taking a step backward.

Me, too. A big step. I said, "We need to retrace her day. She may be drunk as a skunk right now, but we don't know *when* she became this inebriated. It's been hours since the fire started. Plenty of time to down a few cocktails."

Or guzzle bourbon straight from the bottle.

"I agree about retracing her day, but first I need to get her home," Glinda said. "She's going to be of no use to anyone for a while, unless Dennis can sober her up with a spell."

Dennis rubbed his hands together. "I'm game. Let's do it."

At the mention of a spell, I looked around to make sure no mortals were nearby. We seemed to be alone in this little plot of woods, thank goodness, because I still didn't have any memory cleanse handy.

"No!" Dorothy wagged her finger again, this time in Dennis's general direction. "Don't touch me."

Even though some of those words were slurred, they were perfectly understandable.

Dennis folded his arms across his chest. "Well, if this doesn't prove she's faking all this . . . I'd be able to prove with one touch if she is really as drunk as she seems. Or we can wait for one of Nick's officers to arrive with a Breathalyzer. I refuse to let her walk away without knowing for certain she's not faking."

Her refusal did seem a bit . . . convenient. Why not let him work his magic?

"Dennis is right," I said. "Dorothy should be tested. One way or another. Her choice."

"Just let Dennis help, Mother," Glinda said.

Dorothy dug in her heels. "No."

"Why?" Dennis asked.

"Said so," she answered, drawing her shoulders back and lifting her chin stubbornly.

I saw Nick send off a text message. No doubt, a Breathalyzer was on its way.

"*Hmph*," Dennis said, looking smug. "Can't you arrest her right now, Nick, and interrogate her later?"

"Arrest! What for?" she asked, her voice high as she swayed again.

Dennis snorted. "As if you don't know."

Nick's tone conveyed that he'd rather have been just about anywhere else as he said, "There was a fire at Divinitea. Leyna Noble was murdered."

Clearly startled, Dorothy's face blanched. But then she started laughing.

"Mother," Glinda said sternly.

Dorothy kept on laughing and muttered something about karma. Abruptly, she quieted and put her hand on her stomach. "Sick." She lurched toward the walnut tree and started retching.

Talk about karma.

"This day just keeps getting better and better," Glinda said, her tone dark. "There are days I wish I'd been the one she gave up for adoption."

It was a wish I couldn't grant. I couldn't turn back the hands of time, no matter how often I longed to do so.

Glinda's older brother, Vince Paxton, had learned only last year that he was Dorothy's biological child. She'd given him up at birth to a mortal family. It had been quite the bombshell when we all learned the truth. Glinda's younger sister, Zoey Wilkins, a mortal, had been adopted at birth by Dorothy and her second husband, also a mortal, who had passed away years ago. Sadly, Zoey was currently in prison on kidnapping and attempted murder charges. She should have been in prison for murder, but her husband had confessed to crimes she had committed in desperation to save his life. She hadn't succeeded in the latter regard.

Dysfunctional didn't even come close to describing the Hansel family.

Concern was etched on Glinda's face, in downturned lips, eyebrows pulled low. "Can you help her with the nausea?" she asked Dennis.

"I can't." His voice held a note of true regret. "I'm prohibited from helping a witch who has refused treatment. She said no."

"She's clearly not of sound mind," Glinda protested.

"Take it up with the Elder," Dennis said, now sounding as though he was losing patience. "My hands are tied."

Little did Dennis know that by this time next week, *Glinda* might be the Elder. Have mercy, as my aunt Ve would say.

"Mom?" Glinda called out. "Are you okay?"

Dorothy kept retching.

Glinda winced.

My stomach started rolling with sympathy nausea as I asked, "What do we do now?"

"I can't arrest her like this," Nick explained. He didn't take his gaze off Dorothy. "She needs to be sober to understand her Miranda rights. The station doesn't have a drunk tank. I'd have to take her into protective custody and then drop her off at a treatment facility. I'm hesitant to do that without any solid evidence whatsoever that she was involved with what happened this afternoon."

"So what do we do?" I asked.

Nick dragged a hand down his face. "We wait for the Breathalyzer. If she's drunk, Glinda will take Dorothy home, sober her up, and will meet me at the station tomorrow morning at eight AM sharp. If Dorothy's faking, I'll take her there right now."

Dennis muttered under his breath, then said, "Dorothy could be halfway across the world by tomorrow morning."

Glinda nodded. "She'll be there. Even if I have to hog-tie her . . ."

"She won't run," I said.

Dennis frowned. "You can't know that."

I glanced at Glinda—she and I both knew Dorothy wouldn't leave this village. Not now, not with the Elder's renewal coming up. But we couldn't say anything about that in front of Dennis—he had no idea what was going on behind the scenes in our witchy little world.

Glinda said, "I'll stay by her side all night long. I won't let her go anywhere."

Dennis threw his hands in the air. "Am I the only one thinking rationally here? She killed Leyna. She shouldn't have the luxury of sleeping in her own bed tonight."

"Actually, your love for Leyna is clouding your rationality," Nick said, his eyes narrowed with intensity. "You're thinking like a *mortal*. You cannot dismiss the spell Andreus cast on the cottage simply because you want to. Dorothy couldn't have been the one to kill Leyna. I might only be a Halfcrafter, but even I know that."

Meaning, he'd once been mortal. A Halfcrafter was half mortal, half witch. When in a committed relationship, a witch had the option of revealing the truth of the

Craft to the loved one. Usually it was a romantic relationship, but in rare cases it applied to friendships as well. But there was a high price to pay to reveal the truth in that all the witch's powers were revoked. Nick's former wife, Melina, had been a Wishcrafter like me. She'd lost her abilities when she told him, but her powers lived on in Mimi. Because Nick had become part Crafter through marriage, he was able to make sure Mimi nurtured her gifts, and he could be fully involved in the magical world they lived in and privy to many of its secrets.

Glinda straightened. "I'd forgotten the cottage had a spell on it. Who cast it?"

I quickly filled her in on Amanda and Leyna's visit to Andreus.

She said, "And they used Dorothy's hair? Then there's no way she passed through those doorways. No wonder the vandalism stopped so abruptly."

That was true—it had.

"Which proves Dorothy was behind the vandalism," Dennis pointed out. "So arrest her for that."

It seemed he had a one-track mind when it came to Dorothy. He was getting on my nerves at this point, since I thought Nick had made it quite clear why he couldn't make an arrest right now—any arrest.

"There's no hard proof about the vandalism," Nick said, exhibiting more patience than I. "I'd never get a conviction. I can't tell the DA about a spell, now, can I?"

Dennis faced me. "Then what about punishment for abusing the Craft?"

I said, "She didn't use any Craft to commit the vandalism. There's nothing the Elder can do."

Anger infused his features, narrowing his eyes and coloring his cheeks a deep red. "Seems to me that

Dorothy's found the perfect loophole between the magical and mortal worlds, hasn't she?"

None of us had a response to that—because it was true. She'd danced in and out of that loophole for a long time now.

He went on. "I'm positive once Dorothy realized *why* she was blocked from the cottage, she found a way around Andreus's spell."

"Impossible," Glinda said. "*No one* gets around Andreus's protection spells. Don't you think Darcy's house would have gone up in flames by now otherwise?"

I frowned, not wanting to think about that.

With a stubborn set to his chin, he said, "If anyone could, it's Dorothy."

A chill went through me at his words, because I feared they were true. Dorothy was as smart as she was malicious.

Dorothy stumbled back to us while trying to open her clutch purse. She tripped on a root, sending the contents of the clutch flying. Nick grabbed Dorothy before she hit the ground and helped her stand up.

She sneered at him. "You should've married Glinda."

Once upon a time, Glinda's sights had been set on Nick. I tried not to think too hard about those days.

"Kill me now," Glinda muttered.

Dorothy went on. "I bet she'd have babies with *you*. Did you know she and Liam don't want babies? Ridiculous. If only Zoey had been a witch. We wouldn't be going through this. How are we to keep the Eld—"

"Enough, Dorothy," Nick said, his voice like steel.

I shouldn't have been surprised that Dorothy would bring up her family lineage at a time like this, but I was. Glinda and her husband, Liam, weren't planning on having children, a decision that had almost gotten Glinda disowned. If it hadn't been for Dorothy's grand plan to install Glinda as Elder, I had no doubt that Dorothy would have cut her off completely.

Dorothy kept talking as though she didn't have putrid-colored slime dripping down her chin. "I mean, I suppose they could adopt witchy bastards, or I suppose Vince could have ki—"

"Is that Sylar I see?" Glinda asked abruptly, squinting at something in the distance.

Dorothy silenced immediately and starting tugging on her dress and adjusting her cleavage for best viewing. "I need some lipstick. Hand me my lipstick! He can't see me like this. He'll gloat, the old pig."

I glanced around but didn't see him. Despite the name-calling, did she still care for him?

"Oh, my bad," Glinda said. "It was just a shadow."

Dorothy glared at her.

Glinda gave me a sly smile when I looked up at her. Apparently Glinda could push Dorothy's buttons just as well as Dorothy could push hers.

Crouching, I started picking up Dorothy's purse contents. Thin wallet, cell phone, lipstick, breath mints, and hairpin.

Hairpin.

I picked it up, studied it. It was made of beautiful amethysts in varying shades of purple. "Where did you get this?"

Dorothy blinked as though seeing me for the first time. Her eyes darkened with hatred and her lip curled into a snarl. "Bug off, Darcy Merriweather."

"*Mother,*" Glinda said with a sigh.

"She's a peach," Dennis said. "No wonder Sylar filed for divorce."

Dorothy lunged at him, but Glinda held her back.

I kept staring at the pin. "Where did you get it, Dorothy?" I asked again.

"What is it?" Nick asked me.

"A hairpin. It's identical to one Leyna owns. I saw it in her hair just yesterday."

Glinda stared at the hairpin. "I saw it in her hair, too. Earlier *today* at Divinitea. It was sticking out of Leyna's hair bun. I don't understand . . . how did it get in my mother's purse?"

In my head, I saw the image of Leyna being carried out of Divinitea. Her hair had been down, nearly dragging on the ground.

"Where did you get this hairpin, Dorothy?" Nick asked.

Dorothy shrugged. "Never saw it before," she said, the words jumbled together.

Dennis snorted and rolled his eyes. "I told you she did it. The proof is right there in your hand."

My stomach ached. How was this possible? Dorothy couldn't have possibly been inside Divinitea . . .

Nick's jaw jutted as he said, "Looks like Dorothy's coming with me right now."

"No way." Dorothy shook her head.

"This time you don't have a choice, Dorothy," Nick said. "I'm taking you into custody. Once you're sobered up, you're going to be arrested for the murder of Leyna Noble."

Chapter Six

Twenty minutes later, I'd dropped off the fascinator and the hidden seed at home, let Higgins, our Saint Bernard, outside for a few minutes, updated Harper and Mimi via text messages as to what was going on, and then went straight back out. I was exhausted all of a sudden and longed for a nap, but I had things to do that I couldn't put off. I headed out to do a little snooping. Dorothy might have been taken into custody, but I wasn't wholly convinced she was guilty. The thought that there might be a killer on the loose in the village was eating at me. I needed to find more proof. Somehow. Some way.

"Darcy!"

Dennis jogged toward me along the brick sidewalk. Behind him, I saw Amanda helping Laurel Grace into the back seat of their car parked at the curb. "We were just on our way home when I saw you."

I stepped up to meet him. "Is everything okay? Do you need something?"

He set his hand on the fence and looked me in the eye. "I wanted to apologize. For earlier. I acted like a jerk . . ." He looked away, then back at me. "I get caught up sometimes."

I knew. His nickname, Dr. Dreadful, was quite fitting. He had little tact and often spoke his mind. Even when he was upset and angry.

Especially when he was upset and angry.

"We all do," I said. "Don't worry about it."

"Will you do me a favor?"

He'd saved my life, and Harper's too. I'd known him and his family since the first week I'd moved to the village. Cherise was like another aunt and Terry like an uncle. They were family. "Name it."

There was an impassioned plea in his eyes as he said, "I know you're working the case for the Craft, but could you work it as a friend of mine as well? Leyna was family . . . I want the truth of what happened, wherever it leads."

"You don't think Dorothy is guilty after all?" This was a complete one-eighty if I ever saw one.

He dragged a hand down his face. "I don't know what to think. I'm *angry*. I know Dorothy made threats. But I also recognize that it's easy to blame the murder on her because of that anger. I need someone impartial to look at the facts. All the facts. The only person I trust to do that is you."

I had the feeling he didn't hand out his trust very often. I put my hand on his arm. "I'll do everything I can to figure out what happened. I promise."

"Thank you, Darcy."

With that, he turned and went back to his car.

I looked both ways, crossed the street, and stepped onto the village green.

While I wasn't convinced of Dorothy's guilt, I wasn't sure about her innocence, either. It was all so very murky. Nick hadn't had any other choice than to take Dorothy into custody. Between the threats she'd made and her possession of Leyna's hairpin, the circumstantial evidence was stacked against her. His reputation in law enforcement would have been shredded if he hadn't taken action. His hands were tied.

But the fact remained that there *had* been a spell on Divinitea that should have prevented Dorothy from entering the premises.

Should have . . .

But had it?

It was a subject to discuss with Andreus, and I was suddenly quite grateful Nick and I were having dinner with him tonight at Ve's.

The Firelight festival was still going strong on the village green, the fire at Divinitea not dampening the crowd size in the least. I looked for Hildie among the booths, but she was nowhere to be seen. There was a line of people queued up in front of Feif Highbridge's tent, waiting for a reading. I walked over, getting close enough to see him sitting inside at a round table draped in purple and red cloths, his hand on the wrist of a woman who kept nodding, her eyes wide as though she was in a trance.

I needed to find out about the *misunderstanding* between Feif and Leyna, and if they'd had another confrontation after he'd sneaked back into Divinitea.

One thing was for certain—if he was mourning Leyna, he wasn't showing it. He'd changed out of his wet clothes and looked perfectly calm and at peace.

I wasn't altogether sure how I was going to question him about Leyna, since he was a mortal, and I couldn't reveal that I worked for the Craft. If my life hadn't been so complicated at the moment, I'd have posed as a client and tried to ask him questions while he read me. But these weren't ordinary times, and I couldn't risk my secrets being exposed.

After a moment of watching him work, I decided that interviewing him was something to worry about later. Right now, I had another mission. I needed to find Vince Paxton. Why had he been at Divinitea this afternoon? Did it have to do with his mother?

As I turned toward Vince's apartment, on the second floor above his shop, Lotions and Potions, I saw the woman with red hair who'd been crying in front of Divinitea earlier. She was one of many people walking among the Firelight booths.

I hesitated for only a second before going after her. I wanted to know who she was and how she'd known Leyna. I would figure out *how* to get that information once I caught up to her.

I dodged and weaved through the crowd, finding it hard to walk quickly on the congested pathways. By the time I could make any forward progress, I'd lost sight of the woman.

I spent fifteen more minutes searching for her before giving up. My head pounded, and I really just wanted to go home. Instead, I turned toward Lotions and Potions, determined to speak with Vince.

The shop was packed with tourists happily picking through baskets of handmade soaps, lotions, and balms. Vince wasn't around. His shop manager told me he'd gone upstairs to his apartment not ten minutes before, but she'd balked when I asked if I could use the rear staircase to get up to his apartment.

Back outside, I cut through the alleyway that separated Lotions from Spellbound, Harper's bookstore, and took a hard right into the wide alley that ran behind the shops. The scent of the fire lingered in the air, blending with the pungency of a half dozen dumpsters parked along a tall wooden fence line. I tried to breathe through my mouth as I pressed the buzzer for Vince's apartment.

Stepping away from the brick facade, I glanced upward. There was no indication that he was home other than what his employee had said.

I buzzed twice more before deciding I was wasting my time. If he was home, it was clear he wasn't planning to answer.

Which made me wonder if his shop manager had been mistaken about him being upstairs . . .

Or if he was avoiding me.

My phone rang, and I pulled it from my pocket, hoping it would be Vince, calling me to come back.

No such luck.

Amanda Goodwin said, "I just had a call from Nick. He said that we could get into Leyna's apartment after five. Are you free then?"

Tracking Vince down was going to have to wait a little bit—meeting with Amanda took precedence.

"I'll be there," I said, glancing across the square to the line of shops that housed All That Glitters. I looked at the apartments above the jewelry store, and wondered which was Leyna's. I'd find out soon enough. "I'll meet you in front of the shops."

After hanging up, I turned toward the Sorcerer's Stove, known as the Stove to locals. Glinda had mentioned this morning that in the last few months she'd received many calls from the restaurant about Dorothy's drunkenness. I wanted to find out if Dorothy had been drinking there earlier today.

I waved to Angela Curtis, who was manning the register inside Spellbound as I passed by. As manager of the bookshop, Angela had been a godsend these last few months, going above and beyond to help Harper keep the store afloat in the weeks after Harper had been diagnosed with a chronic illness. Angela and her partner, Harmony, who owned the Pixie Cottage, felt like family.

The Stove was half a block away, give or take, from Divinitea, which still had fire personnel and equipment parked in front of it. The white tent was gone. Leyna's body was now on its way to the medical examiner's office in Boston, where an autopsy would take place. Yellow police tape remained behind, waving in the breeze.

I slowed in front of the Bewitching Boutique with the thought to stop inside for a quick conversation with Godfrey Baleaux, a Cloakcrafter and family friend, or Pepe and Mrs. P, mouse familiars who lived in the walls of the shop. The store was dark, however, with a CLOSED sign hung on the door.

Odd.

Godfrey rarely closed the shop during business hours. Even though he didn't have any employees other than Pepe, who worked clandestinely in the back room, he'd managed to keep the store open seven hours a day, six days a week for as long as I'd been in the village.

I glanced around. A long line of cars and tour buses were slowly making their way along the main road entering the village. Every parking spot around the green was taken, and the lot at the end of the square looked full as well.

I'd seen Godfrey just this morning while I was out for my morning run, and he'd been in good spirits, smiling and joking about my running attire. He despised workout clothes. Unless he'd suddenly become ill, it didn't make sense that the boutique would be closed.

Then Ve's words from earlier came back to me.

She's in meetings all day with some of the Coven of Seven members.

I'd long suspected Godfrey was one of the Coven members. As such, his duties would certainly outweigh keeping his boutique open on a busy shopping day.

And if there was any witch who'd go above and beyond to find a way to keep Dorothy from becoming a de facto Elder, it was him. It buoyed my spirit, knowing he'd have my family's best interests at heart.

I pressed on, passing the Trimmed Wick, a candle shop. I skirted the line of people that trickled out of the Gingerbread Shack's door. Evan Sullivan used his Bakecrafting skills to create the most delectable mini desserts. The wait had to be at least thirty minutes, but I knew from experience that it would be worth it.

I didn't see Evan at the counter but could easily picture him working his magic in the kitchen at the back of the shop. As much as I wanted to go inside to watch him work—and breathe in the soothing scents of vanilla and chocolate and hazelnut—I kept walking. I needed to nail down Dorothy's timeline for the day.

The Stove, with its steep rooflines, faux thatched roof, stone exterior, and center chimney, looked to me like a cottage straight out of merry old England. I shimmied past those waiting in the vestibule and blinked, trying to adjust to the restaurant's dark interior. Sunspots lingered in my eyes as I sidled up to the bar top and waited for one of the barkeeps, Ula Blackstone, to glance my way.

It didn't take long.

Piped classical music played softly, barely audible over the din of the diners, as Ula wiped her hands on an apron. Her short black hair was tied back in a stubby ponytail, showing off six piercings in each ear. "Darcy, hi. Your usual?" she asked loudly.

My *usual* was a banana milk shake that wasn't even on the drink menu. Ula had created the concoction for me after learning how much I loved bananas but didn't keep them at home, because Mimi was allergic. I drank a shake almost every time I came in for lunch, but this afternoon I didn't have time to indulge. I raised my voice to be heard above the din and said, "Hi, Ula. Just a club soda with lime today, please."

I'd known Ula, a Manicrafter—a witch good with her hands—since I'd moved to the village. She'd worked here on and off for two years while pursuing a master's degree from Boston University. Through bartending, she made enough in tips to put herself through school without loans. An amazing feat these days.

When she came back with the drink, I handed her a five-dollar bill and said, "Was Dorothy Hansel Dewitt in here earlier?"

"It wouldn't surprise me. Seems like Dorothy's always in here." She dropped her voice a bit. "She's taking the divorce hard, which is strange, since it's no secret that she wasn't happily married."

It was no secret because the village, as a whole, had loose lips. Everyone—except, perhaps, Sylar—knew divorce papers had been stashed away in Dorothy's lingerie drawer for nearly a year. What no one knew, however, was why she'd never actually given them to Sylar. Or why three months ago, Sylar had suddenly decided he'd had enough of his marriage and had his own papers filed.

I couldn't help but wonder what had been his tipping point. Or why it had taken him so long. I wouldn't have lasted a day married to that woman.

I suspected Dorothy's behavior of late—the drinking, mostly—was because Sylar had struck first. Dorothy hated looking like a fool, and it was obvious she'd been blindsided by his leaving her. And since she always wanted things she couldn't have, it was entirely possible that she now wanted him back.

While I could have sat and gossiped about Dorothy's marriage all afternoon, I tried to stay on point. "You didn't see her?"

Ula held up a wait-a-second finger while she tended to a new customer. She returned quickly and shook her head. "Dorothy wasn't here when I came in at one. I haven't seen her since last night, when she was eating dinner with Vince. And let me tell you, for a broad who's in here drinking every day, she really can't hold her liquor all that well. Two martinis and she was three sheets, if you know what I mean."

Maybe Dorothy had been telling the truth about having only one or two drinks this morning . . . had she also been telling the truth about never before seeing the hairpin? "Do you know if there's anyone around who would know for certain if she was in here this morning or early afternoon?"

"Most of the early-shifters have already left for the day." Ula glanced around, her dark eyes searching the recesses of the dining room. "Let me ask around. Give me a few minutes."

I drank my club soda and waited, trying not to wince at the growing noise levels. The late-lunch crowd was loud and my head ached.

My gaze eventually made its way to one of the private rooms behind me, where I'd once taken a cooking class taught by Zoey Wilkins, Glinda's younger sister. It had been an ill-fated class, though some benefit had come from it. It was where Harper and I had gotten to know Angela Curtis and Harmony Atchison, and also where Harper had started falling for Marcus.

As I thought about Zoey, I wondered if she was the reason Dorothy preferred to drink here, at the Stove, rather than at the Cauldron, the local pub down the street. Did she feel closer to her youngest child here? Connected, somehow, because this had been a place Zoey loved? She'd been an executive chef here when I knew her.

The more I thought about it, the more I doubted the theory. As far as I knew, Dorothy had been just as horrible a mother to Zoey as she had been to Glinda. Worse, even. A true narcissist, Dorothy had little maternal instinct, if any, and despised most mortals, despite having married two of them. She hadn't told either of the Craft, however, so she still had her full Craft powers.

I often thought she had married mortal men to feel superior, secretly knowing she had abilities they could only dream of. Why they had married *her* was beyond me.

It had been Dorothy's second husband who'd wanted to adopt, and poor mortal Zoey had probably never stood a chance at holding her mother's affections. As far as I knew, Dorothy had never even visited Zoey in prison. She'd cut her off completely after the arrest.

But they'd never had much of a relationship to begin with. Zoey despised Dorothy. An old friend of Zoey's had once told me that Zoey never felt like she belonged within her family, but I wondered if she'd simply never been welcomed by anyone but her father. And after he'd died . . .

I couldn't imagine what it had been like to grow up with Dorothy as a mother. It had been difficult enough for Glinda, who was a full Crafter. But Zoey? As a mortal? I could understand why she had never felt at peace within the family.

"Darcy?"

I turned back to the bar, nearly spilling my drink. "Sorry. I was lost in old thoughts about Zoey Wilkins."

Ula whistled low. "That was a bad time, wasn't it?"

"Horrible."

"You know, for a while I was wondering if that was why Dorothy spends so much time here."

"I'd been thinking the same thing."

Ula wiped the counter with a rag. "I actually brought it up to her once."

"You did? What did she say?"

"It was strange. It was like she was repulsed at hearing Zoey's name. Told me to never mention her again. She's a piece of work. Dorothy. Not Zoey. Zoey was just . . . misguided. Dorothy then snottily informed me that she drinks here because we're open all day and the Cauldron doesn't open until five. After that she ordered another Bloody Mary and told me to mind my own business or she'd take her money elsewhere. I try to avoid her as much as possible, if I'm being honest."

"I don't blame you. I do the same thing." And I wished I could have said I was surprised at Dorothy's reaction to hearing Zoey's name, but I wasn't.

"Anyway, Joelle, the hostess, said that Dorothy got here at a little after ten this morning and became sloppy drunk by noon. Stef called Vince to come pick up his mother, but Dorothy left before he arrived."

Hmm. Vince had been inside Divinitea at 12:50 with *Stef* when the sprinklers went off. How had they ended up together? And where had Dorothy been during that time? "Is Stef here now?"

Ula knew I was an investigator for the Craft, so had probably deduced why I was asking all these questions.

"Nope."

Was she still with Vince? Was that why he wasn't answering his door?

Ula leaned in, setting her elbows on the bar top. Her voice was barely a whisper as she said, "Are you looking for Dorothy because of the fire at Divinitea? Because every witch in this village knows Dorothy wanted to burn that place to the ground. We're just surprised it took her so long. And poor Leyna Noble . . ." Moisture made her eyes shiny. "I'm feeling a little guilty about that."

"About Leyna's death? Why?"

Slinging the dishcloth over her shoulder, Ula crossed her arms and hesitated only a second before saying, "Because I thought she was just blowing off steam."

"Leyna?"

"No, Dorothy."

"I'm confused," I said, trying to make sense of what she was telling me.

"Dorothy was tipsy, and I thought she was only blowing off steam, so I didn't report it when . . ."

"When what?"

Pain flashed in Ula's eyes, and with a deep sigh, she said, "Two days ago, Dorothy sat right here at this bar . . . and threatened to kill Leyna with her bare hands."

Chapter Seven

I was watching kittens play in the big bay window of the Furry Toadstool when I saw Amanda approaching in the glass's reflection.

"How're you holding up?" I asked after giving her a quick hug.

She drew in a deep breath. "I'm . . . I don't even know. I think I'm running on pure adrenaline."

It sounded to me like she was in a state of shock, and I hoped that Dennis and his miracle calming cures would be nearby when the shock wore off and Amanda came crashing down. "If there's anything I can do, please let me know."

"You're already doing it, Darcy. Knowing you're looking into the matter helps set me at ease. I know you won't let up until you find the truth of what happened to Leyna."

A lilac scent wafted off her—some sort of lotion or perfume—but it couldn't quite cover the hint of smoke that clung stubbornly to her skin. Her damp hair was twisted into a braid, and her long dress swirled around her ankles as she walked over to a nondescript door located between the pet shop and the jewelry store.

"I'll help any way I can. Are you ready to go up?" I asked.

With a deep inhale, she nodded.

The raised wooden sidewalk that ran along this bank of shops creaked underfoot as I walked toward the door, feeling a flash of regret at leaving the kittens behind. There had been something so calming about watching them tumble and play.

We zigzagged up multiple sets of stairs until we reached the top floor that housed two apartments. Leyna's was the rear unit that faced the woods behind the building. Amanda unlocked the door and slowly pushed it open, allowing me to go inside first.

Vanilla scented the air as I took in the tiny living room and an even tinier kitchen. Off the living space, there was a small bathroom and a bedroom that fit a queen-size bed but left no room for a nightstand.

"How long has she lived here?" I asked.

Amanda closed the front door. "Four months, give or take a week or so. I know it looks like she hasn't moved in, but she was a minimalist. She didn't believe in clutter."

Clutter . . . furniture. Tomatoes, *tomahtoes*.

There was only a sofa and a hanging TV in the living room. I spotted the TV's remote control tucked into one of the couch cushions. There was no cable box, no DVD player. There were no books, no houseplants, and no tables.

Two stools sat next to the kitchen's peninsula. The countertops were bare. On the stove was a small pot full of dark liquid and vanilla bean pods. Homemade potpourri.

I opened a cupboard door and found a stockpile of metal tea canisters, a silver infuser, two mugs, and an electric teapot.

"Did she love tea?" I asked. "Or is all this simply to practice reading tea leaves?"

"She did love tea, as do I. That shared passion is why we decided to open Divinitea. It had been a dream of ours since we were little girls having tea parties with pink plastic teacups. Leyna knew how to read tea leaves even back then—she taught me how to do it."

I turned to her. "You know how? Really?"

"I'm not nearly as good as she was, but I can hold my own."

"So you could reopen Divinitea one day if you wanted."

"I could, but I don't think I will. It wouldn't be the same without Leyna, plus I'll always be worried about Dorothy coming after me."

"There's time to decide the shop's fate, so please don't make any decisions yet. And as for Dorothy . . . I'm not convinced she did this."

This being the murder.

"I'm trying to keep an open mind," she said somberly, "but it's easier said than done."

I opened a few more cabinets and found only the barest essentials. The immaculate bathroom had a utilitarian white shower curtain, white towels, and a white ceramic toothbrush holder and soap dish.

Leyna's bedroom was painted a light beige, and unsurprisingly she had a white comforter. The only thing keeping it from feeling like an institution was a set of crystals hanging in the window. Afternoon light sent rainbows arcing across the room. I opened the closet door and saw that her clothes were hung by coordinating colors. There was a single photo taped to the inside of the closet door of her and Amanda in front of Divinitea, hammers in hand, that I assumed had been taken when they started renovations. In my quick search of the apartment, I found no other photos.

"Leyna never spoke of close friends? Associates with the festival? Dating?"

"No. As I said before, Leyna keeps—kept—to herself. She wasn't a sharer." Amanda gave me a sad smile. "I'm the opposite. Get me talking, and I'll chat your ear off. I *like* clutter. I could never live . . . like this. It would make me insane. But differences are what make the world go round, right? Leyna was brilliant. And generous. She didn't have to share her gift with the world, but she did. She liked helping people—it made her happy. It helped them heal, mentally and physically, and now she's gone. It's not fair." Amanda's eyes misted.

"No, it's not," I agreed.

I poked around a few minutes more but found nothing that helped explain who might have killed Leyna.

This visit had showed me only one thing.

Leyna's gift of helping others might have brought her happiness, but it had also forced her to live a very lonely life.

Which made me wonder if it was a gift at all . . . or more of a curse.

* * *

"It's *impossible*," Andreus Woodshall said emphatically as he shook a bottle of soy sauce over his plate, his black eyes glinting in the abundant light of Ve's kitchen.

In his early fifties, Andreus had the unusual ability to change his appearance in relation to his surrounding illumination. In regular lighting, he was old-school movie star handsome. Debonair, even, with his slicked-back black hair, high cheekbones, and aristocratic nose. Cary Grant meets Clark Gable. In darkness and shadows, however, he morphed into a monster from a terrifying horror film. Dracula meets the Crypt-Keeper. Crepey skin, hollowed cheeks, evil eyes, sinister scowl. He had earned himself the nickname Mr. Macabre long before I arrived in the village.

Andreus's personality often shifted with his exterior change as well, matching his appearance. Benevolent versus malevolent. He'd threatened me more than once, but he'd protected me from harm even more. He was an odd, complex man.

When I'd arrived tonight, I'd turned on every light of the first floor of Ve's house.

A witch couldn't be too safe.

Andreus used chopsticks to push lo mein noodles around his plate. "Dorothy could not have been the one inside Divinitea today. She did not set that fire. She did not kill Leyna Noble. She might have wanted to, yes, but she did not. *Could* not."

"There's *no* way around the spell you cast other than what we've already ruled out?" I asked.

"No."

It was just after seven. I had hoped to enjoy dinner, then ease into the whole Dorothy situation. But easing was not meant to be. As soon as we sat down and loaded our plates, Andreus jumped into the investigation with both feet.

I hadn't said one word about the doubts surrounding the efficiency of his spell to either of them, so I assumed one of the Goodwins had filled them in. My guess was Cherise—she and Ve were best friends.

I tapped my plate with my fork—I'd yet to master the art of chopsticks—while trying to work through my thoughts. I wished Nick had been here to give his insight as well. But he was still at work, piecing together with his colleagues what had happened today between the fire and murder and how Dorothy fit into that puzzle.

Ve said, "There has to be a way Dorothy slipped inside. She threatened to kill Leyna, she loves fire, and she had Leyna's hairpin." She topped off her glass of wine. "Darcy, did Ula have anything else to add about the threat Dorothy made on Leyna's life?"

"Nothing that makes much sense," I said, waving off the bottle Ve held out. "That's one of the reasons why Ula didn't take the threat seriously. She said Dorothy came in Thursday afternoon, huffing and puffing, all worked up about something, mumbling and cursing under her breath. When Ula asked her what was wrong, Dorothy said something about Leyna playing mind games with her. That's when Dorothy added something along the lines of 'If Leyna's joking, I'll kill her with my bare hands.'" I used air quotes and dropped my voice to mimic Ula's.

Air quotes were vastly underrated, in my opinion.

"Joking about what?" Andreus asked, refilling his wine glass.

"No idea," I said. "According to Ula, Dorothy ordered a gin and tonic and a sandwich and didn't say anything more about it. She ended up falling off her stool that night, and they had to call someone to pick her up."

I pulled a piece of pork from the fried rice and handed it down to Missy, an adorable gray-and-white mini Schnoodle, who eagerly lapped it up. Her stubby tail wagged as she licked her lips.

Though technically Missy was my dog, it had become clear to everyone that Missy wanted to live with Ve. Thanks to a ramp that connected our backyards, Missy was free to come and go between the two homes at will, but she hadn't spent the night at our house in almost six weeks. However, she still popped in some afternoons for a quick visit, mostly after Mimi came home from school. Those two had an undeniable bond.

I gave Missy another piece of pork and patted her head as I glanced around for Tilda, Ve's almost-always cranky Himalayan. As usual, I found her at the top of the back staircase. Her blue eyes were closed, as though she wasn't paying the least bit of attention to us, but her tail swished side to side, giving away that she was awake.

"The evidence against Dorothy is undeniable," Andreus said. "But I know my spell. Dorothy could not breach Divinitea, and that is that."

I tended to agree with him, but I couldn't deny the mounting evidence either. I set my fork on my plate. My stomach had been upset most of the day, and I couldn't force myself to eat, even though Chinese food was usually a favorite.

"Are you unwell, Darcy dear?" Ve asked when she saw me push my plate away. "You've barely touched any of your meal. Should I ask Cherise to stop by?"

"Thank you, but there's no need for that. Just a little headache and upset stomach," I said. "It's been a long day of seemingly talking in circles about Dorothy. I've lost my appetite."

"Dorothy tends to make me nauseous, too," Ve said wryly, "so I commiserate."

"The evidence is quite compelling," I said. "Maybe she did get past Andreus's spell."

"Are the two of you not listening to me?" he asked, a hint of outrage in his tone. "She could not get past that spell. You do believe me about the spell, do you not?"

"Of course," Ve assured him. "It's just that Dorothy is devious. She could have found a loophole."

"She's famous for loopholes," I said. "And it doesn't look good for you that you're friends with the Hansel family. I thought Amanda was going to keel over when she found out you were Glinda's godfather."

"And who, pray tell, told her?"

I coughed and slid a finger down the side of my water glass. "That hardly matters."

"I do not like my impeccable character being challenged. Why are you smirking, Darcy?"

"Impeccable?"

"Is it not?"

I tried not to fidget under his scrutiny. "You've lied to me plenty of times."

"Have I?" he asked, his eyes suddenly twinkling.

"Well, to name a few occasions, there was the time you acted as though you had no idea who Dorothy was, even though you're a close family friend—and had been for decades. The time you flat-out lied about breaking into Patrice Keaton's house. Let's not forget that you have a sister you conveniently never bothered to tell anyone about, and I vote that we don't even get into the whole diamond thing. Yes, you've lied."

He chuckled. "So I may have misled you a *few* times. But," he added, all traces of humor vanishing, "my Craft reputation is impeccable, and it takes precedence over any friendships. I am not lying about that spell. Dorothy did not set that fire or kill Leyna. I stake my reputation as a Charmcrafter on it. Not only that, I stake my life. Ve's life, too."

"Hey now!" Ve said, dropping her chopsticks. "Why're you bringing me into this?"

He patted her hand. "That's how serious I am." He looked my way again. "You're going to have to trust me on this situation, Darcy, or someone is going to get away with murder."

"Have mercy," Ve murmured, reaching for a fortune cookie.

In times of stress and strife, dessert was a balm for the women in my family.

That usually included me as well. But not right now. My stomach was a mess.

I held Andreus's gaze.

Trust him.

Could I do it?

After much thought, I nodded. I reminded myself that the times Andreus had lied to or threatened me had only been cases where he benefited. He had nothing to gain from Divinitea burning down or from Leyna's death. "I'll trust you on this."

His eyebrow went up. "And only this?"

I managed a smile. "Trust once lost . . ."

"You're a wise, young witch," he said with a wink that should have been creepy but wasn't.

In his debonair persona, he was also quite charming.

I heard the sound of a rooster crowing, and immediately stood up to let Archie inside. The crowing was his version of ringing the doorbell. Missy barked and ran alongside me.

In the mudroom, I pulled open the back door, and a blur of red, green, and blue feathers flew past. "Greetings. Darcy!" Archie said with his English accent and deep baritone timbre as he swooped past me, heading toward the kitchen. "I dearly hope you've saved me a spring roll."

Missy raced after him, yipping her hellos. I winced.

Perhaps a visit from Cherise to cure this headache of mine wasn't such a bad idea. But no . . . it was too risky with all I had going on in my head. *Secrets.* I sighed, wishing I could be more transparent with those I loved. Like Cherise. And Ve. And even Harper.

Taking a deep breath, I tucked my secrets into a dark corner of my brain and then returned to the kitchen. I noticed Tilda starting to creep down the steps as I cut up a spring roll for Archie.

"You're in a good mood for such a dark day," Ve said to him.

He landed on the curved backrest of the counter stool, his black talons gripping the iron scrollwork, his long tail nearly touching the floor. "'Tis a bittersweet day."

"We know of the bitter," I said. "What is the sweet?"

"Word has spread that Dorothy Hansel Dewitt is in the pokey and shall undoubtedly be locked up for a long time to come. Perhaps life imprisonment," he said, pressing a wing to his chest. He lifted his beak, and his voice thundered as he added, "It is as though a great black cloud has lifted. Light is shining on this village. The angels are singing. *Hallelujer!*" He flapped his wings.

He'd been on a *Madea* kick lately.

We all stared. Tilda twined herself around my ankles as she watched the vibration of Archie's tail. In one quick move, she swatted, pulling out a feather.

"Yow!" he exclaimed.

I quickly scooped up the cat and set her in my lap. "Sorry. She must have felt moved by the spirit."

Archie glanced around moodily and said, "Your collective silence on the matter of Dorothy is deafening. What am I missing? Besides a few feathers." He glared angrily at Tilda.

She swished her tail—somewhat smugly, I thought—as I said, "We don't think Dorothy could have done it."

Archie eyed the wine bottle. "I am going to need something stronger than wine, Velma."

Ve shimmied off her stool and reached for the bottle of tequila in the cabinet above the stove.

Andreus explained how we'd reached the conclusion while I petted Tilda. She was being exceptionally affectionate tonight, for which I was grateful, but I was still on high alert—I'd been on the receiving end of her sharp claws more than once. To say that she had mood swings was putting it mildly. She could turn on me in an instant.

"Are there any other suspects?" Ve asked me as she set a shot of tequila in front of Archie. He liked his liquor.

"Feif Highbridge," I said.

"Hubba-hubba." Archie fanned his face. "That's a bridge I wouldn't mind crossing."

"Hear, hear," Ve said, raising her glass of wine.

"*Hello*," Andreus said. "I can hear you."

It was her turn to pat his hand. "Have you seen Feif?"

Andreus rolled his eyes, then said, "What business did he have with Leyna?"

"That's unclear," I said. "I need to question him."

Ve raised her hand high. "I volunteer to accompany you."

"As do I," Archie said, lifting his wing.

Andreus refilled his wine glass and swallowed the liquid in one big gulp.

I said, "But what I don't understand is if Dorothy wasn't involved with what happened to Leyna, why did she have Leyna's hairpin?"

Aunt Ve dunked her spoon into a bowl of egg drop soup. "It might be time to consider that Dorothy had a partner in crime. Since she knew she could not go near Divinitea, she sent someone in her stead. That person must have given Dorothy the pin after the hit job was complete."

Someone like her son, Vince? The thought didn't sit well.

"In my experience," Andreus said, "Dorothy is not one to delegate. If she was set on destroying Divinitea, it would be done by her own hand."

That was my experience with Dorothy as well, but people changed.

And by all accounts, Dorothy had changed a lot in these past few months.

"There is another theory," Archie said. He cleared his throat, a sure sign he was about to test me with our movie-quote game. "'This whole thing's a setup, a scam, a—'"

"'Frame job,'" I said excitedly, cutting him off to complete the quote. "And it's *Who Framed Roger Rabbit.*"

Archie huffed. "Spoilsport."

"Framed?" Ve echoed. "Someone is framing Dorothy?"

"Now *that* makes sense," Andreus said.

It did. There wasn't a person in this village who was unaware of Dorothy's hatred for Divinitea, Amanda, and Leyna—or her proclivity for fire.

"But by whom?" Archie asked. "By someone who hated Leyna? Or Dorothy?"

"Or both?" Ve added.

I wasn't sure—and I wasn't ready to let go of the partner angle quite yet either, but I felt a bead of excitement that told me we were on the right track.

One way or another, I *was* going to figure out who had killed Leyna Noble. And why.

As I thought about where to go from here in investigating this case, I instinctively knew I needed help—a cover. And I knew just the witch to ask for help.

Chapter Eight

I woke up the next morning feeling stiff and out of sorts. I rolled over and squinted at the bedside clock. Fuzzy red numbers informed me I'd slept in—it was twenty of eight. The house was eerily silent. Nick's side of the bed was cold, and our cat, Annie, a beautiful black RagaMuffin, was curled up on Nick's pillow, watching me with her big amber eyes.

Sunlight filtered into the room through sheer curtains as I scratched Annie's ears, enjoying the commencing purrs. The headache I'd been fighting was much better, but I could feel its remnants lying in wait behind my left eye, ready to pounce at a moment's notice. Staying in bed all day suddenly sounded like a wonderful idea. Even though I'd had a full night's sleep, I was still tired.

If only I didn't have eight thousand and three things to do today, that number being only a slight exaggeration. The first thing on my to-do list was figuring out where Nick had gone. Was he off to work already? It wasn't like him to leave without saying goodbye. Then I realized Higgins wasn't in his doggy bed by the door and figured the two were together.

Throwing back the covers, I reached for my glasses. I yawned my way into the bathroom, where I brushed my hair and teeth, took two acetaminophen tablets to help fight off the lingering headache, and skipped putting in my contacts until after my shower later on. I slipped into my robe and took a moment to open my sock drawer. I pulled out a pair of hiking socks. From between the folds of the thick wool, I retrieved a small velvet pouch. From that pouch, I shook loose a small green seed.

I stared at the seed, willing it to whisper its secrets. Why had it been given to me? What was it for?

Hildie's voice went through my head. *Keep it safe until you need it. You'll know when the time is right.*

The seed grew warm in my palm as I held it, but it rudely revealed nothing.

I tucked it back into the pouch and decided that the sock drawer was not a safe enough hiding place. Gripping the pouch, I whispered a spell I knew by heart and threw the pouch into the air—where it disappeared.

It would reappear when I called for it. But how I was supposed to know *when* I needed it was beyond me.

I was beginning to question the whole concept of faith as I walked down the hallway. I peeked down over the catwalk's railing, my gaze sweeping across the family room, dining room, and what was visible of the kitchen.

The scent of coffee wafted upward, beckoning.

Ignoring the siren call for now, I looked out the huge two-story windows in the family room, into the backyard. Except for a few finches flying around, all was quiet. The garage at the rear of the yard was closed tight, the lights off, so I knew Nick wasn't in his workshop.

I glanced out the front windows and smiled when I spotted Higgins taking Nick for a walk on the village green. Dragging him, really. I took a moment just to watch their antics, then moved on down the hallway. Mimi's bedroom door was open, her bed still made from the day before, as she'd spent the night with Harper.

There was a framed sketch of her mom, Melina Sawyer, on her desk. It was one of my sketches, done solely from Mimi's memories. We'd worked long and hard on making sure the drawing lived up to the beautiful woman it featured. The oval face, the lips that always tended to curl upward at the corners. Her shoulder-length, straight dark hair. Her expressive dark eyes. Melina had died of cancer long before I moved to the village, yet I felt as though I knew her.

I hoped she somehow knew how much I loved her daughter.

Unfortunately, Mimi had no other pictures to remember her mother by. Until recently, Wishcrafters had been unable to be photographed or videotaped. On film, we showed up as bright starbursts. A little over a year ago, a special spell had been commissioned for Wishcrafters, enabling us to finally be shown on film. It had changed our lives. No more fake IDs, driver's licenses, or passports. We could now document important milestones in our lives. Harper would have baby pictures of her little boy. I'd have wedding photos. It was a gift we'd never take for granted.

In the room directly across the hall, I pushed open the door and looked inside. I'd been using the room as my art studio, but in the past month it had also become a storage area for wedding supplies. One day, it would be a nursery. I already imagined the mural I wanted to paint—the night sky with a bright moon and silver stars bursting with warmth and love.

I stood in the doorway a long time, before finally giving in to the alluring coffee scent.

In the kitchen, I poured cream into the bottom of the mug, then added coffee and stirred. I took a sip and frowned. I'd been trying to cut back on my copious caffeine intake and had created a custom "Merri-weather" blend of half decaf, half full-caff.

I missed the caffeine.

A lot.

And I had no doubt my lingering headache had to do with the loss of what I considered an essential nutrient.

I questioned just how bad too much caffeine was for a person. I figured it couldn't possibly be worse than what I was drinking.

I set my mug on the counter and walked to the freezer, where I pulled out a silver-wrapped peppermint patty. These little circles of cool chocolate-mint goodness were my favorite go-to stress relievers.

I let the chocolate melt in my mouth as I opened the back door to let in the cool morning air. Glancing upward, I hoped to see a mourning dove coming in for a landing, but I saw only fluttering finches and a brilliant deep-blue sky.

I'd become accustomed to my mother dropping in for coffee most mornings, but she'd been a no-show for several days now. And I couldn't go see her, either. This week the Elder's meadow, deep in the Enchanted Woods, was off-limits due to emergency Coven of Seven meetings ahead of the Renewal.

Leaving the door open to let in sweet rose-scented air, I grabbed my mug and went into my office, sat in my desk chair, and pulled out my phone. I sent Vince Paxton a text message.

COFFEE LATER ON?

Vince had always possessed a closed-book, evasive persona, but I'd come to know him fairly well. If I asked him flat-out, I'd be able to tell if he'd had anything to do with the fire and Leyna's murder.

Or at least I hoped I'd be able to tell.

Maybe I'd be able to tell.

I wasn't sure at all.

Sighing, I held the phone, waiting for response bubbles, but none appeared. *Hmm*.

I then texted Glinda.

COFFEE LATER?

Immediately the bubbles appeared.

GLINDA: TEN @ WITCH'S BREW?
ME: GINGERBREAD SHACK? NEED CHOCOLATE THERAPY.
GLINDA: GOOD IDEA. SEE YOU THERE.

I set the phone aside for now and glanced at my day planner. My gaze skimmed across the to-dos for the week, of which there were many. I had my final wedding dress fitting tomorrow afternoon and Harper's birthday party that night. On Tuesday, I had a phone conference in the afternoon, and then there was Harper's actual birthday and the renewal ceremony. I had a meeting on Thursday at the Stove to finalize the reception menu and an appointment on Friday with the Black Thorn florist shop.

The Midsummer Ball, a huge event in the village, was to take place this weekend, and next weekend . . . I was getting married.

I looked again at Tuesday's calendar block, to the ink circle around the afternoon hour penciled inside the square, the time scheduled for the phone conference. I stared so hard at that circle that it started to blur.

Then I realized it was blurring because of the tears in my eyes.

Secrets.

I was keeping a big one that, at its heart, had nothing to do with the witch world . . . but could change it forever.

Don't think about it.

I looked away, turning my attention to the painting of a magic wand above the fireplace. The blue and silver colors soothed, while the swirl of the wand reminded me of the magic in my life.

With a heavy sigh, I turned my attention to the binder on my desk that housed all the wedding particulars. I needed to call the rental company to confirm the chairs I'd ordered for the ceremony, which was going to be held in the backyard.

Nick and I had gone back and forth many times on where we should marry, but it all came down to one deciding factor for me: my mother. I wanted my mother to be there, in her human form, preferably. But that would depend on the outcome of the Renewal, of course.

The wedding date had been set before we knew about the Renewal and its possible consequences. Once we'd found out, we'd debated changing the date of the wedding, but it had been my mother who'd insisted we didn't.

We needed something joyous on the calendar to look forward to, she'd said.

I suspected she also wanted me distracted with wedding planning to keep me from worrying about the Renewal.

She'd clearly forgotten that I was a great multitasker.

No matter what happened at the Renewal, she would be at my wedding, and for that I was grateful. Her presence, however, meant severely limiting the guest list to witches—and beyond that, to witches who knew the truth about my mother being the Elder. Which was why there would be fewer than twenty people at the ceremony.

An electronic ding from the alarm system let me know Nick was home before I heard the mudroom door close. I smiled at the sound of a loud metallic drumbeat—Higgins's tail hitting the dryer repeatedly. He was like a one-dog marching band.

I quickly closed the binder, grabbed my phone and coffee cup, and shut the office doors behind me. I had the cup safely on the island before Higgins noticed me and started galloping through the kitchen at full speed.

"Sit!" I said as he charged forward. I held my hands just so, like the dog-obedience instructor had taught me.

Higgins slowed but didn't stop and drop. Drool flew as he raced toward me.

As I plastered myself to the island and braced for impact, I was thinking we should ask for our money back from those doggy lessons.

"Cookie!" Nick yelled.

Higgins abruptly applied the brakes, his feet skidding on the wood floor like something you'd see in a cartoon. He executed a perfect one-eighty, spotted Nick's hand gesture for sit, and immediately dropped into a sitting position. His tail flew back and forth, sweeping the floor.

Nick handed him a doggy biscuit and he slurped it down, crunching and slobbering.

"Good save," I said, wiping drool from my glasses. "Cookie bribery usually works with me, too."

"Duly noted," he said with a smile as he came around the island and kissed me. "How're—"

I held a finger to his lips. *Uh-uhn.*

"But—"

"We made a deal." *Secrets.*

His thick eyebrows dipped into a dark V shape. "You don't even know what I was going to say."

I lifted an eyebrow and stared him down.

His grin crept back. "Deals are meant to be broken?"

"Nope."

"Not even for a cookie?"

I brought his head down and kissed him again. "Not even for a cookie."

"Two cookies? I'm sure Higgins would share."

At hearing his name, Higgins's tail went from swishing to thumping. He licked the floor clean of crumbs, then galloped out the open back door to chase the birds.

"Tempting. But no."

"So much for cookie bribery."

"Next time, try something other than dog treats."

"Duly noted," he said again, this time with a laugh.

He was wearing his uniform, minus the gun. "What time do you have to leave?"

"Ten minutes. I'm glad you're up—I didn't want to wake you to say goodbye." His gaze shifted to the back door. "Did your mother stop by?"

I shook my head, stared at the dreadful coffee in my cup, and forced myself to take a sip—desperate times being what they were.

Nick said, "I'm surprised she didn't come by this morning, considering everything going on with Leyna and Dorothy."

Normally my mother would have been by to discuss the case with me. After all, she was my boss. "Me too."

He nudged my chin. "She'll be by. It's a busy time for her."

I knew. "It's just that . . . I miss her."

"I know you do. It's going to be okay, Darcy."

"Promise?"

He paused for only a second before he said, "I promise."

I pretended not to notice his brief hesitation and nodded. If he loved me enough to promise the impossible, I loved him enough to accept it as fact.

Nick went about gathering his badge, keys, and wallet. As he went to get his gun from its locked case in the closet, I tried to shift the focus of my thoughts to why Nick had to work on a Sunday. "You'll be careful with Dorothy? Take extra precautions?"

He clipped an empty holster onto his waistband. "I don't suppose you have a truth spell you could teach me real quick? That would save me some time."

I smiled. "Sorry."

"She's going to be . . . difficult."

I thought that was putting it mildly as the words *fire and brimstone* went through my head.

"I've already gotten two calls this morning from the treatment facility where Dorothy stayed last night. She's raising hell."

"I can imagine. Will you interrogate her there?" Where there were padded rooms nearby—just in case.

"No. I have a team bringing her back to the village as we speak."

"I thought I felt a heat wave coming on."

He laughed. "A circle-of-hell kind of heat?"

"Pretty much." I leaned against the wall. "Are you going to go through with arresting her?"

Despite the conjectures that Dorothy was being framed for Leyna's murder, Nick had a big decision to make. There was a lot of evidence pointing to her guilt, and he had mortal laws to uphold.

"I'll question her, then decide. If I have any wiggle room, I'll probably let her go while we continue to investigate."

"Or maybe you can keep Dorothy locked up for a little while longer. Like, until after our wedding. Or, you know, a decade or so."

He kissed me and smiled. "I'll see what I can do."

After Nick left, I called Higgins inside and once again looked to the skies . . . and found them empty of everything but a few fluffy white clouds drifting over the village.

As I went upstairs to get ready for the day, I tried my hardest to shake the feeling that my mother was avoiding me too.

Chapter Nine

By the time I left the house to meet with Glinda, the village green had gone from sleepy to wide awake. People milled about as the Firelight participants set up for the day. Villagers walked their dogs and streamed into the Witch's Brew. Spellbound's storefront was still dark, as it wasn't set to open for another hour, and I thought about the text messages Harper had been sending me. She was convinced that if Dorothy wasn't guilty, Feif was.

He was high on my suspect list, but I couldn't question him quite yet—not without a good cover story. And for that, I needed Glinda. I did slow down as I passed his tent, however, simply because I couldn't believe my eyes. "Starla?"

She jumped back from the tent flaps and laughed as she covered her heart. "You scared me."

I bent down to pet her dog, Twink, a bichon frise. I wasn't convinced he was actually a dog—he looked more like a tiny ball of fluff. He'd been staying with Evan, Starla's twin, while she'd been out of the country. It was good to see the two of them reunited.

"Why were you peeking inside Feif's tent?" I asked.

"I mean, I wouldn't say I was peeking," she said, her color high. "I was . . ."

"Peeking?"

"*Looking* to see if he was in there," she said, tossing her blonde hair over her shoulder. She wore it down today instead of in her usual high ponytail. "He's not, in case you're wondering."

It seemed to me he was running late—his booth was due to open in less than ten minutes. People were already gathering nearby, queuing up.

"Were you looking for a reading from him? Or a date? Are you wearing *lipstick*?" Normally, she was a lip balm kind of witch. Maybe lip gloss on special occasions. Maybe.

She rolled her eyes and smiled. "All right, you caught me. So what? He's cute. Better than that, he's leaving in less than a week. Win-win."

Starla had been through some heartbreaking relationships over the past couple of years and had decided to take some time off from long-term commitments. It was actually good to see that she wasn't turned off the dating scene altogether. I just wished she'd chosen a better match. "He also might be a killer."

Her face fell. "What? I thought Dorothy . . ."

Twink sniffed my sandals. "It's complicated. Walk with me?"

She threw a look at Feif's tent and sighed. "All right."

As we walked through the maze of tents and booths, I explained the current status of my investigation the best I could.

"What can I do to help?" she asked as soon as I finished.

"Did you take any photos inside Divinitea before the alarms went off?"

"Yeah, lots."

I stepped aside, out of the way of a passing stroller. "Could you get me copies?"

"Sure thing. Anything you're looking for in particular?"

Feeling a pinch of guilt, I shook my head and lied. "I just want to see what I can see. Maybe something will jump out."

I didn't mention that I hoped some of her pictures had caught Vince in the background. If he'd been involved in what had happened in some way, it was possible it had been caught on film. Since one of Starla's heartbreaking relationships had been with him, I didn't want to dump all that on her in case he was innocent. They were trying their best to keep hold of some semblance of a friendship, and I didn't want to put the brakes on that progress unless I absolutely had to.

Being here, in the midst of these tents, reminded me of the redheaded woman I'd tried to chase down yesterday afternoon. "Did you happen to notice a redhead at Divinitea yesterday? I saw her outside, after the fire was out, and she seemed upset. Devastated, actually."

Twink bounced ahead of us as she said, "I saw her. I don't know who she is though, do you?"

I shook my head. "The reaction she had makes me think that she might be a friend of Leyna's. A friend who might be able to give us a little more insight into Leyna's life. Amanda didn't seem to know much at all."

"From what I've been hearing, Leyna valued her privacy. It's amazing how many people knew so little about her."

"Where did you hear that?"

"Here, this morning. Everyone's talking about Leyna's death."

It hadn't taken long at all for the news to spread that the fire had been a cover-up for murder and that Dorothy Hansel Dewitt had been taken into custody.

Starla said, "I have a couple of photos of the redhead from the shots I took outside Divinitea yesterday afternoon. Do you want me to ask around here to see if anyone knows who she is?"

"Definitely. I can use all the help I can get with this case. With the Firelight festival packing up in a few days, the wedding planning, and the—" I broke off, my throat suddenly tightening around the word *Renewal*, refusing to release it.

Starla bumped into me, full body. "I'll help you any way I can, Darcy."

I bumped her back. "Thank you." She nodded and we walked in silence for a few minutes before I said, "Maybe start with Amanda? If Miss Redhead is a friend of Leyna's, then Amanda might know who she is."

"Oh, see, I was thinking I'd start with Feif . . ." Starla batted her long eyelashes.

"Killer, remember?" I singsonged.

She singsonged right back. "Innocent until proven guilty."

I knew she was teasing me, but I also knew her well enough to know that she wasn't going to let the whole Feif thing go anytime soon. "Please be careful, especially if you do see Feif. If he really is psychic, he might be able to tell a lot more about you than your future."

Her eyes twinkled in the sunlight. "Like how I don't normally wear lipstick?"

I laughed. "Exactly."

When we reached the corner of the green across from the Gingerbread Shack, we parted ways, planning to meet up at my house for dinner later. I looked both ways before crossing the street and breathed deeply as I went inside the bakery.

If heaven had a smell, it had to be like this shop. Chocolate, vanilla, hazelnut, cinnamon, coffee. Bliss.

The space was light and airy with sunlight highlighting white beadboard wainscoting and poster-sized close-up photographs Starla had taken of cake slices. A tall glass case displayed all the miniature tasty treats Evan created, each one filled with magic—eating his desserts filled one with peace and contentment. The taste of the tiny brownies, delicate tiramisu bars, fanciful cake pops, and beautiful cupcakes was just a bonus.

There was a line at the register even though the employees behind the counter seemed to be moving on fast-forward.

Glinda sat at a high-top table, holding a paper coffee cup that had steam rising from the hole in the lid. She was chatting with Evan, who smiled when he spotted me.

"I heard there was need of chocolate therapy," he said, pushing a plate of mini devil's food cupcakes toward me.

"I love you," I said to him as I sat down.

"There's a lot of that going around," he said, grinning.

"Oh?" I questioned.

With a wide smile and a pink tint to his fair cheeks, he said, "Scott's finally moving in."

Evan and his boyfriend, FBI agent Scott Abramson, had been dating long distance for more than a year now. "Evan! That's wonderful! When?"

"Two weeks from today," he said, beaming with happiness.

I took a bite of cupcake, suppressed a moan, and said, "Oh, darn, I'll be on my honeymoon and won't be able to help with the unpacking. What a shame."

Evan looked at Glinda. "That's gratitude, after begging me to be the one to preside over her wedding. I had to get certified to do it and everything."

"You *volunteered*," I said, cupping my hand to catch the cupcake crumbs falling from my mouth.

He sighed dramatically. He was involved with local theater productions in his spare time—he knew how to do dramatic to its fullest effect. "And now, she's leaving when I need her most."

"It's almost as if she planned it that way," Glinda said with a smile.

She might be smiling, but she looked like she hadn't slept much last night. Deep-purple circles smudged the skin under blue eyes shot with red. She'd barely touched the bite-sized cheesecake on the plate in front of her.

Evan slid a cup of coffee over to me, then drummed his fingers on the table. "If only Darcy knew someone who could help instead." His gaze slid slowly back to Glinda.

Glinda snort-laughed. "I should have seen that one coming. Well played."

Evan took a bow. "Well?"

"Count me in," she said. "And I'm sure I can get Liam and Will to help as well."

"Look at that, Darcy," Evan said. "Glinda's even throwing in eye candy to sweeten the deal."

"Eye candy you wouldn't have been treated to if I wasn't going to be out of town on that day. You're welcome. You'll have to tell me all about hauling boxes up the long flight of narrow stairs to your apartment in the summer heat when I get back. I'll be sure to send you a postcard."

He said, "Don't make me take away your cupcakes."

I pulled the plate closer and wrapped my arms around it protectively. "I dare you."

He smiled. "I'll let you off the hook this time only because you've been dealing with Dorothy."

Glinda said, "There's not enough cupcakes in the world to deal with Dorothy."

"There's not enough *anything* in the world to deal with her," Evan said.

I completely agreed.

"Speaking of your wedding, Darcy," he added, "everything on my end is going smoothly, so you don't have to add that to your list of worries."

Evan was in charge of the wedding cake, a large towering concoction that I was convinced would feed all of Massachusetts. And the fact that he knew I had a list of worries showed what a good friend he was. "I'm not worried about the cake."

Glinda said, "You've been surprisingly calm about the wedding."

I took a sip of coffee and almost cried with relief, thinking I'd never tasted anything so good in my entire life. "Did you think I was going to be a bridezilla?"

She laughed. "No, but I didn't think you'd be . . ."

"Mademoiselle Mellow?" Evan put in.

I eyed him.

He laughed. "I heard the name from Pepe, so take it up with him."

Pepe, the mouse familiar who lived in the walls of the Bewitching Boutique with his significant other, Mrs. P, spoke with a charming French accent. Both were dear friends.

"But seriously," Glinda said. "How are you so calm? I was a wreck before my wedding."

"Well, you were dealing with your mother."

"There's that," she said, nodding.

"I'm just . . ." I shrugged. "The cake, the dress, the flowers . . . all are wonderful, but the most important thing to me about the wedding are the vows Nick and I are going to make to each other that day. The rest is just a bonus. And I'm not the least bit worried that Nick's going to be a no-show, so . . ."

"No worries at all," Glinda said.

I nodded.

Evan made a retching sound, and I gave him a shove. "Besides," I said, "Harper is doing enough worrying for all of us. She's the one who's done most of the planning. I'm just following through with those plans."

Evan looked at Glinda. "Harper was in here a few weeks ago, checking the list of ingredients for the wedding cake, to make sure I was using only top-notch products. I had to find three new suppliers just to make her happy."

I laughed.

"It's only funny for you because you're not dealing with her," he said to me.

"Hello." I waved a hand. "I pretty much raised her. I've dealt with her for almost twenty-five years." I used air quotes around *dealt*.

He jabbed a finger at me. "Aha! Then this is your fault."

"Don't you have a cake to bake?" I asked with a sweet smile.

"Luckily for you, I actually do have to get back to work," he said, giving us exaggerated waves as he headed back to the kitchen.

Glinda picked at her cup lid. "I'm glad you're not worrying about the wedding, because knowing you, you're doing enough worrying about another *event* coming up."

The Renewal. To say I was worried was an understatement of epic proportions. All I could do was nod.

Glinda lowered her voice. "Has there been any indication that Harper will surprise us all and accept the role?"

She was speaking vaguely on purpose in case anyone overheard us. "Anything is possible, I guess. But she's still adamant she's done with, you know." Glinda would know I was talking about the Craft and how Harper had sworn it off. I went on. "I can't see how she'd accept a role to be in charge of something she wants no part of."

Glinda said, "Put that way . . ."

"Are you ready to take on the role if it comes to that?" I asked, my heart beating in my throat.

"I'm trying not to think about it, if I'm being honest."

"It might be time to start. It's a very real possibility."

She pushed her cup between her hands. "I have faith the Coven will find another option."

Faith. I thought of Hildie and that green seed and wanted so badly to ask Glinda her opinion about them, but knew I couldn't.

I took another bite of cupcake and said, "Have you heard anything from Dorothy this morning?"

"Radio silence," she said. "From Vince, too. He isn't answering my calls."

I was glad to know I wasn't the only one he was avoiding, but he wasn't going to get rid of me that easily. "Does Dorothy have a lawyer?"

"Not that I know of. I really didn't want to get involved with her legal troubles, but guilt got the best of me, so I made a few calls on her behalf. There's not one lawyer in this village willing to represent my mother."

Most of the lawyers in the village were Lawcrafters, including Harper's fiancé, Marcus. I imagined there wasn't enough money in the world that would tempt them to act on Dorothy's behalf. And the other lawyers, well, clearly they had good sense. No one of sound mind wanted Dorothy for a client.

"The court will appoint one if it comes to that."

"Oh yes, I'm sure my mother will be completely open to a mortal representing her."

Her sarcasm wasn't lost on me. "Maybe she won't need a lawyer at all, if the real killer is found before she's arrested."

"There's a lot of evidence stacked against her. It's going to be hard for Nick to bury the case."

"I know, but I can continue my investigation and pass along what I find to him."

"Are there any other suspects?"

I bit into the cupcake, felt contentment wash over me. "So far, there's only one. It's Feif Highbridge."

"Does that tie into him being thrown out of Divinitea yesterday?"

"That's what we need to find out."

She set her elbows on the table. "We? You and Nick?"

"We, *you* and me."

"You and me?"

"I'm hoping you'll partner with me. With your PI license and personal link to this case, we'll be able to question mortals without suspicion."

"I'm in," she said without hesitation.

"I thought we'd start with Feif."

She hopped off her stool. "I'm ready when you are."

I finished my cupcake, took one last long sip of coffee, waved to Evan, and headed for the door with Glinda.

Once we were out on the sidewalk, she stopped and faced me.

"What is it?" I asked. "Are you having second thoughts about teaming up?"

"No, it's not that. It just seems a little strange that we're working together to clear Dorothy's name, especially since neither of us like her very much. There are a lot of witches in this village who'd love to see her rot in jail. I have to admit I'm conflicted as well. She's not a nice person, Darcy—at all—but I don't want her to be railroaded for a crime she may not have committed."

I didn't bring up Archie's glee last night—or the fact that I wouldn't mind seeing Dorothy behind bars, either. Some things a witch knew best to keep to herself.

And I definitely did not point out the fact that Glinda had qualified Dorothy's involvement.

. . . for a crime she may not have committed.

Her use of *may not* told me that, despite Andreus's assurances about Divinitea's spell, Glinda wasn't wholly convinced of her mother's innocence.

Instead, I nudged Glinda forward toward the crosswalk. "I'm not thinking of our work as exonerating Dorothy. We're working to find Leyna's killer. That's where our focus should be."

Wherever it might lead us.

Glinda looked my way. "I like that much better."

"It helped me sleep last night."

The light turned, and as we started across the street, I spotted Sylar Dewitt coming our way—he was looking down at his phone. When he looked up and spotted us, he froze for a moment before spinning around and rushing off in the other direction.

"That's weird, right?" I asked.

Glinda watched him fast-walk away. "Very weird. It almost looks as though he's running away from us, doesn't it?"

It did.

"Why, though?" she added. "Guilty conscience?"

I wasn't sure. But because of his squirrely departure, I added Sylar to my suspect list.

Chapter Ten

"What is this about?" Feif Highbridge asked, forty dollars and almost an hour later.

Glinda and I had stood in line, not-so-patiently waiting our turn with the psychic. He charged twenty dollars per ten-minute reading, and even though we'd tried to tell his handler we weren't there for a reading, there was no getting around each of us paying the fee.

We'd already wasted several of our twenty minutes with Feif trying to explain why we were there.

He was playing dumb.

If Harper were here, she would have shredded him on the spot.

During the time we'd spent in line, we learned from those among us that Feif's method of reading people's energy came from touching the pulse point on their wrist. That news had come as a relief to me. As long as I kept my hands to myself, my secrets would be safe.

"We're investigators hired to look into the death of Leyna Noble," Glinda said again.

Remarkably patiently, I thought. In fact, she gave off the vibe that she didn't care what he said or did. Her limbs were loose, her shoulders relaxed, her face blank. Meanwhile, my shoulders were so tight they ached, my fists were clenched, and the headache pulsing behind my left eye was starting to sound just like Higgins's tail hitting the dryer. My eye twitched, and I was clenching my teeth.

Feif was scraping my last nerve raw.

Glinda had already showed him her credentials. While I technically had a PI license too, I wasn't comfortable using it, since I'd kinda sorta obtained it magically. Glinda had obtained hers the old-fashioned way. The *legal* way.

For this interview and any others that involved mortals, however, I was acting as Glinda's apprentice. It gave us the cover we needed to ask questions without coming off as busybodies. After talking with Feif, we planned to find Stef Millet to see if she knew when Dorothy had left the Stove the day before.

Feif's dark wavy hair was slicked back, and his high forehead wrinkled as though he didn't understand a word she was saying. "Private investigator?"

I tried not to sigh at his arrogance. "What was your relationship with Leyna?"

"Did I have a relationship with Leyna?" he asked.

Glinda turned to me. She lifted her eyebrows and said dramatically, "Maybe we should just let Nick handle this. Can you give him a call? I'm sure Feif, here, wouldn't mind spending the rest of the day at the police station."

"I agree," I said, knowing she was trying to force his hand. "Feif's fans might be disappointed—and his bank account as well by the looks of the line of fans outside—"

"Clients. Not fans," he interrupted.

"*Clients*," I said, fumbling for my phone in my tote bag. "But you might be right, Glinda. A long afternoon in an interrogation room might loosen Feif's tongue a bit. Do you have a lawyer?" I asked him. "You might want to give them a call, because we know you were in Divinitea when the fire broke out—which was *after* you were thrown out by Amanda Goodwin."

"I'm sure there's a perfectly good explanation for the discrepancy," Glinda said to me, as though we were alone in the tent.

Just two friends chitchatting.

"Oh, surely," I said. "Nick will sort it out."

"Nick?" Feif asked, not so much as blinking.

Cool as a cucumber, this one.

"Nick Sawyer," Glinda said. "The village's chief of police. He was with the state police for years before that. Wasn't he in the military, too?"

"Yes. And he's also my fiancé." I smiled and flashed my diamond ring. "We're getting married next weekend."

"My felicitations," Feif said dryly.

I pulled out my phone, and he held up a hand.

He said, "I don't think that's necessary."

Glinda leaned forward, narrowed her eyes, and sharpened her voice as she said, "What was your relationship to Leyna?"

His eyes flared at her sudden personality shift, before he went back to being too cool for school. "Business," he said breezily. "We'd had great success when she was with the festival, and I was encouraging her to come back. She was stringing me along, playing me for a fool."

"How so?" I asked.

"For one, we were supposed to meet up on Friday at the local coffee shop to discuss details of her return to the festival, but she stood me up."

I stiffened at the mention of the coffee shop. "What time were you supposed to meet with Leyna for coffee?"

"Eleven," he said easily. "I brought the paperwork for her return to the festival. I should have known she wouldn't show."

"Being that you're a psychic?" Glinda asked with a smile.

He mocked her smile. "Being that she liked to play mind games."

He was a good liar. If I didn't know the truth, I would've believed him about being stood up. But I'd been there, inside the Witch's Brew, with Leyna. She'd been waiting for someone.

Feif had been the one who stood *her* up.

Why was he lying? I was debating calling him out on it when he said, "For another, she called, apologizing for missing the coffee meeting. She asked me to meet her at Divinitea on Saturday to sign the contracts."

"You thought she was jerking you around, but you still went to the Saturday meeting?" Glinda asked.

"I place business before my ego. Her talent was remarkable—the festival wasn't the same without her." He blinked, his eyes softening. "I know *I* won't be the same without her."

I tried not to gag at the line he'd fed us. I didn't believe for a second that he cared for Leyna in any capacity, other than dollar signs. I decided to hold back on calling him out for lying about the Witch's Brew. If he was supposed to be meeting with Leyna but had stood her up, where had he been during that time? It had to be somewhere important if he was crafting such an elaborate lie. I didn't want to tip his hand too soon.

"We know you two argued on Saturday," Glinda said. "Was it about the contracts?"

"It was," he said. "She reneged on our deal at the last minute and had me thrown out like common trash."

The comparison fit, I thought. "But you went back in."

He acceded with a nod of his head. "I thought if I could just get her to listen to me . . . really listen . . . I went around to the back door and into the kitchen. I was hiding in an alcove, waiting to sneak down the hallway and into the office again when the alarms went off. I evacuated. The end."

Glinda rolled her eyes. "Can anyone verify that story?"

"It's not a story," he said. "It's the truth. And I don't know. I didn't see anybody, but that doesn't mean they didn't see me. No, wait. Someone did see me. She was coming back from the bathroom. I don't know who she is, though. Blonde hair, blue eyes. Pretty. She smiled at me. I smiled back."

Starla? I wondered. But no, she would have mentioned seeing him. The sooner I could get that guest list Amanda was putting together, the better. Because if what he was saying was true—and that was a big if— then he had a solid alibi.

I rather doubted he was telling the truth. About any of this.

His forehead furrowed. "Isn't there already a suspect in custody?"

"New evidence exonerates that suspect," I said, bending the truth. "Which means there's still a killer out there."

Glinda said, "Do you know of any enemies Leyna may have had? Someone who could have done this to her?"

"Have you spoken to Carolyn Honeycutt?" he asked, leaning forward.

"No," I said. "Who's she?"

"She's Leyna's stalker. Oh, I'm sorry. Carolyn prefers the term *groupie*." He used air quotes.

Suddenly I didn't like air quotes very much anymore.

He went on. "She has followed Leyna from town to town for years now. Leyna tried to distance herself, but the more she withdrew, the more determined Carolyn became." He tapped his temple. "She's not right in the head."

"Is she here, in the village?" Glinda asked.

He nodded. "I've seen her several times. Most notably in front of Divinitea yesterday as the place burned."

Immediately, I thought of the redheaded woman. "By chance, does she have red hair?"

"Yes, she does. Red hair and sociopathic tendencies. Be careful when you're dealing with her. She's unpredictable."

"Do you know where we can find her?" I asked.

"Unfortunately, yes. She's staying in the same B and B as me, the Pixie Cottage. Now. If you two don't mind, I have fans waiting."

I stood up. "Don't you mean *clients*?"

Anger infused his handsome features, turning them into something ugly. "Good day, ladies."

As we walked outside, Glinda said, "I don't like him."

I blinked against the bright sunshine. "That's because he's a lying liar who lies." As we walked toward Stef Millet's condo, I told Glinda about the incident at the Witch's Brew and how Feif had been the one to stand up Leyna.

"But," Glinda said, "is he lying about *everything*? Is Carolyn Honeycutt really a crazed stalker?"

"Only one way to find out. Are you up for a trip to the Pixie Cottage after we talk to Stef?"

She nodded. "Definitely."

*   *   *

The air was filled with the sounds of summertime as we walked across the village, headed to Stef's. A lawn mower hard at work, children laughing, birds chirping. Two young girls rode past us on bicycles, talking loudly about the Midsummer Ball this weekend—an event that was always planned around the solstice.

"I keep thinking about Sylar and how he ran away from us this morning. Have you had much contact with him since he and Dorothy separated?" I asked Glinda.

I'd texted Starla about the redheaded woman and had given her an abbreviated version of what Feif told us. She texted back that she was still planning to ask around. I had the feeling she was hanging around the festival to *accidentally* bump into Feif.

I also texted Harper and Mimi, giving them an extremely condensed version of the morning's events. I'd be able to tell them more later on, during our Sunday supper.

"Not much contact," Glinda said. "I've seen Sylar a few times while grocery shopping—and he always stopped to chat. Most recently, he called me to come get Dorothy out of the tree. He was nice. Cordial. I don't know why he's had a sudden about-face."

A literal about-face.

She looked my way. "Maybe it's *you* he's scared of."

I laughed. "I know, I'm so terrifying. So he's been cordial with you, but how's he been with Dorothy?"

"It's been an ugly split," she said. "Sylar pretty much blindsided Dorothy with those divorce papers."

"I would think she'd be happy to be free. She's wanted to be rid of him for a while now."

"On her terms," Glinda said. "Not his. He made her look like a fool, so she's been on a quest to bring him down. She's hitting him hard where he hurts most—in his wallet. She kicked him out of his own house and withdrew all but a few hundred dollars from their joint account."

So much for my theory that she might want him back. She just wanted to make the split as painful for him as possible. "The house is only in his name?"

Glinda nodded. "He never got around to adding Dorothy to the deed."

Which made me wonder if he had seen the writing on the wall all along.

She said, "I'm not sure how Dorothy's getting away with keeping him out the house, but she is."

"He's probably afraid of her. I can't say I blame him."

"Me either."

I said, "I want to feel badly for him, but he had to know what he was getting into when he married Dorothy."

"Love is blind," she said. "And in Sylar's case, deaf and dumb as well."

"Something opened his eyes, though, since he filed for divorce. What?"

"Your guess is as good as mine. All the papers said was 'irreconcilable differences.'"

I'll say. "Do you think he's capable of killing someone just to frame Dorothy?"

"I don't know," she said after taking a long moment to think about it. "I certainly don't want to think so."

Neither did I. Sylar could be a pompous blowhard, sure, but I'd never considered him evil.

We turned the corner onto Stef's street, and I tried to put thoughts of Sylar out of my mind for now.

Stef lived in a two-story condo on a picturesque, tree-lined cobblestone lane not too far from the village center. The row of colorful condos had been designed in a Victorian style that always reminded me of San Francisco's painted ladies. Stef's place was painted a cheerful coral pink and had purple flowers spilling out of twin window boxes. The garage door was closed and no lights were on as we climbed the steps.

I surreptitiously peeked in the window by the front door as Glinda knocked. I didn't see the flicker of a TV or spot anyone moving around. Everything was neat and tidy, from the pillows on the sofa to the gold photo frames on the table. All of which seemed to hold pictures of Stef and her husband, Adam, who'd passed away some time ago after a battle with leukemia. She didn't speak of him often, but when she did, I could hear only the immense love she had for him. Not too long ago, she'd been dating Vince casually and had told me she wasn't interested in anything long-term. Soon after, they'd gone their separate ways and Vince had started dating someone else. Yet he and Stef had been together at Divinitea. Were they back on?

My phone chimed, and I pulled it out of my tote as Glinda knocked again.

"It's a text from Nick," I said. "Dorothy's refusing to answer questions without a lawyer present."

"That's not surprising," Glinda said. "She has to know that hairpin makes her look guilty, not to mention the threat she made on Leyna's life, and of course, the vandalism . . ." She frowned. "If she was framed, she made it easy for someone, didn't she?"

If. There she was again, qualifying. "I'm not sure she could have made it easier. Maybe if she'd actually been caught holding the match."

My phone chimed again. "Nick says they're waiting for an attorney to show up."

"Court appointed?"

I texted Nick the question and waited. "No. Personal, he says."

"Where did she find a lawyer?" Glinda asked.

"Good question." I texted it to Nick and waited. "He says it's somebody Vince found."

"*Vince*," Glinda said on a sigh. "I really need to talk to him."

"Me too." I had questions for him about his presence at Divinitea yesterday.

Glinda nodded at my phone. "Is Vince at the police station?"

My fingers flew over the keys. "Nick says no." I glanced at her. "Since Stef doesn't seem to be home, maybe we have time to stop by Vince's place before going to the Pixie Cottage to question Carolyn Honeycutt?"

"We can make the time," she said as we headed down the steps.

As we walked back toward the village square, I couldn't help thinking that perhaps we might find Stef at Vince's place as well.

Chapter Eleven

"What?" Vince said through the intercom system connected to the buzzer in the alleyway.

"Good morning to you, too," Glinda said. "I'm here with Darcy. We have a few questions."

Morning. It was hard to believe it wasn't yet noon. "Lots of questions," I amended.

His voice crackled. "I can barely contain my joy."

The buzzer sounded, the door made a clicking noise, and Glinda pulled it open. "He gets his charm from Dorothy."

"Clearly."

We went up the steps, and I was overcome with memories of another murder case that had taken me up this staircase a long time ago. A case that had involved Vince. A lot had changed between Vince and me since then. And a lot had stayed the same.

Sunlight streamed through the open door and onto the oak landing at the top of the steps, spotlighting years of wear and tear. I followed Glinda into the apartment, fully expecting to see Stef sitting on the couch, but Vince was alone. He stood in the kitchen, wiping his hands on a tea towel. A dish rack next to the sink held one bowl, one glass. He'd eaten breakfast alone.

He said, "I have fifteen minutes before I have to be downstairs to open the shop. You're on the clock."

Vince was in his early thirties, but he had a boyish look about him that made him look years younger. With longish brown hair that could only be described as floppy and big blue puppy-dog eyes blinking out from behind a pair of glasses, he gave off an air of innocence that was misleading.

Truth be told, he was one of the most dangerous witches in this village, thanks to his dabbling with the dark arts, which focused on malevolence and could be performed by anyone—not only witches. The practice was the complete opposite of the Craft and everything it stood for. Darkness versus light. I hadn't witnessed or heard about any incidents involving his use of sorcery lately—and hoped it stayed that way.

As I looked around, I tried not to dwell too long on how badly off the mark my hunch about Stef had been. Before I could ask about her, however, Glinda launched right in with a question of her own.

"Why aren't you answering our calls?" Glinda narrowed her gaze on him.

"Did you call my cell?" he asked.

"Yes," she said. "Called and texted."

"I only texted," I added, jumping into the conversation.

His apartment was bright and surprisingly clean. It had elements of a stereotypical bachelor pad—mismatched, worn living room furniture, no curtains, no kitchen table, no artwork. But there were a few homey touches, such as the vase of wisteria, the scented pillar candle nestled in a glass container full of colorful rocks, and a snapshot of Vince and Noelle pinned to the fridge door with a magnet.

"Then that's the issue," he said. "My cell is somewhere in Divinitea. Probably melted beyond all recognition at this point. It fell out of my pocket in the rush out of the cottage. It's been kind of liberating not having it, to tell you the truth."

"Where did you find a lawyer for Dorothy?" Glinda asked him. "I could barely get any of the ones I called to call me back."

"I know people," he said with a grin.

"Is he a mortal lawyer?" Glinda asked.

"Is *she* a mortal, you mean? Don't be so sexist, Glinda." He walked over to his open laptop on the coffee table, powered it down, and closed the lid.

"Don't make me push you out a window," she threatened.

He looked at me. "Glinda gets her charm from Dorothy."

I couldn't help smiling. "Clearly."

Glinda rolled her eyes as she sat in a ratty wing chair that looked like it might collapse under her weight. "Seriously, though. Where'd you find the lawyer?"

"I saw the name on the side of a passing bus." He pulled sneakers out from beneath the couch and slipped his feet into them.

"*Vince*," she said. "I wasn't kidding about the window."

"Calm yourself," he said, motioning for me to sit. "The lawyer is a mortal who does a lot of work for Noelle. She's doing me a favor."

"Noelle or the lawyer?" I asked, bypassing a rickety-looking chair next to Glinda to sit down on a threadbare love seat that was surprisingly comfortable. My gaze darted around the room. It seemed like every flat surface had a stack of books on it. Everything from the latest bestseller to Mark Twain's *Life on the Mississippi*.

Vince sat on the sofa, his long legs bumping against the coffee table. "Both," he said with a grin, and then threw me a wry glance and reached over and closed the album.

"Is that . . ." Glinda motioned to the photo album. "It is! Hand it over."

Vince didn't look like he was going to, so I reached over and picked it up.

"Did Dorothy give you this?" she asked him.

He pretended to pick something off his khaki chinos. "I may have borrowed it one of the times I dropped her drunken self off at home."

Glinda opened the album, and her gaze skimmed the photos. "I should have thought to make copies for you. Sorry."

"It's not a big deal," he said.

"Yeah, no big deal. You only stole the photo album because you're a closeted klepto. Good to know."

He crossed his arms. "We all have our hobbies."

She gave him a smile.

He added, "I really just wanted to see what you looked like with buck teeth and glasses."

I leaned forward. "Really?"

She rolled her eyes. "No. That's Zoey. She went through an awkward phase in her teens, but she was the cutest baby."

I risked life and limb by switching seats. I sat in the wobbly chair next to Glinda and leaned over the armrest for a better look.

Her finger hovered over a newborn baby photo—
Zoey, I presumed. She *was* adorable, with a shock of
the whitest blonde hair that stuck straight up like a
troll's hairdo. She was asleep in the photo, looking as
peaceful as peaceful could be.

I hoped she was—because I knew that later in life
she'd carried around a tortured soul.

Vince said, "I don't have time for this walk down
memory lane, ladies."

Glinda shut the album with a thump. "I'll be sure
to get you copies of all the pictures I can find. And, if
you wouldn't mind, I'd like copies of yours from growing up, too."

"To throw darts at?" he asked.

"Of course," she said.

He hid a smile behind a cough, and I couldn't help
feeling like I wanted to hug him. I resisted.

As I went back to the spot on the love seat, I
noticed the stack of books under his laptop. Witchcraft
books. I'd seen them before, actually. They'd come
from Harper's old collection—the one she'd had before
giving up the Craft. "Where did you get those?"

He followed my gaze. "Where do you think?
Harper."

Harper probably didn't quite think of Vince as the
pesky brother I did, but only because she had dated
him briefly when we first moved to the village. Very
briefly. After overcoming a few personal obstacles,
they'd formed a solid friendship.

"I thought Harper is off the Craft," Glinda said.

Vince had recently learned all about the
Renewal, the coup attempts, and my family's role in
the Craft. My mother had told him everything in
hopes that he too would become a secret agent for

the Craft. She had believed that taking him into her confidence would help sway him toward the side of good, not evil. He, however, had declined her offer, choosing to stay neutral on the situation. Like I said, Vince was a wild card. While I felt there was good within him, I didn't know if it was enough to make him shy away from the darkness. Or put his relationship with his mother in jeopardy, even if it was the right thing to do.

"She is," he said. "But it's not stopping her from trying to get me on board with it. A bit hypocritical of her, don't you think?"

A thread of hope went through me. Maybe Harper wasn't as off the Craft as she'd have liked us to believe. I noticed that many of the books had sticky notes marking certain pages. Harper might have led Vince to the water, as it were, but he seemed to be drinking it of his own free will.

I wanted to do a happy dance.

I resisted that urge as well.

"So, you and Noelle?" I asked, steering the conversation away from Harper. "You're still dating?"

He looked at me oddly. Almost . . . panicked. "Have you heard otherwise?"

"No, it's just that you were with Stef yesterday at Divinitea."

His shoulders relaxed. "We weren't together, *together*. Stef was doing me a favor by going with me. You do know a man and woman can dine together without it being romantic, don't you?"

I smiled, realizing he liked Noelle. A lot.

"What's that dopey look on your face?" he asked me.

"Oh, nothing."

"Well, knock it off right this minute." He shook his head and said, "Noelle and I had reservations at Divinitea for lunch, but she got a call from a client and had to bow out at the last minute. That's right around the time Stef called me about Dorothy being drunk at the Stove . . . again. By the time I arrived, I found Stef trying to corral Dorothy outside—apparently she thought she would drive herself home . . . in someone else's car."

Good heavens.

"After Stef helped me get Dorothy home, I invited her to join me at Divinitea so I didn't have to cancel the reservation. I had to twist Stef's arm. She actually doesn't like tea."

"Why didn't you want to cancel the reservation?" I asked.

He said, "You're nosy."

I shrugged. "I've been called worse. By you, in fact."

"That's very true," he said.

"You said you took Dorothy home. To her house or here, to yours?" I asked.

"Hers. I made some coffee, put on a Bogart movie, and told her I'd check in with her later. Stef and I went straight to Divinitea from there. We'd barely been there five minutes when the fire alarm went off."

"Is there any chance Dorothy followed you there?" I asked.

"No way," he said emphatically. "She was too out of it."

"Yet she eventually wound up in the woods behind Third Eye," Glinda said. "Any ideas how she ended up over there?"

"Let me clarify," he said. "She was too out of it to sneak into Divinitea unnoticed, strangle someone without anyone seeing anything, and light a fire to cover her tracks. She was not, however, too drunk to stumble over to Third Eye to spy on Sylar and pass out. She's been spying on him for months now, looking for ways to blackmail him."

That bit of information should have been more surprising than it actually was.

He bent to tie a shoe, and I pressed on. "You never did say why you didn't want to cancel your reservation."

He pushed his glasses up his nose. "You'd think you'd take the hint."

I glanced at Glinda. "Why do I like him?"

She shrugged. "You have issues?"

"*Clearly*," Vince said, smiling at us. A genuine smile.

It faded when I asked, "Were you at Divinitea because my bridal luncheon was being held there? It's rather coincidental you were going to be there at the same time."

"You, you, you," he said in a high-pitched voice. "Did you ever stop to think that maybe I like tea and ridiculously small sandwiches and that particular time was when the tea cottage had a reservation open?"

"No," I said sarcastically.

"Did Dorothy ask you to spy on Harper and Darcy?" Glinda asked.

"No," he said, echoing the tone of my sarcasm.

I wasn't sure what to make of that. Had he or hadn't he been planning to spy on us? With the Renewal coming up, I wouldn't have put it past

Dorothy to spy on us right up until the very last minute.

"Did you notice anything strange while you were there?" Glinda asked. "Anyone out of place?"

"I didn't see anything out of the ordinary. It all seemed like a perfectly normal afternoon until all hell broke loose." He stood up. "I think we're done here. I need to get to work. Come on, up with you both."

Vince herded Glinda and me to the door and said, "If you need me, don't call. I'm not sure when I'm getting another phone. Stop by. Or use smoke signals. Or something."

As I passed by a bookcase, I noticed several shelves stuffed full of books on black magic and the dark arts. Dozens more than he had on the Craft. The spines were worn, the pages dog-eared. It was obvious they'd been read many times.

Which made me wonder why he was reading about the Craft at all.

Was he studying our ways to learn them?

Or to use them against us?

Chapter Twelve

My phone chimed as Glinda and I made our way down the alleyway toward Pixie Cottage. I slowed to a stop behind the Black Thorn flower shop and fished the phone from my bag.

"Nick?" Glinda asked.

"Yeah. He says Dorothy's lawyer arrived, and they're talking privately before he formally questions Dorothy. He'll update us when he can."

I kind of wished Dorothy would find herself in lockup for another night. It was rather freeing knowing she wasn't roaming the village, scheming against my family.

Well, she was probably still scheming. But the whole not-roaming part was reassuring.

Glinda and I exited the alley on a side street, about half a block from the Pixie Cottage. The scent of honeysuckle from a nearby vine floated around us, strong enough to cover the smell of fried dough that seemed to permeate the air.

Sun shining on Glinda's hair made it look as if she had a halo as said, "That was interesting news about Harper and the books she gave Vince, no?"

"I wonder why she's never said anything to me about giving them to him."

"I don't know," Glinda said, "but I think it's a hopeful sign, don't you?"

"I think so, too, it's just . . ."

"What?" she prompted.

"Is it too little, too late? Harper's not going to appreciate being ambushed on her birthday and forced to make a life-changing decision on the spot. While she can act rashly at times, it's usually on *her* terms. Even if she's easing her way back into the Craft by helping Vince, someone else telling her to decide right that minute if she wants to govern all witches? That's only going to set her on edge, raise her hackles, and I wouldn't be surprised if she cusses out the Coven. I wish there was some way we could warn her."

"You know I don't have the abilities to grant that wish."

"I wish you did."

She laughed.

"The worst of it is, I think if Harper knew what was at stake and had time to think it through, she'd make the right decision."

Glinda slowed to a stop. "The right decision for who, though?"

"What do you mean? For everyone."

"For *Harper*?" she questioned.

I studied Glinda's face, looking for signs of subterfuge and found none. "You don't think Harper would be a good Elder?"

"I'm sure she would be. But is it what *she* wants? Or is it what everyone else wants . . . because of what's *at stake*?" she said, tossing my own words back at me.

What was at stake. My mother dethroned, a family legacy forced to end, and Mom having to turn into a familiar forever.

And with that thought, I knew Glinda was right. I wasn't looking at this situation objectively. I was reacting because I was scared. I absently looked both ways before crossing the street. "I see what you're saying."

"I didn't mean to upset you," she said, jogging to catch up with me. "I'm sorry. It's just that I kick myself for not standing up for Zoey more, for what she wanted in our family. *Needed* from our family. I think things might have been so different if someone had just listened to what she was trying to tell us. I could have protected her more from Dorothy's mental abuse . . . I *should* have."

I put an arm around her. "You were a kid who was also dealing with Dorothy's abuse."

She squeezed my hand and gave me a sad, placating smile. "We can't change the past, right? We can only learn from our mistakes to change the future."

And she was sharing her so-called mistake with me so I could learn from it as well. "That sounds easier said than done."

"It sucks, honestly. It's painful."

I could understand why.

Because if I *listened* to Harper, truly listened to what she wanted and what was going to make her happy, then I was going to have to come to terms with the fact that the Craft might soon have a new Elder.

* * *

Colleen Curtis was manning the registration desk at the Pixie Cottage and smiled when she saw us come in.

"Are you here about your reservation block for next weekend, Darcy? I was just pulling that information together for Harper. We were able to set aside five rooms for your guests."

In her early twenties, Colleen was one of the hardest-working people I knew. She was due to graduate college next year and worked part-time at the local library, at the bookshop—her mom, Angela, managed Spellbound—and here at the Pixie Cottage, where she'd pretty much grown up. Her mom and Pixie Cottage's owner, Harmony Atchison, had been a couple for more than ten years.

"Five, really? I'm surprised, what with this being your busy season."

Nick and I didn't have many out-of-town guests coming to our reception—mostly old friends and distant relatives of Nick's—but enough that we wanted a nice place for them to stay. There wasn't anywhere nicer than the Pixie Cottage, with its charming decor and extensive gardens. Not to mention it also had Cookie, the Nigerian dwarf goat, and Scalawag, the mini donkey, who pretty much had become village mascots over the past year.

Colleen tucked recently dyed purple hair behind her ear. "A few people may have been bumped." She leaned in and whispered, "You didn't hear that from me."

"Hear what?" I asked Glinda.

Glinda shrugged. "I didn't hear anything."

Colleen grinned.

"Well, thank you for the rooms," I said. "Nick and I appreciate it. I didn't actually come here to check on the reservations, but we're hoping you can help us on another matter."

"What's up?" she asked.

"Glinda and I are looking into the Leyna Noble case," I said.

Colleen knew us well enough that I didn't need to bother explaining why we were snooping. In fact, her mom and Harmony had helped me solve a case or two in the past, and everyone in the village knew Glinda's colorful history as a former cop turned PI as well.

"I heard Dorothy's in custody," Colleen said. "The whole village is talking about it. There's a betting pool going around on whether or not she'll shank someone in prison. No, uh, offense, Glinda."

"None taken," Glinda said on a sigh. "If she remains in custody, my money would be on yes, by the way."

"Everyone's money is on yes," Colleen said.

It was an easy bet to make, really.

As far as I knew, Colleen was mortal, so I had to choose my words carefully. "Glinda and I both have personal ties to this case. The Goodwins are close family friends of mine, and there's been some evidence found that suggests Dorothy might be innocent. We want to make sure we do everything we can to ensure Leyna's killer is brought to justice, whether that turns out to be Dorothy or someone else. It's a no-stone-unturned kind of thing."

Colleen slid a sympathetic gaze to Glinda as though she had already decided Dorothy was guilty as charged. "What can I do to help?"

"We're looking for Carolyn Honeycutt," I said. "Midthirties, long red hair."

Colleen leaned forward. "You think she had something to do with Leyna's death? I saw them together a few days ago. Leyna met Ms. Honeycutt for breakfast here on Thursday. They looked friendly to me. Not, like, at each other's throats or anything."

"We don't know if she's involved or not," I said, storing away the tidbit she'd offered. "We're just fact-gathering."

"Do you know if Carolyn is currently in her room?" Glinda asked.

"I'm really not supposed to say," Colleen said, shaking her head vigorously. Then she jerked her chin toward the back of the building. "You might want to stop and say hi to Cookie and Scal while you're here."

Cookie and Scal, who lived in an enclosure behind the inn.

"We'll do just that," I said. "Thanks, Colleen."

Glinda said, "Oh, and one more thing. Feif Highbridge. Can you confirm that he's staying here, too?"

"He is." Colleen looked left, then right, and nodded. "Funny you should mention him."

"Why's that?" I asked, glad he hadn't lied about absolutely everything.

Colleen said, "Because I saw Leyna Noble with him, too."

"At that same breakfast?" Glinda asked.

Shaking her head, Colleen said, "It was Thursday night, when he was checking in. I was headed out to the library and passed them on their way in—they were talking about going out to dinner. Harmony might have more information, since she was working the desk that night."

Dinner. Odd that Feif hadn't mentioned that.

"Is Harmony around?" I asked.

"She had errands to run all day," Colleen said. "She should be back tonight."

We thanked her again, and Glinda and I followed the hallway to the back terrace, which opened up onto a stone patio. Cookie, a beige-and-white dwarf goat, and Scal, a dark-gray miniature donkey, were in a large fenced play yard, surrounded on all sides by shrubs and flower bushes. Cookie was bouncing around stacks of brightly colored tires, *mehh*ing happily, while Scal stood on one end of a teeter-totter like he was king of the world.

Dressed in shorts and a low-cut tee, Carolyn Honeycutt was lying on a lounge chair, her face to the sun, her eyes closed. Her long hair was pulled into a loose bun on the top of her head.

"Ms. Honeycutt?" Glinda said.

Carolyn sat up with a start, blinking against the sunshine. "Yes? Who're you?"

I grabbed two deck chairs as Glinda gave Carolyn the spiel about being a private investigator and finished with, "We heard you and Leyna were friends."

I thought it smart of Glinda not to mention that Feif had called the woman a sociopathic stalker.

I'd learned over the years that sociopaths came in all shapes and sizes and from all walks of life. If I'd passed Carolyn on the street, I wouldn't have noticed anything off about her, necessarily, other than the sadness in her eyes.

I quickly added, "If so, then we're sorry for your loss."

"Thank you," she said, dabbing her eyes with a tissue she pulled from her bra. "Leyna and I have been best friends for almost three years."

Best friends? Could it be true? Or was she believing her own lies?

"Are you a psychic, too?" I asked even though I knew the answer. I wanted to hear how she described her role with the festival.

"No, sadly," she said. "It would be amazing to have that kind of ability. I started out with the festival as just a devoted follower. Even back then Leyna was always so very kind to me. Warm and welcoming. She really took the time to get to know me. A lot of the others wouldn't really give me the time of day, not until Leyna was able to land me a job as a publicity assistant for the festival. I've been working with them since. That was about eighteen months ago."

Funny how Feif had failed to mention that Carolyn worked for the festival, too. He might have lied by omission as much as he had lied to our faces.

He'd really played up the stalker angle, but why would Leyna find Carolyn a job with the festival if she was trying to distance herself, as Feif had told us? It didn't jibe.

Carolyn dabbed her eyes again. "It was a sad, sad day when Leyna announced her retirement. I still can't believe she left the group."

Glinda said, "We heard Leyna retired because she was tired of the travel. Is that true?"

Carolyn swung her legs over the side of the lounger and put her feet on the ground. "Maybe somewhat. Traveling takes its toll. But the main reason she left is because of Feif Highbridge, that sneaky, weasely snake. I hate that man."

Glinda and I shared a look. I said, "Feif? What did he do?"

Carolyn's face hardened. "He broke her spirit is what. When she started talking about being tired of the traveling, he wooed her. Sweet-talked her into staying. Turned on all his charms. And, like a fool, she fell for it. He kept up the act for a while until she kept pushing him to set a wedding date."

"Wait—they were engaged?" I asked, unable to keep the shock out of my voice.

"For a few months," she said. "He's an excellent con man."

A lying liar. I sighed, thinking he deserved to have Harper sicced on him.

"Was she the one who broke it off with him?" Glinda asked.

"Yeah. Like I said, she was pushing for a wedding date. She wanted to quit the festival and settle down. She was dreaming of a cute house, brown-eyed babies, a picket fence, the whole nine yards."

In my mind's eyes, I suddenly saw Leyna sitting at a toddler-sized table with a little girl who looked a lot like she did. They were having a tea party with little pink cups and saucers.

Taking a deep breath to ease the sudden ache in my chest, I tried to refocus on what Carolyn was saying.

"Leyna didn't see the light until Feif got her tipsy one night and tried to get her to sign a business contract, tying her to the festival for another ten years. You see, he owns the festival. He knew Leyna, his most renowned psychic, was the moneymaker. He wanted to be her partner, all right—her business partner. She was heartbroken. Crushed. She packed up and left."

Wow. I'd known he was slimy, but I hadn't realized quite how much. "I'm actually glad you two stopped by," Carolyn said. "I heard on the news that someone was taken into custody, but I think they have the wrong person. I think it was Feif who killed Leyna."

I scooted to the edge of my seat. "Why do you think so?"

"And do you have proof?" Glinda asked.

"Hard proof? No," Carolyn said on a sigh. "But I know Feif was up to his old tricks. Wooing Leyna, trying to win her back. He told her how sorry he was and how much he missed her, blah, blah. I warned her about his motives, but she wanted to give him the benefit of the doubt. She met with him on Thursday, after he got to town."

"We heard they went to dinner," I said.

"It was more than dinner." Disgust crept into Carolyn's eyes. "She ended up spending the night here with him. I happened to see her sneak out of his room early Friday morning."

Happened to? Or had she been spying on them?

Maybe she did have some sociopath in her after all.

Carolyn looked off in the distance. "He played her but good."

Sneaky snake was an apt description.

"She was crushed yet again when she learned the truth—that he was just trying again to get her back on tour."

"When did she find that out?" I asked, thinking it was rather amazing that it wasn't Feif who'd turned up dead.

"On Friday afternoon, he went to see her at Divinitea with a contract in hand, spinning an elaborate excuse for missing their morning meeting."

"Do you know why he stood her up?" I asked.

She shook her head. "Leyna didn't give his excuse, but she did tell me he ran down all the reasons they should go back on tour together. Just the two of them this time, playing big arenas. Leyna told him no, demanded he leave, and told him never to come back.

I think," Carolyn added, "it was then that she realized
he'd been manipulating her with his affections.
Again."

"No wonder Leyna had him thrown out of Divinitea on Saturday," Glinda said. "He was back to his old
tricks."

Carolyn nodded. "And it's why I believe he snuck
back in and killed her."

Chapter Thirteen

"Since Vince gave us the timeline for Dorothy's adventures at the Stove yesterday, I don't think we need to go back to Stef's," I said. "And I don't think I'm up for another round with Feif today. My stomach can only take so much of him."

"Yeah, no," Glinda said. "Tomorrow is soon enough."

Before leaving, we'd promised Carolyn we'd share the information she'd given us with the police and promised to look into Feif's alibi a little deeper.

I pulled open the gate and stepped out onto the sidewalk. "Then I vote we call it quits for today and regroup in the morning."

Glinda shifted nervously from foot to foot. "We could. Or . . ."

"Go on," I said.

"Or you could come with me to Dorothy's house. I want to get those photo albums to make copies for Vince, and I don't want to go alone. That house gives me the creeps."

"Because your mother lives there?"

"Probably."

That made perfect sense to me. "I'll go, as long as we're quick about it. The thought of being in Dorothy's house is already giving *me* the creeps, and we're a block away."

She smiled wide. "I owe you, Darcy."

"No, you don't. You're the one doing me the favor with this case."

"That's right, I am." She laughed and grabbed my arm, tugging me down the sidewalk. "It shouldn't take long at all. Go in, grab the albums, get out."

"Are we even sure I'll be able to get in? I know Dorothy has a hex on her house that hurts trespassers." My little mouse friend, Mrs. P, still had the scar on her tail from the time she'd tried to sneak in to do some reconnaissance.

"You're not a trespasser," Glinda said. "You're my guest."

"Are you sure *you're* not considered a trespasser?" She and Dorothy weren't particularly on the best of terms.

Glinda paused for a second, then kept walking. "I have a key. Trespassers don't have keys."

She sounded sure of herself, but I could see concern on her face, in tightened lines and pressed lips. I said, "I'm sure it'll be fine."

"Now I'm kind of worried. Dorothy has been acting so strange lately. Paranoid. She probably has that house hexed to the hilt. I really don't want boils."

I was starting to think that going inside the house was a bad idea. "Me either. It's too bad we can't text Vince to find out."

"We could always swing by Lotions and Potions on our way."

Lotions was hardly on the way, but the detour might be worth it. Then another thought came to me. "Or, you know, the phones in his shop work just fine."

She laughed. "I should have thought of that myself."

"It's been a long day."

"Yeah, it has." Glinda pulled out her phone and dialed.

While she did, I checked my phone for any updates from Nick I might have missed. There were none from him but three from Harper, demanding a progress report. I told her I'd tell her everything at supper tonight.

She texted back an angry face.

I texted back a kissy-face emoji and dropped my phone into my tote bag.

Glinda said, "Vince says we won't get boils. At worse, there will be a little zap. Less than a Taser, more than static. But in all likelihood, since I have a key, we'll be fine."

I was still wondering how on earth I was going to get out of going into the house when we rounded the corner and it came into view. It was a small bungalow, well kept, with a wide front porch and freshly mown lawn. In the middle of the front yard, a fountain in the shape of a large green frog spit water into the air.

"That's strange," Glinda said. "There's smoke coming out of the chimney."

That wasn't the only strange thing. "The front door is open."

I panicked, thinking Dorothy had been released and Nick had forgotten to tell me. I had visions of her lying in wait inside the house, ready to pounce.

"Come on," Glinda said, grabbing my hand.

"But—" I didn't even have time to lodge a proper protest before we were up the front steps and through the front door.

No zaps, thank goodness. And no Dorothy, either. At least not at first glance.

"Hello!" Glinda called out.

My gaze flew around the room, trying to take in everything. The air was heavily scented with the smell of burning wood—and something earthy. Sage. Nothing looked disturbed, no furniture was overturned, no tables upended.

I didn't like the bad juju, as Harper would have called it, so I slowly backed toward the door, certain Glinda wouldn't mind if I waited for her on the porch.

The door behind me suddenly slammed, and I spun around in time to get soaked with *something*. Liquid flew onto my face, and I tried not to panic that I was going to get boils in my eyes as I furiously swiped at my skin with my hands, trying to dry it.

"Deliver us from evil!" a blurry man shouted.

I wiped my eyes clear just in time to see Glinda deliver a solid punch to the man's solar plexus.

Sylar Dewitt gasped for breath as he sank to the floor like a deflated balloon. As he grabbed his chest, he dropped the small container in his hand.

I picked it up.

"What in the actual hell?" Glinda asked as she wiped her face with the hem of her shirt and then took the bottle from my hand.

The bottle had a small cross with golden letters written beneath it. The mystery liquid wasn't a hex to give us boils.

It was holy water.

* * *

"If I had a gun on me, I could've killed you. What in the world were you thinking, ambushing us like that?" Glinda asked Sylar as she handed him a mug of hot tea.

He'd finally caught his breath, but he didn't look well at all. His hand shook as he took the cup. His face was pale, and perspiration beaded on his forehead.

Of course, he could have been sweating because it was approximately three thousand degrees in the living room—thanks to the roaring fire—but the paleness and shaking were disturbing.

"I was casting out the devil," he said as the cup rattled against its saucer. "You know, doing an exorcism."

For a moment, I thought about pulling out my phone to record this conversation, because I knew without a doubt that Harper was going to want a detailed recounting of every word spoken.

I couldn't blame her—if the roles had been reversed, I'd have wanted the same.

An exorcism.

Have mercy, as Ve would have said.

He said, "You just came in at a bad time. I couldn't be too safe."

I skipped the tea. "Why don't you start at the beginning? What's with the devil stuff? And the holy water? And I'm guessing that's a sage smudge I smell?"

He nodded and his glasses bobbled on his big nose. "I read about it online, how sage cleanses the house of bad energy. That's where I bought the holy water too—online."

"You can buy holy water online?" Glinda asked.

"You can buy anything online," I said to her. Harper had taught me that a long time ago.

Glinda skipped the tea, too, I noticed, as she said, "Doesn't it seem a little, I don't know, sacrilegious to get holy water from the Internet?"

Sylar gave up on trying to hold the mug and set it on the coffee table. "If it works, I don't care where it comes from. I'm a desperate man."

He looked it, his eyes bright with fervency. He ran a hand over his thinning white hair, swooping it across the top of his balding head. Sweat kept the hair in place better than hair spray ever could. He pulled a hanky from his pocket, and his hands shook as he took off his glasses, wiped them, and set them back on his bulbous nose. He dabbed at his face with the white cloth, sopping up the moisture, and then put the hanky back into his pocket.

"What brought all this on?" Glinda asked, her arms sweeping wide to encompass the fire, the bottle of holy water, and the general craziness of it all.

"Dorothy, of course." He made the sign of the cross. Twice.

Glinda's eyebrows were practically in her hairline as she looked my way. I shrugged and said, "I didn't know you were a particularly religious man, Sylar."

He said, "You find religion real quick when you're dealing with the devil."

Glinda's eyebrows stayed up. Way up. "The devil being . . ."

"*Dorothy*," he said, as though we were thick in the head.

"Is this little exorcism why you ran away from Darcy and me earlier?" she asked.

He nodded. "I'm sorry for being rude, but I'm a lousy poker player. I didn't want you to know what I was up to. I couldn't risk you warning Dorothy before I could get the house cleansed."

"What exactly makes you think Dorothy is"—I coughed—"possessed?"

"I don't *think* it," he said. "I *know* it. It all started when she brought those books into the house four months ago."

"What books?" Glinda asked.

He motioned to the fire. "The ones that are burning."

Glinda and I both looked toward the fireplace. Sure enough, I could see the remains of *something* mixed in with the wooden logs.

"Books about black magic and sorcery." He shuddered and reached for the holy water. This time, he doused himself. "I feel tainted just talking about it."

They had to be books from Vince's collection. What was Dorothy doing with them?

"That's about the time she started to change," Sylar said. "She became obsessed with those books. She wasn't eating right. Not sleeping. She lost weight. Her hair started falling out. This *stuff* was making her sick, and she refused to hear it. The more I tried to tell her, the more snappish she became. Mean as a snake, she was."

I personally thought that was her regular personality—she'd probably been putting on an act for Sylar for years. Making herself sick, however, told me she'd taken the obsession a little too far.

"I started to see strange things around the house that couldn't be explained. Like this," he said, scooting aside to reveal a burn mark in the sofa. It looked like a cigarette burn, only bigger. "There are random burns all over the place. The walls, the ceilings, even."

I glanced up. Sure enough, there was a charred circle on the ceiling. A perfect sphere.

"Then one day we got into a fight over her obsession, and she waved her hand in my direction, and I went mute. Mute! My lips were moving but nothing was coming out. Dorothy insists I had a ministroke, but I know what I saw. That glare in her eye . . . It was the last straw. And now she's in jail for *murder*? I should have seen it coming, with the way she was talking crazy on Friday night."

"You saw her on Friday?" Glinda asked.

"I found her up in the damn tree again. She was rambling on and on. Verbal vomit is what it was."

I could've done without that imagery.

Sylar went on. "Her strange behavior has been escalating for months—I should have had her committed. That poor Leyna woman . . ."

"There's a chance Dorothy is innocent," Glinda said. "New evidence has come to light—"

"What?" He jumped up and spun left, then right. His voice went up an octave as he said, "She's being let out? I thought she was gone for good. I need to get the house cleaned up before she gets home."

"Seems to me," Glinda said, "you might want to get the locks changed."

I wasn't sure that would stop Dorothy, but it might make Sylar feel better.

Out came the hanky again. He mopped his face. "I need to *leave*. Leave this house. Leave this village. I've been thinking about finally retiring and moving south. Florida, maybe. Or California. Somewhere far, far away."

I said, "Dorothy's still being questioned by the police, so you don't have to leave this very minute."

"But you do think she'll be set free?" he asked.

I nodded. "Eventually."

He sank down onto the couch, deflating again.

"You said the muteness was the last straw. Is that when you filed for divorce?" Glinda asked.

"Hell yes!" he cried, and then coughed. "I mean, *yes*. I put up with a lot from Dorothy over the years, but she crossed a line I couldn't overlook when she turned into a demon. A man has his limits."

A bubble of laughter rose in my throat, and I pressed my lips together to keep it from coming out. This situation wasn't the least bit funny. Yet . . .

A man has his limits.

My eyes started to water, and I covered my mouth because my lips were failing me.

Sylar must have seen the tears in my eyes, because he reached over and patted my arm. "I know, I know, Darcy. It's tragic to lose such a fine woman to the devil."

I risked a look at Glinda, but she was doing her own version of the lip pressing. I took a deep breath and said, "We should probably go."

She nodded, quickly gathered some photo albums from the built-in bookshelves next to the fireplace, and we left with a quick goodbye. We were barely down the sidewalk before we started laughing. Great big gales of laughter that had us doubling over. We sat on the curb and tried to collect ourselves.

When we finally came up for air, it didn't take long for the reality of the situation to sink in.

This went beyond Sylar mistakenly believing Dorothy had become some sort of devil woman.

Way beyond.

The fact of the matter was that Dorothy was practicing black magic. I wiped my eyes and said, "We're going to have to talk to Vince again."

Glinda swiped tear-stained cheeks with the back of her hand. "I can't believe Dorothy's practicing the dark arts. It's beyond reckless. What does this even mean in terms of the Craft?"

"I don't know," I said.

All I knew was that Dorothy wasn't just practicing black magic.

She was using it to play with fire.

Chapter Fourteen

"Better the devil you know?" Archie said, his beady eyes shimmering with delight.

"Better than the devil and the deep blue sea," Ve said, chuckling.

"Speak of the devil!" Starla said.

Andreus scratched his chin, puckered his lips, and then snapped his fingers. "The devil's in the details."

I shook my head. "I'm out." I couldn't think of one more devil idiom to save my life. We'd been playing this game for nearly fifteen minutes now.

"We probably shouldn't be making fun," Starla said. "But I just keep picturing Sylar tossing holy water at you and Glinda, and I can't help but laugh. That poor man."

"I mean, I can't blame him for filing for divorce after all that. I'd probably draw the line at Satan as well," Ve said. "Unless he looks like the actor that plays Lucifer on that one TV show. Have mercy. He's a beautiful man. I might sell my soul for that."

Andreus rolled his eyes.

"Tall, dark, and handsome? Yes, please," Starla said as she shaved Parmesan into the salad bowl.

"Seconded," Archie said from his driftwood perch next to the island.

I was starting to think I should have canceled Sunday supper. I'd started the tradition a couple of months ago to have a few friends and family over on Sunday nights. It was a nice way to wrap up the week and almost always ended with full bellies and smiles on our faces. *Almost always.* There was one time when Archie had almost choked on a sunflower seed and proclaimed we'd all been in no rush to save him. It took hours and a game of Scene It to soothe his ruffled feathers.

Ve said, "You can't say Sylar didn't give Dorothy a fair shot. I wonder what he'll do now."

"He talked about moving south," I said. "Somewhere warm."

"Probably not *Hades*," Andreus deadpanned.

I rolled my eyes as everyone else laughed.

Archie cleared his throat. "'Have you ever danced with the devil in the pale moonlight?'"

"*Batman*. And I'm starting to get the heebies from all the devil talk," I said. "Can we change the subject?"

"That was a gimme, and you're a party pooper," Archie said, cocking his head in faux outrage.

I stuck my tongue out at him and wished Nick were here. He'd texted earlier that he'd be late for dinner and not to wait for him, but he hadn't said anything else about Dorothy. Curiosity was driving me crazy.

Ve glanced at her watch. "No word from Nick still?"

Andreus said, "In the five minutes since the last time you asked?"

Ve made a sour face at him, complete with a pucker.

Curiosity was fairly killing us *all*, not knowing what was going on with Dorothy.

Andreus bent and kissed Ve's pucker, and a collective "Ew" went through the kitchen.

"I might hoik," Archie said.

Starla took a big step away from him.

A buzzer went off, and from the oven I took two loaves of garlic bread, one plain and one covered in bubbling mozzarella. I set them on a rack on the counter and threw a look at the clock. Harper and Mimi would be here soon. Godfrey had canceled at the last minute with the excuse that he'd forgotten he had an appointment, which I deciphered as meaning he had an emergency Coven meeting to attend. But we were still missing two small guests.

"I'm surprised Pepe and Mrs. P aren't here yet," I said.

Archie stretched his wings. "It is quite unusual for them to be tardy when there's cheesy garlic bread involved."

"I'm sure they'll be along any minute," Andreus said, trying to reassure us all. "There's been a lot of gossip flying around the village today. They're probably trying to collect it all to share with us."

That made perfect sense to me. Gossip was like a second language to the two of them. Or a third, in Pepe's case.

I lowered the flame on the pasta sauce and stirred. It was a simple recipe of crushed tomatoes, tomato sauce, tomato paste, Italian sausage, and spices. Water bubbled in a large pot on the back burner, waiting for me to add the pasta.

"If only we were psychic like that dreamy Feif Highbridge, we'd know where they are." Archie sighed heavily. "Talk about tall, dark, and handsome."

I turned to face him. "And slimy, and manipulative, and a liar. Not quite what I consider dreamy."

"You have your dreams, Darcy. I have mine," he said, humor lacing his deep voice.

"A liar? Darcy, did you question Feif without me?" Ve thumped her hand on the counter. "I wanted to go with you."

Archie puffed his chest. "As did I."

Both stared.

"I was on official Craft business when I questioned Feif," I explained. "The two of you drooling over him would have been distracting."

"For him or for you?" Archie asked. "Methinks you might have been a bit selfish in leaving us behind."

I jabbed a finger his way. "You're about to lose your portion of cheesy bread to Higgins."

Archie clamped his beak closed.

Higgins stared forlornly into the house from his spot on the patio. I was waiting until we were all seated at the dining table before I let him in. Missy sat by the front door looking out a sidelight as though she knew Mimi was on her way home.

Starla said, "For what it's worth, everyone at the festival I spoke to speaks highly of Feif."

"He's their boss. I doubt they'd speak out against him if they want to keep their spot on the tour." I gave them a quick wrap-up of what Carolyn Honeycutt had told us about the man.

Starla tossed the salad. "Everyone I spoke to also said that Carolyn was an odd duck and if not for Leyna acting as a benefactor of sorts, Carolyn wouldn't be welcome at all. She makes people uncomfortable."

That description fit with what Carolyn had told Glinda and me—how the other participants of the festival had treated Carolyn badly. On one hand, I felt terrible for her. On the other, if she was a sociopath, were they right to keep their distance?

"Are you sure this Carolyn is trustworthy, Darcy?" Ve walked around the dining table, laying down silverware. "Seems to me she threw Feif straight under the bus."

"Honk, honk," Archie said.

I stirred the sauce. "I don't have reason to doubt her, and it's a pretty detailed story to be made up, don't you think?"

"The best lies are elaborate lies," Andreus said. "No one doubts a story with many details."

Feif's recounting of being stood up by Leyna at the Witch's Brew had been an elaborate lie. One I wouldn't have questioned if I hadn't known Leyna had been at the coffee shop—and Feif hadn't been.

"You must ask yourself why Carolyn would lie," Andreus said. "What does she have to gain?"

"On the surface, nothing." I set the spoon on its rest. "She seems only like a woman mourning her friend."

"But, dear," Ve said, "didn't you just tell us that Feif said she was a sociopath?"

I nodded. "Yes, but you're forgetting that Feif is a lying liar."

"But is Carolyn one, too?" Starla asked. "What if she wasn't as close to Leyna as she made you believe?" She snapped her fingers. "Ooh, what if she offed Leyna because Leyna had refused to have anything to do with her anymore?"

Offed. I tried not to smile at Starla's enthusiasm, because she was dead serious as she threw out theories.

I swore that if the Elder ever planned to hire any more investigators, there'd be a stack of applications. Starla's would be on top.

"Yes!" Archie cried. "Their relationship definitely has shades of *Single White Female*."

I said, "But Colleen Curtis saw Leyna and Carolyn having breakfast together. Laughing. Very friendly."

"Damn," Archie said. "I'd forgotten that."

I cleared my throat. "'The satisfaction of me being right and you being wrong is more than enough for me.'"

"*Definitely, Maybe*." He bowed. "Thank you, thank you. I'll be here all night."

I smiled, not telling him that quote had been a gimme as well. The bird knew every Ryan Reynolds movie by heart. I just loved pointing out when Archie was wrong, even more when the message was delivered via a movie line. "But, you know," I said, "Feif did say someone could prove his innocence. Supposedly, a pretty blonde-haired woman returning to the dining room from using the restroom saw him hiding in the hallway of Divinitea right before the alarms went off." I faced Starla. "Was that you, by any chance?"

"Not me. I'd remember seeing Feif." She snapped her fingers. "Hold on. I think we can find the answer."

"Isn't this intriguing?" Ve asked as she abandoned setting the table and walked back to the island.

Starla stepped into the mudroom, where she dug through her handbag and came back with a mini iPad. She set it on the island, and within seconds, a photo popped up on the screen. It was a shot of Divinitea's interior, specifically the table that had been reserved for the bridal luncheon. I stuffed down a sudden tidal wave of emotion as my gaze swept over the delicate linens, the fanciful teapots, cups, and saucers, and the flickering flame on the hand-blown glass candle centerpiece.

It was all so beautiful, so perfect. Amanda and Leyna's attention to detail was evident in everything from the crease in the cloth napkins to the shine on the silverware. Suddenly I mourned more than just Leyna's passing—but the death of the dream she and Amanda had shared. Amanda had mentioned that she wasn't likely to reopen Divinitea, but even if she did, it would never be the same without Leyna.

Starla used the pad of her finger to swipe through the images on the tablet. "Here," she said, tapping the screen. "This is what I was looking for. As we were waiting for you and Harper to arrive, Darcy, I was taking shots of the room and caught this. It would have been around the right time to verify Feif's alibi."

The image caught Stef Millet, who was indeed pretty and blonde, walking from the direction of the hallway toward a table for two. The back of Vince's head was easy to identify, with his long, wavy hair.

"Oh, sure," Ve said. "Stef was waiting in line for the restroom when I came out of it. We took a second to chat about Darcy's wedding. It slipped my mind in the chaos afterward."

This was good information to have. "If Stef can give Feif a solid alibi, then I can cross him off my suspect list for good."

Starla kept swiping until we had examined all the photos for any other clues about what had happened to Leyna. We found none with the shots from the interior, but when Starla swiped through the exterior shots she had taken, Ve spoke up.

"Wait, wait, go back a picture, Starla dear," Ve said. "There. Who is that woman?"

The photo was a close-up of Carolyn Honeycutt, taken shortly before Leyna's body had been brought out of Divinitea. "That's Carolyn," I said. "Why?"

Ve's eyes clouded over with concern. "*That's* Carolyn?"

"Do you know her?" I asked.

"No, I don't," she said. "But I've *seen* her, Darcy. When I went to use the powder room at Divinitea that afternoon, I spotted her lurking in the doorway of Leyna's reading room. When she saw me, she scurried inside the room and sat down."

My jaw dropped. Carolyn had been inside Divinitea?

Ve continued to stare at the photo. "Carolyn was the *client* waiting for Leyna yesterday afternoon. I recognize that red hair. Did she not tell you that she was there during the fire, Darcy?"

"No, she didn't," I said, feeling foolish for not asking for her alibi.

Starla said, "That seems like a rather big detail to omit."

"But, look." I pointed at the screen. "Carolyn isn't dripping wet—she couldn't have been inside Divinitea when the fire broke out."

Ve patted my shoulder. "Who's to say she didn't kill Leyna, then hightail it out of the shop before the sprinklers went off?"

Andreus nodded. "Archie may have been on to something with his *Single White Female* reference."

Archie's chest puffed up, and in his haughtiest tone, he said, "'The satisfaction of me being right and you being wrong is more than enough for me.'"

I so hated having my own quotes thrown back in my face. But as much as I wanted to argue his point, I couldn't. Because it was looking more and more as if Carolyn Honeycutt *was* a liar, too.

And with that, I moved *her* to the top of my suspect list.

Chapter Fifteen

"Why do you keep looking at me like that?" Harper asked as she stuck a spoon into a pint of cherry ice cream.

It was nearing nine o'clock. Mimi was upstairs doing homework with the help of some furry companions, and everyone else had gone home. There had been no further word from Nick, and I was trying not to worry. There had been no contact from Pepe and Mrs. P, either, and a call to Godfrey to check on them had gone unanswered. Were they all at a Coven meeting?

"You're cute?" I said, waving a spoonful of butter pecan ice cream toward her. We were sitting side by side on the sofa, our feet on the coffee table. The patio doors were open, letting in a warm breeze and the scent of roses.

The smell reminded me of Hildie's booth and the seed she'd given me. I fought a surge of apprehension as I recalled what she had told me and tried to keep my focus on this moment, right here and now.

"Stop it," Harper said. "You're freaking me out."

I was staring because I'd been thinking about what Glinda had said earlier, about taking into account what Harper wanted versus what had been planned for her by others.

It had stirred a memory of my father and how he'd often said to believe what people said the first time they told you. From day one of arriving in this village, Harper had made it clear that she was unsure about the Craft.

Not much had changed since.

I crossed my eyes and made fishy lips. "I can't help it if you're cute. You were born that way."

Just as she'd been born a Crafter.

A Crafter who was the rightful heir to the Eldership.

It was a title she hadn't asked for, and it wasn't right to blame her if she didn't want it.

"Are you okay?" she asked. "You've been acting strangely lately."

"I call you cute and you call me strange? How is that fair?"

She smiled. "Strange *and* a master of diversion. You're deflecting, trying not to answer the question about being okay."

"I'm hardly a master if you caught me doing it."

She spoke around the spoon in her mouth. "That's true. You need to work on your diversion skills. So?"

I sprinkled more jimmies into my pint and set the shaker back on the table. "So what?"

"You. Strange. Why?"

"Born that way?"

"*Darcy.*"

"I have a lot on my mind. The wedding . . ."

She shook her spoon at me. "Uh-uhn. You're calm about the wedding. Too calm, if you ask me, but I digress. And we already talked through all the new leads with Leyna's death, so I don't think it's that. It's as though . . ." She raised an eyebrow. "You're keeping secrets from me."

Ha! If she only knew how many.

"Is this about my birthday?" she asked. "You know I don't want a big to-do."

The surprise party we were having for her tomorrow night was going to be a *little* to-do, so I didn't feel guilty by saying, "Noted."

We'd opted to hold the party the night before her birthday, because shortly before sundown on her actual birthday, she'd be summoned to see the Elder and the Coven in the Elder's meadow.

There, she was going to get the shock of a lifetime.

Harper was going to flip her lid.

"And Mom?" she asked, wheedling. "She knows I don't want anything big, right?"

"I can't speak for Mom." I stuck a big gob of ice cream in my mouth to keep from accidentally saying anything incriminating.

"I'd ask her myself, but with all these Coven meetings she's having this week, she's been incommunicado. Has she said anything to you about the Renewal?"

I started choking, and as I coughed and sputtered, she pounded my back until my throat cleared. "I'm okay," I said after a second. "I apparently tried to inhale a jimmie."

"Is this another diversion tactic? Better method, by the way, if it is."

"I'll remember that, but no. These jimmies are dangerous. Delicious but dangerous."

Harper leaned back against the couch cushions and picked up our conversation as though she hadn't almost had to perform the Heimlich maneuver. "Mom's Renewal is coming up in two days. It's actually the night of my birthday, since it falls on Midsummer's Eve this year. I'm surprised she hasn't said anything."

In the midst of all my worrying, I'd forgotten that Harper knew about the Renewal. Not everything, of course. Only that it existed. She'd found the information in a witchcraft book a long time ago.

"I'm sure Mom would talk about it if she could. It's probably one of those persnickety Craft rules."

She spooned more ice cream. "Are you worried at all?"

Down to my very soul. I tried to sound surprised by the notion as I said, "Worry? Why?"

"Do you remember when we learned about the Renewal? How it's actually called the Renewal or Renaissance? What's the Renaissance part?"

I thought about faking choking to avoid saying anything, but instead said, "I'm not sure. The secrets within the Craft can be so frustrating."

"Agreed," she said. "I could never be Elder. I'd lose my mind if I had to keep track of every rule and violation."

My heart sank. I'd suspected she felt that way, but to hear her speak the words clear as day nearly took my breath away.

"You know what, though?" she asked, waving the spoon.

"What?" I asked, trying to keep my voice from cracking.

"I'd love to be part of the Coven. I want to be the one to *make* the rules. Our laws need a complete overhaul. How do I get *that* job, because I'm ready to start tomorrow. First up, more transparency. Why are there so many secrets within the Craft? Especially about the Eldership? And yeah, yeah, I understand there's a danger present, but come on, we're witches. Surely we can come up with protection spells for the Elder's family. I think in general it's stupid."

My head was swimming. There was a lot to sort through in what she'd just said, but one thing jumped straight out. "I thought you were done with the Craft?"

"I didn't mean *forever*. Gosh, Darcy. You take everything so literally."

"You *literally* said you were done with it forever."

She smiled. "I'm pregnant. It was the hormones talking."

My phone chiming with a text message was the only thing that stopped me from wringing her neck. "You are so lucky I love you."

"I know," she said, licking her spoon.

I picked up the phone. "It's Nick—he's on his way home."

"Nothing else? How can he leave us hanging like that?" she asked. "What's happening with Dorothy? Is she walking into a sage-scented house right now only to be doused with holy water? I bet she melts, by the way."

It wouldn't have surprised me if she did. "You know as much as I—"

I was cut off by a creaking sound coming from the floor. Harper and I leaned over the couch arm and watched as one of the oak floorboards lifted upward. A small white mouse popped up and out, followed by a chubbier brown mouse.

"Hiya, dolls!" Mrs. P said, straightening her pink velour dress. "Have you heard the news?"

"What news?" Harper asked. "We haven't heard anything other than Archie waxing on about Ryan Reynolds."

"Do you blame him?" Mrs. P asked. "I don't!"

"What news have you brought, Mrs. P?" I asked. "Hi, Pepe."

"*Bonjour, mes amies*," he said as he dropped the floorboard back into position.

"The news about Dorothy!" The fur sticking up between Mrs. P's big ears fairly quivered with excitement. "We've been keeping our eyes on her all day."

Pepe tugged at the hem of his red vest. "Wait, wait, *s'il vous plaît*. There is a more pressing matter at hand at the moment than Dorothy."

"What's that?" I reached down, and both climbed into my palm. I set them on the arm of the couch. "I can't imagine what's more pressing than Dorothy right now."

Pepe pressed his tiny hands together. "*Ma chère*, please tell me you saved some cheesy bread. I've been dreaming of it all day. It's the only thing that saw me through listening to Dorothy and her mumbo jumbo. The woman is . . ."

"She's off her rocker, that's what." Mrs. P laughed, a sound that always reminded me of the way Phyllis Diller had laughed—it was more of a joyous bark.

"More than usual?" Harper asked. "Because we all know she's never been sane of mind."

Mrs. P said, "Enough so that she's finally been carted off to the loony bin."

"*Mon amour*, I do not think that is the technical term for the institution in question." He tapped my arm. "The bread, *ma chère*?"

"The loony bin?" I asked. "As in a psychiatric hospital?"

Mrs. P rubbed her hands together. "Yes indeed."

Harper's jaw dropped. "Has she been involuntarily admitted to the hospital for an evaluation?"

"*Oui*, for seventy-two hours. The bread?" Pepe asked again.

I smiled at him. "It's keeping warm in the oven. I'll make you two a plate."

"Wow, Dorothy in a psych ward," Harper said. "I'm going to need *all* the details. Do not leave anything out."

As I bustled around the kitchen, I listened in as Pepe explained what had happened at the police station during the day—but my mind was already jumping ahead.

Seventy-two hours.

That would put Dorothy's release date the day *after* Harper's birthday.

Dorothy was going to miss the Renewal.

* * *

"It was Dorothy's own lawyer who suggested the psychiatric hold?" Starla asked early the next morning as we jogged around the village. "Is she already trying to set up an insanity plea?"

"Maybe," I said, kicking a pine cone off the path. "Nick said that Dorothy was truly behaving erratically. Cursing. Flailing. Slurring her words. Spitting."

Still not feeling all that well, I'd almost canceled our usual morning jog, but I'd thought the fresh air might do me some good. So far, running had chased away some of my nerves, but my stomach wasn't having it, tossing and turning to the point where I'd had to stop to walk a few times and had finally decided to cut the run short. Jogging slowly, we were on our way back to the village.

"Spitting?" Starla made a horrified face.

"I know, right?" I shuddered. I could deal with cursing and flailing, but get saliva involved, and it gives me the heebies. "She threatened Nick, me, the lawyer, and to burn down the village. She said we were all framing her. She started pulling her hair out and eventually had to be restrained."

My heart rate kicked up just talking about the threat to burn down the village. Had it been an empty threat? I wanted to think so. But those scorch marks at her house suggested otherwise.

I also left out the part where Dorothy had said we were framing her to keep her from taking over the village—Starla didn't know about the Renewal. And the statement had been vague enough that the mortal lawyer hadn't needed a memory cleanse.

"Was she acting?" Starla asked. "Because she wasn't drunk anymore—she'd spent the night drying out, right?"

"Right, and I don't know if she was faking it. All I do know is that Dorothy's lawyer suggested the psych hold and Nick was relieved to agree to it. He didn't want to have to arrest Dorothy, and it was looking like that was the only option after she didn't deny the threats to Leyna or come up with a logical solution for being in possession of the hairpin. Not to mention, an arrest was in order for attacking a police officer at the station and making threats."

I kept thinking about how Glinda had said Dorothy seemed off lately and how Sylar had said her personality changed. I was beginning to wonder if she'd actually had a mental breakdown.

Starla's blonde ponytail swung as she jogged. "Her out-of-control behavior only bolsters the theory that she's planning an insanity plea, doesn't it?"

"I can see her lawyer thinking so, but I can't imagine Dorothy believes she'd ever be found guilty of anything. Nick said Dorothy went berserk after arriving at the psychiatric facility. They had to sedate her when she learned she was going to be there for three days."

Because she was going to miss the Renewal.

"Maybe she really has lost her mind," Starla said. "What happens in three days when she's released?"

"Nick mentioned that it's possible her stay could be extended if deemed necessary."

We turned a corner, and I looked ahead to the Pixie Cottage. Dew on the roof sparkled in the early-morning light.

Before Pepe and Mrs. P had left last night, I'd asked a favor of them that involved sneaking into Feif Highbridge's room, and I wondered if they'd had a chance to complete their mission yet. I planned to meet up with them later today for a full report on what they might have discovered.

Something incriminating, I hoped.

"Well, hidey ho," Starla said. "There's Feif."

He crossed the street toward the Pixie Cottage, a cup from the Witch's Brew in one hand, a pastry bag in the other.

"Good morning, ladies," he said when he spotted us.

I smiled and kept jogging, only to find that Starla had stopped to chat. With a groan, I doubled back, giving her the evil eye the whole way. Which was completely lost on her, as she had eyes for only Feif.

Googly eyes, at that.

"It's a shame," he said, "that I have only a few days left here in the village. I wouldn't have minded running with you. Such a great form of exercise."

His gaze drifted down Starla's legs, and I wanted to smack him upside his head.

I bit my tongue to keep from saying he hadn't been invited to run with us, but Starla said, "You have a few days left. You can join us tomorrow morning."

And now I wanted to smack *her*. What was she thinking?

He smiled her way, all warm and charming. "Thank you, I think I'll take you up on that."

I said sternly, "I don't think that's a good idea. Feif is a subject of an investigation."

Feif raised his eyebrows at me. "I thought I was cleared?"

"We haven't verified your alibi." I folded my arms.

"It's all but said and done, right?" Starla said to me. "Once you talk to Stef . . ."

"Stef?" he said. "Is that the woman's name?"

Starla nodded. "Stef Millet. She works at the Sorcerer's Stove. I actually have a picture of her coming back from the restroom that verifies your story."

"You were there that day?" he asked. "You're my savior." He tucked the bag under one arm and picked up Starla's hand to kiss it.

I bit back gagging noises. "*Nothing* is verified yet," I said, fighting the urge to yank her hand away from him. "Just because Feif said that he saw Stef doesn't mean she saw him. Glinda and I are going to talk to her this morning. We'll see what *she* says."

"Oh, she saw me," he said.

Ugh, his arrogance irritated me to no end. I said, "Just like you waited at the Witch's Brew for Leyna on Friday?"

The red tea tag sticking out of his cup fluttered in the breeze like a warning flag. "I didn't?"

"No, you didn't. I know this because I was at the Witch's Brew and saw Leyna there. Who I didn't see was *you*."

"Oh, I'd forgotten about that lie," Starla said, taking a step away from him.

He lifted a shoulder in a half shrug. "I might've had the times wrong."

"I don't think you did. I think you stood *her* up. Why, though? Where were you when you were supposed to be meeting with her?" I asked.

He took a sip of his drink. "It doesn't matter."

"I think it does," I countered.

"Fine, if you must know, I was here," he said, gesturing to the Pixie Cottage. "And if you need verification on *that*, you can ask Carolyn Honeycutt. We were together. In bed."

My jaw dropped.

"Now, if you ladies will excuse me, I have things to do." He pushed open the gate and started up the path.

Starla yelled, "The offer to run with us is officially rescinded."

He didn't comment as he pulled open the front door and went inside.

"Did he just say he slept with Carolyn Honeycutt?" I asked.

"Yeah, he did. Didn't he tell you she was a sociopath?"

"And didn't she say she hated him?"

"It's looking like they're both lying liars who lie," Starla said as we kicked into a jog again. "I always had a bad feeling about that Feif."

I slid her a glance. "You did, did you?"

"I'm a fabulous judge of character." She grinned and sprinted ahead.

I glanced back at the Pixie Cottage. As much as I wanted to go pound on Carolyn's door to see what she had to say for herself, it was too early to go barreling in there. Plus, I should wait for Glinda.

But as I ran to catch up with Starla, I couldn't help thinking about all the lies told between Carolyn and Feif. Why? Was it because one of them had killed Leyna?

Or because it had been *both* of them?

Chapter Sixteen

"It's possible they were working together to get rid of Leyna," I said forty minutes later as I frowned at the full pot of Merriweather blend coffee, willing myself to pour a cup. My stomach had settled a bit after a couple of pieces of toast.

Nick came up behind me and kissed my neck. "Why not just have one cup of coffee a day that's full-strength caffeine rather than suffer through a few cups of that horrid decaf blend?"

"You don't know what you're asking of me. One single cup?"

His lips lingered. "Maybe you should cut coffee altogether. Have you considered herbal tea instead?"

"Considered and dismissed."

Annie sat on a counter stool, watching us. Nick went over and rubbed her ears. She pushed her head against his palm and purred. He said, "I hear water is quite satisfying."

"Are you *trying* to get turned into a frog?"

"Do no harm, remember?"

"Frogs are cute. No harm there." I poured cream into my cup, added coffee, tasted it, and then added more cream and a pinch of sugar.

Nick laughed at the dour look on my face. "One cup . . ."

"*Ribbit.*"

I was about to pick up the topic of Carolyn and Feif but held back when Mimi came into the kitchen, her backpack slung over her shoulder. Her hair was still damp from a shower, and curls hung around her face in tight black spirals.

She kissed the top of Annie's head and then dropped her backpack on a stool and yawned. "I hate Mondays."

I put my arm around her. "As much as I hate this coffee?"

She eyed the mug. "Probably not. I'm starting to think cutting back on caffeine has been more harmful to you than helpful. Maybe you should think about going back?"

She had no idea how I really, really wanted to. "Doing what's best isn't always easy."

"That's a good life lesson," Nick said as he shook cereal into a bowl.

Mimi rolled her eyes. "It's Monday and way too early for life lessons." She went into the mudroom to fill Higgins's and Annie's food bowls.

Nick laughed. "It's never too early for life lessons."

I took another sip of coffee and winced. "Maybe one cup a day isn't such a bad idea." I pointed at Nick. "Do not say I told you so."

He stuck a spoonful of Cheerios in his mouth.

Shaking my head, I said, "Mimi, do you want to pack your lunch today? Or buy?"

I adored these little moments, the snapshots of our life together. The *normal* moments. The times when our thoughts weren't preoccupied with the Craft or with murder or other police work. Just us. Life. Family. Love.

"I'll buy." Mimi crossed the kitchen to wash her hands before letting Higgins inside. "It's pizza day, the only good thing about Mondays."

I went to get my tote from my office to give Mimi some cash for lunch. My day planner was opened to this week's tasks, and my gaze went straight to tomorrow's full block, including that afternoon phone appointment. Taking a deep breath at all I had going on, I headed back to the kitchen. I had to dodge Higgins, who had a one-track mind as he galloped toward his food bowl. I spun around to avoid getting run over, and something flew out of my tote bag and clattered on the floor. Annie leapt off the stool, ran over to investigate, and started batting whatever it was around. I bent and picked her—and the object—up.

I carried Annie to the laundry room and set her down on the washer next to her food dish—which we had to keep up high, away from Higgins and his voracious appetite.

I came back into the kitchen looking at the item in my hand.

"What's that?" Mimi asked.

"I'm not sure. Maybe a charm?" I rubbed my thumb over the beautiful blue stone and its golden veins. Oval shaped, it was glossy yet textured. It looked familiar, but I couldn't place why. "I don't know where it came from."

"A protection charm? It certainly doesn't look like any ordinary rock," Nick said. "Maybe Andreus slipped it to you at dinner last night?"

If the stone had been harmful or hexed, it wouldn't have made its way into the house. I often joked that our home was more protected than Fort Knox—except its security came from magic, not armed guards.

"I'll ask him about it." But why wouldn't Andreus have just given it to me? Why hide it in my tote bag? I certainly wouldn't have turned down any extra protections these days.

Until then, I said a spell and tossed the rock into the air. It disappeared.

"Magic is so cool," Mimi said.

It wasn't long before Nick and Mimi had to leave. Nick for work, Mimi for school. On his way out the door, Nick set a time to meet up with me for lunch.

I was on my own with investigating for the time being, since Glinda was at the hospital, hoping to see Dorothy. We'd get together later today to go over what I'd found.

My first stop of the day was to find Stef Millet to see if she could verify Feif's alibi. After that, I needed to track down Carolyn again to ask her about her relationship with Feif.

Tangled webs, I thought as I threw a load of laundry in the washer.

I had put aside thoughts of the case while cleaning up the kitchen and was thinking about my dress fitting later on. I couldn't wait to see Godfrey and Pepe's finished design. I had given them only vague ideas of what I wanted, and they'd assured me they knew exactly the dress I had in mind.

A flash of movement outside the window caught my eye—a mourning dove coming in for a landing on the patio. In a blink, I saw the bird turn into my mother.

I smiled, dried my hands, and hurried to the back door. Dressed in a white blouse and wide-legged white pants, Mom had her hand raised to knock on the door when she spotted me and smiled.

Higgins barked as I flipped the lock and let her inside. I said, "You don't even know how glad I am to see you. Wait. Are you *sinking*?"

In her human form, Mom didn't walk—she floated. I stared at her feet, which were always bare for a reason she had never disclosed. I'd always figured it had something to do with the Eldership, and now I was sure of it. Her feet were a good inch closer to the ground than normal.

Her long auburn hair was pulled back in a French braid, and her bluish-brown eyes clouded over as she said, "I was hoping you wouldn't notice."

"Higgins, down!" I said, tugging on his collar as he put his big paws on her shoulders and slurped her face.

"Hi, Higgins." Her laughter echoed through the room.

I enjoyed the sound of it for a moment before asking, "*Why* are you sinking?"

She sighed, and for a second I thought she wasn't going to tell me. But finally she said, "My Eldership powers are waning ahead of the Renewal. It's perfectly normal and nothing to worry about."

Not worry. I wasn't sure I knew how.

"What happens if your feet do touch the ground?" I'd asked her the question numerous times before, but she'd always dismissed it. Now that it was clear there was a chance her feet might touch down, I hoped she would answer.

Much to my surprise, she did.

She said, "If my feet touch, it means I've lost all my power as Elder. If or when that happens, I have two choices. I can stay in this world as a familiar, or I can choose for my spirit to cross into the beyond."

If or when. I took a deep breath. She'd already told me that if the worst was to happen, she would take on her mourning dove form. I wasn't losing her again. She was just . . . changing.

Mom petted Higgins's head, waved her hand, and produced a rawhide bone. His tail slashed the air as he grabbed it. He carried it to his dog bed, where he plopped down and started chomping happily.

Suddenly, she gave me a big hug as if sensing I needed it, and then held me at arm's length. "Something's different. Let me look at you."

I said, "It's been less than a week since I saw you last. What could possibly be different?"

She tapped her chin. "I'm not sure. It's something, though."

"Probably my caffeine deficiency. Come on in. I'd offer you coffee, but I love you too much to subject you to that swill."

"How about some of the good stuff?" She waved her hand again, and a coffee cart appeared.

Annie, who'd been lounging on top of the fridge, bolted. The poor kitty wasn't as enthused with magic as Mimi.

"One cup," I said, smiling. How I was going to make it through the rest of the day was anyone's guess. Maybe I'd pick up a banana shake at the Stove later on to see me through. "How're the meetings going?"

"They're going," she said as she poured coffee into a mug. "I honestly thought we were onto something with Mimi, but the Coven vetoed."

"With Mimi?" I sipped the coffee and sighed.

"It was proposed that if you adopted Mimi, then Mimi would become the youngest witch in the family, but some in the Coven argued that if we were to keep the *hereditary* monarchy, it should be a bloodline relative who takes over. A consensus couldn't be reached."

All avenues, Ve had said.

The heat from the mug warmed my hands. "I'm grateful the Coven is looking at every option, but I'm not sure I would have been comfortable with that proposal. As much as I love Mimi and would adopt her in a heartbeat, I wouldn't want to force the issue on her, and I certainly wouldn't want her to think that I was trying to replace Melina in some way."

Mom's eyes softened. "No one would ever think you were trying to replace Melina. Even Melina wouldn't think that."

I sipped the coffee slowly—trying to make it last. "We can't know that."

Mom arched an eyebrow, and I noticed a slight smile behind the rim of her mug. Before I could question her about the odd reaction, she said, "What is the latest with the murder of Leyna Noble?"

I leaned against the island. "You know everything going on with Dorothy, I presume?"

"I do."

"And that she's going to miss the Renewal . . ."

"A blessing, truly."

"Doesn't she need to be there if, you know, Harper declines to make the promissory vow?"

"If it comes to it," she said, her words measured, "Dorothy's presence is not needed for her agenda to move forward."

"But if she's one of the Coven . . ."

Mom said, "I cannot divulge who . . ."

"Yeah, yeah, I know." I rolled my eyes. "You can't tell me, blah, blah, blah."

She smiled. "However, I can tell you that if a Coven member is found to be practicing black magic, then she would be summarily dismissed from the Coven, reprimanded, and have her powers suspended for a period of one month."

I nearly dropped my mug. "Holy bombshell! Dorothy was kicked out of the Coven?"

"Did I say that?" Mom asked, a playful gleam in her eye. "Now, tell me about Leyna."

I stashed away the thoughts of Dorothy being ousted for the time being. Mom and I talked for nearly half an hour about the case, going over every detail that Glinda and I had learned so far. "If what Carolyn told us was true about Leyna being used by Feif, how did she not know he was using her? As an Emoticrafter, Leyna should have been able to read his true motives."

"Sometimes even witches see and feel what they *want* to see and feel."

"What you're saying is Leyna might have been too taken with him to see his true motives?"

"Love is a powerful blindfold."

As images of Leyna's apartment went through my head, the sparseness, the air of loneliness, I thought about her and Feif having dinner the other night . . . and how Leyna had stayed over with him. "That might explain why she was willing to give him a second chance as well."

Mom nodded. "It sounds as though you're on the right track with Feif and Carolyn, but let me remind you that time is of the essence. The festival is due to leave town on Wednesday." She waved her hand, and the coffee cart disappeared. "I should get going. I have meetings all day."

I wasn't ready to let her go quite yet. "About tomorrow night . . ."

"I'd rather not talk about it," she said. The light drained from her eyes, and she suddenly looked worn and drawn.

"I know, but *Dorothy*. I think we need to have a plan in place—"

She floated toward the back door. "Dorothy won't be in the village tomorrow."

"But the black magic . . . can she work it from far away?" I had questions about the kind of power Dorothy had at her fingertips. Could she *escape*? I shuddered at the thought.

Mom took a deep breath and then cupped my face in her palm. "Darcy, my darling, don't worry about Dorothy, okay? I've taken precautions. I'll see you soon."

Precautions. Thank goodness. "Will you be at Harper's surprise party?"

"I might be late, but I'll be there." She kissed my cheek, opened the door, and the second she stepped over the threshold, she turned into a mourning dove and flew off.

I watched her soar above the trees at the back of the yard until I couldn't see her any longer. Telling me not to worry about Dorothy was like telling me not to breathe. It wasn't going to happen.

Chapter Seventeen

"'Poor devil had his tongue cut out, so he trained the parrot to talk for him.'"

I'd been walking down the driveway when I heard Archie call out. He was in the side yard, perched on the iron fence that ran along the property line I shared with the Goodwins.

I crossed over to him. "I thought we were done with the devil quotes."

Archie tilted his head. "Do not try to change the subject. Cough up the answer or confess you don't know."

Dew brushed against my ankles as I leaned on the fence. "Fine, I don't know."

"Aha!" He laughed with maniacal glee. "*Pirates of the Caribbean: The Curse of the Black Pearl.*"

I should have known—it was one of his favorite movies to quote.

"Good morning, Darcy," Terry Goodwin said with a nod and a curl of his upper lip. He had on a large straw Panama hat and sunglasses while watering flower beds.

Terry even *sounded* like Elvis. It was why he was a recluse, rarely leaving the house without a disguise— with the exception of Halloween. On that day, he went all out with his Elvis-ness. Last year, he'd even held an impromptu concert on the green.

"Darcy!" Cherise said as she came around the corner with a flat of flowers in her gloved hands. "It's taken everything in me not to knock on your door first thing this morning. You must tell us everything about Dorothy. Inquiring minds need to know."

Archie pressed his wings together like he was praying. "Please make this old bird's day and tell me they put her in a straitjacket. Please, please, pretty please?"

"I wish I could," I said, "but I don't know." I gave them the quickest rundown imaginable on Dorothy, then said, "How's Amanda doing?"

Cherise set the flowers at her feet and leaned against the fence. "About what you'd expect. She's in shock, the poor dear, and so far hasn't had much time to grieve. Because of the nature of Leyna's death, Amanda's been thrust into insurance purgatory. Fortunately, Leyna's brother is flying in from Arizona to take care of the funeral plans, so Amanda doesn't have to worry about taking care of those as well. Dennis has been giving her around-the-clock calming spells, and Terry and I have been helping take care of Laurel Grace as much as possible."

Her gaze narrowed on me. "How are you faring, Darcy? You look"—her brows knitted—"anxious."

"Have you been talking to my mother?"

She laughed. "Derrie stopped by this morning with some concerns. But seeing you for myself, I do agree with her that something is off."

"I'm fine," I said. "I promise."

"You do have a lot on your plate these days. The wedding, the investigation, the Renewal . . . I'd be more than happy to give you a calming spell."

Archie said, "I suggest accepting the offer. You don't want to look like an old hag on your wedding day."

I frowned at him. "Thanks for that image."

"I live to serve," he said, lifting off the fence. "I shall be in my cage should anyone need me." He soared over the rooftop and disappeared from sight.

Honestly, a spell would have been wonderful right about now, but I couldn't accept one. When I thought of *why* I couldn't, I shoved all the secrets I was keeping into a dark closet of my mind, slammed the door, and padlocked it. I forced a smile. "You're very kind, Cherise, but I'm okay. I recently cut back on coffee and am living to regret the decision. In fact, I think I might swing by and pick up a nice big cup from the Gingerbread Shack," I lied, rambling along so she would believe all was just fine and dandy in my little world.

Elaborate lies of my own.

She rested her hand on mine. "Perhaps a wise decision would be to cut back on your coffee intake when life is a bit more settled, eh?"

"A very good idea." I knew she couldn't read me through my hand, so I didn't flinch at her touch. "Could you possibly do me a favor?"

"Anything."

"If you talk with Amanda today, could you find out what you can about Vince's reservation at Divinitea the day of the fire?" His presence at the tea shop nagged at me. Why had he been there? Good or evil?

"Is this about Leyna's murder?"

"It could be, but I'm thinking it has more to do with the Renewal."

"Oh dear," she said. "I'll be sure to find out."

"Thanks, Cherise." I glanced at my watch. "I need to get going. I'm off to see if Stef Millet can verify Feif's alibi."

"You be careful out there investigating."

"I will, thanks." I started walking away.

"And Darcy?"

I glanced back at her.

There was a sly smile on her face as she said, "Don't forget that big cup of coffee."

Which made me think that perhaps she knew I'd been lying about the coffee.

Which then made me think she'd been able to read me through that touch on my hand, after all.

If that was true, I hoped she'd keep my secret better than I could.

But as I walked away, I hoped even more that I was imagining her reaction.

It was safer that way.

For both of us.

* * *

The Sorcerer's Stove was busy with the breakfast crowd when I arrived a little after nine o'clock.

Joelle, the hostess, asked, "Table for one?"

I said, "Actually, no, I'm not here to eat. I'm looking for Stef Millet."

"Stef's a popular one this morning," Joelle said, "but she's not here yet."

"Popular?" I asked. "How so?"

Joelle said, "Yeah, some guy was in here earlier looking for her. He was pretty insistent about it, too. After I told him she wouldn't be in until ten, he asked me where she lived. I didn't tell him, of course—that would be against company policy." She fanned herself.

"But I wouldn't mind if he was looking for me, if you know what I mean."

Why did I have the sinking feeling I knew just who she was talking about? "Tall, dark hair, dark eyes, charming smile?"

"How'd you know?" she asked, and then waved a hand. "Better question is, who is he? I might need an introduction."

"Feif Highbridge."

"The psychic?" she asked. "Is he really psychic? Because if so, wouldn't he have known that Stef wasn't here?"

I started to explain his psychic abilities and then decided better of it. "I don't know," I said. "All I know is that he's a slimy womanizer, so don't be deceived by the pretty packaging."

Her face fell. "Damn." Then, after a moment, she wrinkled her nose and softly said, "Might still be worth it . . ."

On that note, I said my goodbye. I wanted to find Stef before Feif did so he didn't have the chance to influence her statement about the events on Saturday. I could just see him trying to charm her into going along with his alibi.

I headed back outside, and in my rush, I nearly smacked straight into Carolyn Honeycutt, who had her phone in one hand and a takeout cup from the Gingerbread Shack in the other.

She spun herself around, slipped her phone into her pocket, and started fast-walking away from me.

At Carolyn's guilty reaction, I instantly decided that Stef could wait. With a kick to my step, I caught up to Carolyn quickly. "Lovely day for a walk, isn't it?"

"Beautiful," she said as she kept up her fast pace.

I matched her steps. "I could walk all day. I don't have anything else planned," I said, lying through my teeth.

I really had to cut back on the lies. They were starting to come much too naturally.

"Fancy running into you," Carolyn said on a heavy sigh, slowing to a stop in front of the village playhouse when she realized she wasn't going to be able to lose me easily. "Feif mentioned that he ran into you this morning."

"Mentioned to you," I said, "or warned you?"

The corner of her lip curled upward before she took a sip of the coffee. Dark liquid dribbled down the side of the cup as she said, "Warned."

"Why didn't you mention your relationship with Feif yesterday?" I asked.

Carolyn pulled her braid forward and started picking at its end. "Well, for one, I was embarrassed to tell you. But mostly it was because I wanted you to take a serious look at Feif. I think he's guilty. He's a snake—"

"And a weasel," I cut in. "And you hate him."

"Yes," Carolyn said emphatically. "This is what I'm saying."

I said, "But yet you slept with him? Are you two dating?"

Carolyn's face morphed into one of disgust. "Dating? No. *Gross.* He's not even good in bed."

I knew quite a few people who were going to be disappointed to hear that.

"And it was only the one time," she said. "I took one for the team, as they say."

"Please explain this all to me," I said to Carolyn. "As concisely as possible, because it's already been a long day even though it's barely past nine, and I haven't had nearly enough coffee."

"It's like this," she began. "I tried to tell Leyna a million times how awful Feif was, but she just wouldn't—or couldn't—hear it. And here she was again, falling for his same old tricks. When I saw her sneak out of his room on Friday morning, I knew I had to do something drastic. I couldn't let her be hurt by him again. I had to *show* her how bad he was. So . . . I slept with him. And"—her cheeks turned red—"I kind of video-recorded it."

Oh. My. "Did you show the video to Leyna?" I asked as I tried to pick my jaw off the ground.

"No. It didn't come to that because before I did, Feif showed her the tour contract, and she flipped out on him."

Fool me once, shame on you, fool me twice . . . Leyna hadn't been as blinded by love the second time around. Her previous heartache had given her some clarity, and I'd have bet a frozen peppermint patty that she'd read his energy when he presented the contract. I couldn't help wondering if that energy had also revealed Feif had slept with her friend hours after he'd slept with her.

It was possible. Had she also read Carolyn's energy when she'd shown up at Divinitea the next day? I knew Carolyn had been in the cottage, thanks to Ve's eyewitness account, but when had she left the premises?

"If we're done here, I need to go," she said. "Things to do. People to see."

"Actually, there is something else you can clarify. Were you in Divinitea around the time the fire broke out?"

Surprise filled her eyes—I'd clearly caught her off guard.

She said, "I was scheduled for a reading, but Leyna never showed up . . ."

"If you were so close to her, why would you have to schedule a reading?"

"Leyna only reads people under certain circumstances. Never outside the realm of a business deal. Well, except for that one time last Thursday, and I know she immediately regretted it, even though she was so overwhelmed with the lady's dark energy she couldn't help herself from speaking up."

Dark energy. "Wait, what?" I asked. "When was this again?"

"Thursday afternoon," Carolyn repeated. "Leyna and I crossed paths with a woman near the Sorcerer's Stove, and the woman spit in Leyna's direction. I would have decked her myself, but Leyna has more restraint. *Had.*" She shook her head. "Anyway, Leyna pulled the woman aside and gave her a reading right then and there."

"Do you know who the woman was?" I asked, already thinking I knew precisely whom she was talking about.

"No. It was an older blonde lady in a skintight dress. Big boobs, big hair, lots of Botox, but she didn't look too healthy."

Dorothy. It had to be.

I said, "Did you hear what Leyna told the woman?"

"I couldn't hear the whole conversation, but I did pick up the words *sick* and *doctor.* I mean, which makes sense, because the woman didn't look well at all. When we left, Leyna said she should have just walked on by altogether, but the woman's dark energy wouldn't let her stay silent since dark energy usually means severe illness or impending death."

I recalled what Ula, the bartender from the Sorcerer's Stove, had said about Dorothy's behavior on Thursday afternoon. How Dorothy had said that if Leyna was joking, she'd kill her with her bare hands.

Had Dorothy said that because Leyna had told her she was ill?

Or was there more to it?

There was no way to know, so I pressed on, trying to get more answers from Carolyn. "Why were you seeking a reading from Leyna on Saturday?" I asked her. "What spurred the reading on *that* day, at *that* time?"

She quickly said, "I wanted Leyna's advice on whether I should quit the festival. The job wasn't the same without her, and though I like the work, I wasn't sure it was for me anymore. I thought if she could read my tea leaves, she'd be able to give me some direction. But she never got the chance."

I'd been thinking that was a discussion to be had with a friend, rather than a psychic, right up until she mentioned the tea leaves. The tea leaves gave her story credibility.

"And did you decide?" I asked. "About the job?"

"I'm tendering my resignation today, effective after this week's festival wraps up. I won't be moving on to the next town with the rest of the troupe."

How much of her decision had been made because she'd slept with Feif? I'd guessed it had played a big role, especially if she was being honest about disliking the man.

If.

Carolyn threw a look toward the village green and all the tents. "Speaking of work, I need to go. Do you have any more questions?"

I couldn't think of any right now. I shook my head.

Carolyn said, "Good," and then walked away, her braid swaying.

As I watched her go, I wondered what to believe, because if I'd learned one thing about Carolyn, it was that she never told the full truth.

I believed the videotape part, but wondered if Feif had known he was being recorded (but perhaps not *why*) and had agreed to it.

The part about Dorothy . . . It jibed with what Ula had told me the other day, but I didn't know how to corroborate the theory. After all, there was no one but Carolyn to even confirm that the conversation had taken place. Dorothy hadn't said anything specifically about being ill to Ula, either.

If she's joking . . .

The thing about Dorothy, however, was that she liked being the center of attention. If she had been pulled aside by Leyna and told she was ill, she wouldn't keep it to herself. Couldn't. My instincts told me she'd revealed that conversation to someone.

Since Dorothy had no friends, no job, was semi-estranged from Glinda, and had a husband who thought she was the devil, that left only one confidant I could think of.

Vince.

Ula had said Dorothy had been sloppy drunk on Thursday. Undoubtedly, Vince had been called to collect his mother. I needed to have another talk with him.

But first, I needed to find Stef. If she could validate Feif's alibi, it'd make my job a little easier. I could have kicked myself for the fact that he even knew about Stef in the first place. If Starla and I hadn't run into him this morning and let Stef's identity slip . . .

I glanced back at the Stove, recalling what Joelle had said about Feif showing up, looking for Stef. My original thought had been that he wanted to charm her, to make sure her version of events matched his.

But what if it didn't?

What if Stef hadn't seen him on Saturday? And refused to play along with his plan to give him an alibi? If he'd killed Leyna and thought Stef was the only thing in the way of his getting off scot-free . . .

What would stop him from trying to silence Stef as well?

Nothing.

Instant panic washed over me, and I broke into a run, telling myself she was fine. Just fine. But the sooner I got to her house and saw that she was okay with my own eyes, the better.

Chapter Eighteen

Stef's garage door was open as I jogged up her drive-way. Her car's engine ticked in the bay, the trunk lifted.

When I saw her step out of the doorway leading from the house into the garage, I let out a breath of relief.

When she saw me, she let out a scream.

"Oh my god!" She grabbed her chest. Then she laughed. "You scared me. Is everything okay?"

"Sorry! I was about to knock. Can I talk to you a minute?"

It looked like Stef had been to the gym at some point this morning. She had on workout leggings, a moisture-wicking T-shirt, and sneakers. Her hair was pulled back in a cloth headband. She tipped her head. "What's going on? Are you okay?"

"Oh, I'm fine. Through As You Wish, I'm looking into Leyna Noble's death for the Goodwin family," I said, just going with the flow of the lies at this point, even though that one had a factual foundation. "They want no stone unturned. You were at the tea shop on Saturday, right?"

She nodded and said, "Let me just grab the rest of these groceries, and I'll tell you everything I know."

I went to help, picking up two reusable bags printed with book quotes from the trunk.

"Excuse the mess," Stef said, nodding into the trunk space. "I tend to throw things in there and then never take them out again. It's like a portable junk drawer."

Stef wasn't kidding about the mess. There was a jumble of plastic grocery bags I assumed were meant for recycling, a couple of crumpled blankets, a pillow, a picnic basket, a laundry basket with clothes in it, a few books, and a spatula. "A spatula?"

She laughed. "I should probably take that inside, but I can't bring myself to do it."

"Why?"

"Most of the stuff in here brings back memories of my husband. The spatula is from the last time we went camping together. The blankets and pillow are from when I spent nights at the hospital with him. The clothes, too. I should clean it all out. My therapist would tell me it's past due, but I just can't bring myself to do it yet." She closed the trunk and led me into the house. "I even tried dating again, but it was too soon."

I said, "With Vince, right?"

She nodded. "He's a nice guy, but I wasn't ready, even for a no-strings relationship."

"How long has your husband been gone?" I asked.

"A little less than a year and a half," she said. "The doctors tried just about everything. God, I'd have done anything to save him."

Understandable. I couldn't imagine if Nick faced a similar diagnosis. It made my stomach roll just thinking about it. "I don't think there's a set time on grief. Eighteen months isn't very long at all."

Stef set her bags on the counter, next to a to-go cup from the Witch's Brew. There was moisture in her eyes as she said, "Sometimes it feels like a lifetime."

I fought the urge to give her a hug and instead focused on all the pictures she had stuck to the fridge. "How long were you together? You look like little kids in some of these photos. Is that one from a prom?"

It was one of those matte-finished shots under an arch of blue and maroon balloons. She'd been wearing a long, poofy pink gown, and he'd been in a tux with a pink tie and cummerbund. She stared up at him with adoration in her eyes as he grinned at the camera. Her profile, with her hair pulled back in an updo, reminded me of someone, but I couldn't quite place who.

"We were high school sweethearts and married right after college. It would have been twenty years this year. It's a long time to love someone, and I'm grateful for that. But I just wish there had been more time together."

My skin tingled at the wish, but I couldn't grant wishes for time.

"And no, no kids," Stef added, turning away from the pictures.

"Okay," I said, since it seemed so important to her.

"Sorry. Since people tend to ask, it's become second nature to just tell."

I smiled. "I'm sure that gets annoying."

"Beyond." She took off the top of the cup, poured its dregs in the sink, rinsed the tea leaves stuck to the basin, and then went about unpacking the bags. "Now that I've given you my whole life story, what is it you wanted to talk to me about?"

"Feif Highbridge," I said.

"The psychic? He's a gorgeous man, isn't he? He might be able to convince me to give dating another try."

"No!"

She laughed. "I was just joking. Psychics give me the willies—I don't want anyone reading my mind. That's just creepy. But by your reaction, I'm guessing I should steer clear of him altogether."

I nodded. "Definitely, but that might be easier said than done. He's been looking for you this morning. He hasn't been by, has he?"

"No. I haven't seen him—I've been out since sevenish. I swear one of these days I'm going to find a nice, late-afternoon exercise class. I stopped at the Witch's Brew after the gym, then went grocery shopping. I didn't see him at any of those places, either. Why would he be looking for me?" She set a container of strawberries on the counter. "I don't understand."

"Long story short," I said, "Feif is a possible suspect in Leyna's murder."

"I thought Dorothy is in custody?"

"She *is* in custody," I said, "but she hasn't been arrested. She's on an emergency psych hold."

Stef nodded and carried the strawberries and a sixpack of yogurt to the fridge. "I heard that this morning at the Witch's Brew. I wasn't sure what that meant for the case, though. But now you think Feif might have killed Leyna? Did they even know each other?"

"They had a business relationship that ended badly, and he was inside Divinitea when the fire broke out. His alibi is that he was hiding in an alcove in the hallway when the alarms sounded and the sprinklers went off. He said you could verify his alibi."

Her face clouded with confusion. "Me? He really said that?"

I folded the reusable bag she'd emptied. "He told us he saw you on your way back from the restroom and you smiled at him. Did you? See him, I mean?"

Stef tossed the empty to-go cup in the recycling bin and shook her head. "No. I didn't see anyone but Ve on that trip to the restroom. We talked about your wedding for a minute, but that's it. Why would Feif lie?"

"Grasping at straws. I'm guessing he was planning to use his charms to get you to corroborate his alibi. He's really persuasive, apparently."

"I'm not one to be swayed by charm."

"Well, keep that in mind if he does show up. And call Nick or me, too, if he does."

"But, Darcy, if Feif *is* guilty, what does that mean for Dorothy and her psych hold? Is she going to be let out of the hospital?"

"She still has to complete the seventy-two-hour hold," I said, "but after that she'll be free to go."

"I hope while she's in there she gets the help she needs. She's been acting . . . bizarrely lately. More than just the drinking, I mean."

"What have you noticed?" I asked.

She unpacked another bag as she said, "Strange things like talking to herself, pulling out her hair, swatting at things that are only visible to her. Beyond the mental issues, I saw a lot of the same signs in her I saw in my husband when he was ill. Losing weight, sweating, thinning hair. I asked her once if she'd been to see a doctor lately, and she nearly bit my head off. She doesn't like me."

"She doesn't like anyone," I said. "So don't take it personally."

"I don't," she said. "Everyone at the Stove warned me about her personality. Honestly, I don't know what's going on with Dorothy, but I will say that even some of her mental symptoms troubled me. When my husband's cancer spread to his brain, he wasn't himself anymore."

I stiffened, suddenly worried. I knew of another case with similar symptoms that had drastically changed a man's personality. I hadn't connected the two before, because Dorothy was a naturally cruel person. But if she had a medical issue, the recent, overly aggressive changes in her behavior made a lot more sense.

Stef added, "I hate to say it, but when this is all said and done, I wouldn't be the least bit surprised to find out that Dorothy is gravely ill."

*　*　*

As I opened the door to the Bewitching Boutique, I wanted nothing more than to clear my mind of everything that had to do with murder and evilness to focus on my wedding. To feel only the joy this fitting should bring me.

But I couldn't separate the subjects, because this appointment wasn't just for a dress fitting.

It was also to hear a report on a covert operation.

The boutique was empty of customers, and Godfrey Baleaux greeted me with open arms. "Darcy, my love, let me look at you."

I smiled at him. This was his usual greeting, but his once-over wasn't anything more than a reason to judge my outfit. I took in his as well. As usual, he was dressed impeccably in a tailored suit and tie, complete with a pocket square. He had slimmed down since I'd first met him, but still carried a slight paunch and full cheeks. His white hair was combed back off his face, and his beard was neatly trimmed. Kind eyes assessed me, and a hint of a smile lurked on his lips.

He wiggled his hand side to side. "Fair to middling."

"You've got to be kidding me." I looked down at myself. "What can possibly be wrong with my outfit?"

I had on a pair of cuffed ankle-length jeans and a blouse he'd picked out for me. The sandals were leather, broken in, and so help me if he zapped them away.

"That blouse is so last year. I have something much better." He rushed me into his workshop at the back of the store, closed the drapes behind us, waved his hand, and said, "Ta-da!"

I blinked back tears as he turned me toward the mirror, where a bride stared back at me. I tried to take the dress in, all in one glance. The lace bodice with delicate cap sleeves, the sweeping A-line skirt made of silk and chiffon, a thin silk belt at the waist.

My hands went to the bateau neckline first, gently touching the hand-tatted lace at my collarbones. I turned to the side and gasped at the low-cut open back. "It's perfect," I said on a whisper.

I heard a tiny sob behind me and turned to find Mrs. P on the sewing table, Pepe's handkerchief at her eyes. "Doll, I've never seen anyone so beautiful in my life."

"Aw, thank you, Mrs. P. Anyone could be beautiful in this dress. It's a work of art. Thank you, Godfrey; thank you, Pepe."

"*Ma chère*," Pepe said with a bow. "The dress is not nearly as beautiful as the one wearing it."

I kissed his head, then Mrs. P's.

Godfrey coughed.

I kissed his cheek, too.

I turned back to the mirror, swinging my body left, then right, admiring the way the dress swirled around my legs. I might have leaked a tear when picturing Nick's reaction to seeing me walking down the aisle. "It's perfect. I couldn't have asked for anything more. I can't thank you all enough."

"Seeing you happy is thanks enough," Godfrey said. "It is all we have ever wished for you."

They all nodded, and I blinked away more tears as I thought about the family I'd gained since moving to this village. People who held huge places in my heart, and it didn't matter one little bit that we weren't blood relatives.

"Now," Godfrey said, eyeing me critically, "it seems you've gained a pound or two since I took measurements."

I pasted on a fake smile. "I'm sure the banana milk shakes I'm addicted to aren't helping things any."

There was often a blurry line between secrets and lies, I decided.

"Time to stop partaking in those shakes, Darcy m'dear. If you gain so much as another ounce, you must let me know immediately. That lace bodice is unforgiving."

I laughed. "You're giving me a whole ounce? Very generous of you."

He scratched at his bearded chin. "Okay, *two* ounces."

"I'm surprised he's allowing you a full exhale," Mrs. P said, laughing.

Godfrey threw her a dark look. "I'm not savage."

Pepe twirled his mustache and said, "*Non?*"

Godfrey took a step toward him, fists raised. "Do you want to take this outside?"

Pepe handed his glasses to Mrs. P. "Right here will do."

I stepped between them. "Now, now, I don't want any blood on this dress. You two have been doing so well getting along lately. What's brought on these quick tempers? Is it this dress? Please tell me you haven't been at each other's throats over my gown."

"It's not your gown, doll. It's the—yow!" She turned to Pepe. "Did you just step on my tail?"

"Did I? My deepest apologies, *mon amour.*" He kissed her hand up to her elbow.

I'd have bet this dress that she was going to say something about the Coven meetings or the Renewal. Harper was right about needing more transparency within the Craft. The shroud of secrecy was fine when dealing with mortals, but within the world of witches, there should be more clarity.

Mrs. P batted her eyes at him. "You're forgiven."

"Sucker," Godfrey murmured.

Pepe threw his fists up. I sighed, reached over, and forced them down. He adjusted his vest, gave Godfrey the evil eye, and said, "My apologies."

Godfrey sat on a stool. "You should be sorry, for that show of PDA. *Blech.*"

Pepe's hand-kissing wasn't nearly as nauseating as Feif's, thank goodness, because Godfrey would lose his mind if I hoiked while in this dress. "Now you're just asking for him to take a bite out of you," I said.

"He is simply jealous," Pepe said with a sniff.

Godfrey pouted. "Perhaps a bit."

I patted his cheek. "Someone will come along soon enough."

His eyes twinkled. "I wish it to be so."

I laughed as I cast the wish into the ether. I couldn't grant wishes for love, but there was no rule about finding a girlfriend. It would be my mother, however, who decided the fate of his love life.

"Are you ready to take it off?" Godfrey asked, gesturing to the dress.

I looked back to the mirror, and suddenly next Saturday couldn't come soon enough.

Reluctantly, I nodded. He waved a hand, and a second later, I was back in my normal clothes. My dress was nowhere to be seen. "Where'd it go?"

"I'm keeping it under lock and key," he said.

"And my shoes! Where are they?" My sandals were gone, replaced with leather ballet flats with a pointy toe.

Godfrey shrugged. "Must have been lost in the shuffle. This magic stuff is not a science, you know."

I growled at him, knowing he was feeding me a line. He knew exactly where those shoes had gone.

"No big loss," Pepe said. "They were well past their life span."

"Not you, too!" I turned on him.

He gave a gentle shrug. "Some things must be said that are difficult to hear."

I suddenly felt like Mimi had this morning about life lessons. I pulled up a stool to the sewing table and sat. "Those sandals have seen me through these last couple of days, chasing leads all over this village."

"I'll be sure to give the sandals a dignified burial," Godfrey said. His head came up when the bell on the door chimed and he excused himself.

Mrs. P sat on the edge of the table, dangling her tail. "Is there any news about Leyna's murder?"

"Not much," I said. "Feif and Carolyn Honeycutt seem to be having a competition about who can lie more than the other." I filled them in on all I knew so far. "Now, tell me, how did you two fare in searching Feif's room?" The two of them had gone during the night, while he was asleep. "Did anything jump out at you?"

Pepe said, "Only the portfolio."

I scooted closer to the table. "What portfolio?"

Mrs. P rubbed her hands together. "A brown leather portfolio on the desk had contracts in it."

"Please tell me you read them," I said.

"Indeed we did read it, by the light of the moon," Pepe said.

Mrs. P added, "It was rather romantic, except for Feif's snoring. And the fact that the legal mumbo jumbo made my eyes cross."

She crossed her eyes for full effect, and I smiled. So much for romantic.

Pepe adjusted his glasses and said, "The information within the portfolio was quite enlightening."

"Well, enlighten me, please," I said. "Carolyn told me that Feif wanted Leyna back because the festival's revenue was down without her. Supposedly the new contract was to entice Lenya into going on the road with Feif, breaking with the festival altogether. Did the contract show that to be true?"

Pepe ran his fingers over his mustache, twisting the ends. "Not quite."

Mrs. P's ear twitched. "Miss Carolyn told you Feif owned the festival, did she not, doll?"

"She did."

She jabbed a finger in the air. "Another lie."

Pepe said, "A half lie, really."

"It's still a lie," she said.

They were making me dizzy. "If not that, what did the contract say?"

Pepe rested his tiny hands on his round belly. "The contract stated that yes, in fact, Feif proposed taking his and Leyna's show on the road."

"But!" Mrs. P interjected. "It wasn't just the two of them."

Pepe picked up where she left off. "Feif Highbridge was not the sole owner of the festival. There's an unnamed majority owner, listed as Kindred Tours, LLC."

Kindred Tours? I'd never heard of it. "Any other information? An address? Phone number?"

Pepe's ears jiggled as he shook his head. "*Non.*"

I drummed my fingers on the tabletop, letting my gaze drift over the display of colorful ribbons. "I really wish Feif would show his face. He could answer so many of these questions."

"But, doll, would he answer them truthfully?"

"Doubtful," I answered, and stood up. "I'll ask Nick to look into who owns the LLC."

Mrs. P nodded. "He's much more trustworthy."

He absolutely was.

I kissed Pepe's and Mrs. P's heads again. "Thank you, guys. For everything."

Mrs. P smiled. "Anytime, doll. Just holler."

As I headed back outside, I thought about the LLC and tried to feel more positive about the new lead. But as I futilely searched the green once again for Feif, I couldn't help feeling like I was getting nowhere fast with this case.

Chapter Nineteen

"I knew that Feif was bad business," Harper said as she sliced open a cardboard box with a box cutter. "You need to learn to trust my instincts more."

I didn't know how she hadn't yet cut off a finger. She wielded that box cutter like it was a dull butter knife.

I sat on a couch in Spellbound, willing my stomach to settle. I'd stopped by Lotions and Potions to see if Vince was around, but he wasn't; then I had gone to the Pixie to see if Carolyn or Feif was there and had no luck with that endeavor, either. I'd even tried to find Andreus to ask him about the mystery stone, but he was out somewhere with Ve.

The village was feeling like a ghost town all of a sudden.

Finding myself with some free time before meeting Nick for our lunch date, I'd come by to see Harper. I'd just finished telling her about my morning with Carolyn and Stef. "What I need to learn is to not stop by here to say hello to you. You're giving me a headache."

The bookstore's decor was *Starry Night* meets Tim Burton. Iron bookshelves in the shape of trees covered the walls, and freestanding bookcases were made of raw lumber, most of which still had its bark. Bold blues and yellows blended on the walls, the colors bright yet soothing, powerful yet warm and inviting.

Harper unpacked the latest mystery releases. "You didn't stop in to say hello. You stopped in to kill time. And you've had that headache for days. It might be time to see Cherise about it."

I stretched out my legs. "Killing time *by* saying hello."

"Diversion," she singsonged. "You should see Cherise."

"Maybe I will," I said to appease her.

Harper pointed the box cutter at me. "Are you just saying that to appease me?"

I was well and truly regretting coming here. "Of course."

"You're infuriating."

Sometimes, when the stars aligned just so, our roles reversed and she became the mother hen and I the beleaguered chick.

"But you love me," I said, batting my eyelashes.

"Not at this moment, but usually, yes."

I laughed. "If the headache isn't gone for good by tomorrow, I'll see Cherise."

"Promise?"

"Promise."

"Okay." She nodded as she scanned bar codes. "Now I'm assuming you went by Feif's tent to question him again after Stef didn't corroborate his alibi. What did he have to say for himself?"

"He said nothing, because he wasn't at his tent."

"Really? I thought he was supposed to open at ten."

It didn't surprise me in the least that she knew his hours. "So far, he's a no-show today. After lunch,

Glinda and I are going to go back to the Pixie to see if he's returned. Stake it out if we have to." He could be laying low on purpose. According to his fans in line yesterday, he was notorious for showing up late to his tent, which I thought was a ploy to drum up excitement among those waiting to see him.

No wonder Archie adored him. They shared a flair for the dramatic.

"Will you come back here after you meet with him and tell me what he says?" Harper asked.

"I'll see what I can do."

"Should I remind you that's it's my birthday tomorrow?"

I didn't need the reminder. "Tomorrow. Not today."

"Consider it an early birthday present."

Yep. Definite regret for stopping by. "Fine," I said.

She grinned. Then her smile faltered.

"What is it?" I asked, suddenly concerned.

She looked all around, then came over to me. "I went back and read the section in that book, you know the book, about the Renewal again."

The book. *Witchcraft: A Crafted History.* Harper had found it in the basement last year and had read it cover to cover.

My pulse jumped in my throat. I didn't bother to ask her why she'd picked up the book once again— when her mind was troubled by something, she researched the matter until there was no stone uncovered.

"There's not too much written about the Renaissance, other than it relates to a promissory oath and an heir apparent. It was all so vague." Her big brown eyes were clouded with apprehension. "You don't think it's possible Mom could be replaced tomorrow night, do you? And what is that part about an heir apparent? That's usually reserved for monarchies."

I panicked for a moment, but then I realized this situation fell into yet another Craft loophole. My oath of secrecy prevented me from talking about Renewal traditions with Harper; however, there was nothing forbidding her from figuring out the truth *on her own*. "I don't know," I said hesitantly. "What do *you* think?"

"I'm not sure." She absently ran a hand over her rounded stomach. "But it sounds to me like the next person in line for the Eldership has to make a vow to take over some day in order for the current Elder to be renewed."

I bit back a smile.

"But do we even know how Elders are chosen?" she asked. "This is why we need more transparency in our world. How'd Mom get the job?"

I was saved from answering by a text from Nick. He was finishing up some paperwork, then would be heading out. It was such a beautiful day, we were going to picnic on the green. I texted that I'd pick up lunch at the Stove and be there soon. "I need to get going," I said, holding up the phone.

"I'll keep looking into the Elder thing," Harper said.

I stood up. "Let me know what you find."

"And don't forget your promise."

"To see Cherise?"

She sighed. "To come back here and fill me in about Feif."

"Did I promise that?" I asked with a smile.

She rolled her eyes, and I waved as I headed out the door. As I crossed the street, no one but me probably noticed that my steps were just a little bit lighter.

My heart, too.

For the first time in a long time, I really believed everything with the Eldership was going to work out just as it was supposed to.

Then I checked myself, and nearly tripped over my own feet.

I was doing it again. Putting what I wanted, my hopes, above what Harper might want. Just because she was easing back into the Craft didn't mean she'd accept the Eldership.

And if she didn't want the role, then that was her decision to make. It was her life. Her happiness.

And happiness was all I'd ever truly wanted for her.

Right then and there, I vowed that I would respect and accept whatever decision Harper made.

But I also couldn't help wishing that all this worrying had been for nothing—that the fates had stepped in to save the Craft as we knew it.

Secrets.

I wished it with all my heart.

* * *

I was almost across the green when I caught sight of Vince in the crowd. He was fast-walking toward the other end of the village. I hesitated only a second before deciding to go after him. I wanted to ask him about Dorothy, and if she'd mentioned to him that Leyna had told her she was ill.

As I passed Feif's tent, I saw that it was still closed up tight. I was beginning to suspect he *had* skipped town. Perhaps shortly after not finding Stef this morning.

Hurrying along, I tried to keep Vince's long, floppy hair in sight. He was tall, which made keeping an eye on him easier, but he was walking faster than I was and quickly losing me.

I issued apologies left and right as I bumped into people in my haste, and tried not to breathe in too many fried-dough fumes. I wasn't going to be the least bit sorry when the festival packed up and left town in two days.

By the time the crowd thinned, I'd lost sight of Vince. Disappointed, I glanced left and right, and decided to take my chances that he was getting lunch at the Stove, too. I rushed that way, and was so focused on the Stove's entryway that I nearly ran straight past Vince. He sat on the edge of the village green across the street from a charred Divinitea.

I stopped comically short, flailing my arms before setting myself to rights.

"Graceful," he commented.

I sat next to him on the grass. "I blame the shoes. They're new."

"Cute."

"Thanks. I'll be sure to tell Godfrey. He zapped them onto me earlier and sent my sandals into an early grave."

Vince smiled. "He tried to get my ripped jeans from me once, and we almost came to blows."

"He takes fashion very seriously."

"I take those jeans seriously. It took me nearly a year to get them broken in just right."

"You're preaching to the choir, but I've learned when to pick my battles."

He slid me a look. "I know."

He did know. I'd fought like crazy to nurture our friendship. To try to get him to see the light when it came to the Craft. To realize that he was more than he was giving himself credit for.

I said, "I've been looking all over the village for you. You know what would have been an easier way to get in touch with you? A cell phone. I'm just sayin'."

"I've been running errands all day."

"Where?" I asked as innocently as I could. "I really searched for you. No one has seen you around today."

"I've got one of those faces. I blend in."

"*Vince.*"

"All right, fine. I went to see Dorothy."

My eyes widened. "You did? Did you see Glinda there? She went too."

"Must have just missed her. If I knew she was going, we could've gone together."

"Maybe if you had a cell phone . . ."

He rolled his eyes.

I said, "Well, how is Dorothy? Did she say anything? And by *anything*, I mean did she confess to *this*?" I gestured across the road.

"It was a waste of my time. They didn't let me see her. Said no outside contact while she's under emergency evaluation."

So it had probably been a wasted trip for Glinda as well.

"But," Vince added, "I don't think Dorothy did *this*, for what it's worth."

I glanced at Divinitea. Other than the bright plywood covering the doors and windows and the blue tarp on the roof, it was covered in black soot. "But *could* she have done it? Using black magic?"

He pushed his glasses up his nose. "It's possible but not probable. I knew she'd been dabbling, but I didn't realize how immersed she'd become in the dark arts until yesterday when I heard about Sylar's attempt to give you and Glinda an exorcism. If I'd known, I would have tried to stop her."

"Sylar burned a bunch of sorcery books yesterday—you didn't give those to Dorothy?"

"No. I don't know where she got them. I haven't used black magic in months, but all my books are accounted for."

"So, you didn't teach her anything about black magic? Nothing? She didn't come to you looking to learn?"

His eyes narrowed. "Darcy, you don't understand. You don't go looking for black magic. It finds *you*."

I shuddered. "What does that mean?"

"It's born of powerlessness, rage, and hatred. It grows stronger in tandem with those emotions. And it doesn't leave you until those emotions are resolved."

I was trying to wrap my head around what he was saying and why, exactly, it sounded like a warning. Finally, I said, "Dorothy's going to come out of that psychiatric facility with more sorcery power than ever before, isn't she?"

"I'm afraid so."

"Can she escape if she wanted?" I asked. "Knock out a wall, that kind of thing?"

"I doubt she has the capabilities yet to do that, but I wouldn't put it past her to try. She's not going to sit idly by. Especially not with the Renewal tomorrow night."

I didn't know where to go with that quite yet, so I said, "Why would she turn to black magic now? What pushed her over the edge? Because she's always been bitter and angry and full of hate."

"I'm not sure," he said. "It's like a switch was flipped a few months ago, where the rage and hatred started to consume her. Whether it was marriage issues, stress with the Renewal, or her drinking is anyone's guess."

Or all three, I supposed. That was a lot for someone to take on.

My gaze drifted back to the tea shop. "So, why do you think that Dorothy didn't kill Leyna?"

"A few reasons."

"I'm listening."

"One, Dorothy was hammered Saturday afternoon. I don't think someone can fake drunk like that, but for the sake of argument, let's say she *did* fake it."

"Okay."

"That leads us to reason two. Strangulation. If, like we suspect, Dorothy was so far down the rabbit hole of black magic, she wouldn't have strangled Leyna. She would have lit Leyna on fire like some sort of black-magic effigy and watched her burn."

Oh dear lord.

"Three, there would be no need for an accelerant. Dorothy can shoot fire from her fingertips—that whole cottage would have been up in flames with a flick of her wrist. No oil needed."

He was sticking fingers in the air like Harper had done on Saturday afternoon, except she had been talking about wedding planning and he was talking about something that was making me break out in a cold sweat.

"Four, she would have disabled the sprinklers. Five, she wouldn't have taken the hairpin—and if she did, she wouldn't have kept it on her person to be found by the police. She's not stupid. Six, she would have made sure you and Harper were in the building before she lit it up."

My heart pounded as I reached over and forced his hands down. "I get it."

"That's all I had, anyway."

My heart raced. "Compelling."

"I think so too."

While my brain raked over all his reasons, one in particular stuck out to me.

Six, she would have made sure you and Harper were in the building before she lit it up.

He sounded so sure, as though he'd been expecting it to happen.

I studied his profile as I suddenly recalled how he'd been insistent on keeping his reservation that day. "Did you suspect Dorothy might try to do something to hurt us at Divinitea on Saturday? Is that why you were there at the time of my bridal luncheon? And why you wouldn't cancel that reservation?"

He fidgeted. "Let's just say I wasn't comfortable with you, Harper, Amanda, and Leyna all being under Divinitea's roof at the same time."

I bumped him with my shoulder. "You wanted to be there to *protect* us." It wasn't a question. I already knew the answer.

"Don't make a big deal about it," he said, rolling his eyes. "Women. *Sheesh.*"

I smiled at him.

"Stop that smiling right now."

I thought about the Craft books on his coffee table, and suddenly I heard Hildie's voice echoing in my head.

Out of darkness, there comes light.

She'd been talking about him. I was sure of it—felt it straight to my soul. Vince had found his way out of the darkness and had come into the light. It made me want to cry with happiness.

He said, "Oh my god, if you don't stop smiling at me, I'm going to leave."

I pressed my lips together, but I could still feel the corners of my mouth pulling upward.

He looked my way and shook his head, but I noticed he was holding back a smile as well. I took a minute just to enjoy this moment, because I knew we still had more to talk about regarding Dorothy.

For now, I wanted to bask in this happiness. I closed my eyes and turned my face to the sun, breathing in deep. When a cloud passed by, casting my face into shadows, I opened my eyes, and the first thing I saw was the blackened exterior of Divinitea.

"Could you have stopped Dorothy?" I asked. "If she had attacked us on Saturday?"

"I would have tried."

I nodded. "I appreciate that."

"You and Harper are pains in my backside, but I've kind of grown attached to you both. And don't you start smiling again, so help me."

"Fine." I waited a few seconds and then said, "Is there a way to stop black magic?"

"There aren't ways to stop it, necessarily, but ways to protect yourself from it. There's one talisman in particular that will protect a single person. I heard about it years ago while visiting a hole-in-the-wall black-magic shop in New Orleans. It would be of little help if Dorothy goes off on the whole village."

"So, what else can we do?" I asked, trying not to think of the whole village on fire.

"Our best option is to keep her in the treatment facility as long as possible. Maybe she can resolve some anger issues while she's there."

How did one resolve decades of anger in a few days or weeks? Dorothy had always had the anger in her, but something had released it recently. Was it even possible to go back to the way she was?

I thought about what Stef had said earlier, about Dorothy looking ill. "There's been some talk that Dorothy might be sick. Leyna apparently gave her a reading and warned her to see a doctor. Did Dorothy say anything to you about it? You picked her up from the Stove on Thursday, right?"

He swiped hair off his forehead, but it immediately flopped back. His eyebrows were drawn low, and intensity radiated from his eyes. "When I picked Dorothy up at the Stove that day, she was babbling about Leyna and sickness. I thought she had been hallucinating. Leyna really gave her a reading?"

I explained what Carolyn had told me, and added, "Apparently, despite their feud, Leyna couldn't walk past Dorothy without saying something about her dark energy."

"She shouldn't have wasted her time. The dark energy can be explained by the black magic."

"Except in the world of empaths, dark energy means severe illness or even impending death," I said as gently as I could.

His jaw jutted, and I could practically feel the tension coming off his body in pulsating waves. News like that had to be hard to hear. Dorothy was his mother, after all. Not a particularly good mother, but that hardly mattered to a son who loved her, flaws and all.

After a long minute, he said, "Do you know if Leyna said anything about poison?"

"Poison? No, not that I know of, but Carolyn admitted she couldn't hear the whole conversation. Why?"

"In Dorothy's ramblings that day, she talked about someone poisoning her. She was angry—because she wasn't told *who* was doing it. I thought she was just jabbering—I didn't take her seriously. She's been talking crazy and being paranoid for months. Is it possible Leyna told her that she was being poisoned?"

I thought again about what Ula had told me Dorothy had been muttering at the bar that day.

If Leyna's joking, I'll kill her with my bare hands.

Had she been talking about learning that someone was poisoning her? I sat up straighter. "If Leyna picked up on the fact that Dorothy was being poisoned, she wouldn't have been able to say who was doing it. She would only be able to sense the toxin in Dorothy's system."

"*If,*" he said.

"If," I echoed. "But it does have the ring of truth to it, doesn't it?"

"I'm not sure." He shrugged.

I grabbed his arm. "Oh my gosh, I know how we can find out."

"How?"

"Dorothy's hair."

He wiggled his arm free. "The hospital is not going to give you her hair."

I smiled and stood up. "It doesn't need to. I have another source."

"Do I even want to know?"

"Amanda Goodwin. Long story short, she and Leyna bribed a hairdresser to steal Dorothy's hair for the spell they needed to protect Divinitea. Amanda has extra. Hair, that is."

"You witches are crazy." He stood up in one fluid motion.

"Hey, you're a witch, too."

"Yeah, yeah."

"We need to let Nick know about this right away." And I'd text Glinda as well.

"I'll let you handle that. I'm going to try and find some other ways to protect against black magic. There has to be something mentioned in one of my books."

I needed to know what I was up against, so I took a deep breath and said, "Do you think that Dorothy will try to harm Harper and me? When she gets out?"

He wouldn't look me in the eye as he said, his voice low, "Rage and hatred."

I took that as a yes.

He started walking away. "Be careful, Darcy. Keep an eye on Harper, too. I'll check in with you tomorrow."

"Hey Vince?"

He turned back to me. "Yeah?"

"It didn't escape my notice earlier when you said you hadn't practiced black magic in months."

"It wasn't supposed to escape your notice. What kind of investigator would you be if you missed that?"

I ignored the teasing and said, "So no more rage and powerlessness and hatred?"

He tipped his head side to side as if weighing the question. "No more rage and powerlessness. I'm working on the hatred."

222   Heather Blake

Concern shot through me. "Who is it that you hate, Vince?"

The breeze ruffled his hair, and the sun brightened sad blue eyes hiding behind his glasses. He gave me a weak smile. "You already know the answer to that question, Darcy."

With that, he turned and strode off.

I took a deep breath and willed my heart not to break in half.

I had only suspected, but hadn't known for sure until I'd seen the truth in his eyes just now.

The person Vince hated was . . . himself.

He might have come out of the darkness, but he was still looking for the light.

* * *

As I walked into the Sorcerer's Stove, the soft tones of classical music and the aroma of garlic-tossed french fries and chocolate hung in the air. A large board near the hostess stand proclaimed chocolate torte was today's special dessert—and the fries were one of the Stove's best menu items.

With the way my stomach had been feeling, the combination of aromas should have been nauseating, but suddenly, garlic and chocolate didn't seem a terrible pairing.

My stomach was a fickle beast these days.

Taking a deep breath, I pressed onward, toward the end of the bar where takeout orders were placed. Ula smiled when she spotted me and held up a be-right-there finger as she set a tumbler of golden liquid in front of Sylar Dewitt, who sat at the far end of the counter.

His head hanging low, he was too busy staring at his napkin to notice me.

I felt someone sidle up next to me at the counter. Stef.

She motioned with her chin toward Sylar. "He's been like that for half an hour. That's his third drink."

I hadn't seen him in here in months. Probably because he'd been avoiding Dorothy, who'd made the Stove her primary hangout. I couldn't blame him for dodging her, not really. Especially when he believed her to be a devil woman.

Do you know if Leyna said anything about poison?

Vince's voice suddenly echoed in my head. The more the word *poison* ricocheted, the more I believed that not only was it possible Dorothy had been poisoned but *probable*. The fine hairs on the back of my neck rose. I was learning that witchy instincts were often just as reliable as cold, hard facts.

The sooner the lab tests on Dorothy's hair could be completed, the better, because the mortal world lived by tried-and-true proof. Instincts weren't going to cut it in a court of law. Scientific evidence of poison would turn the case in a different direction, making Dorothy a victim rather than a suspect.

Or, perhaps, both . . .

The questions still remained, however, of who had poisoned her and why.

My gaze slid back to Sylar. He certainly had motive to get rid of her . . .

He glanced up, caught me watching him, and blanched. He looked quickly away, intent on studying the liquid in his glass. As sweat popped up on his forehead, he shifted in his seat as though suddenly uncomfortable.

Stef's eyebrows arched. "He doesn't seem too happy to see you."

"I get that a lot when I'm asking people questions they don't want to answer."

"You've questioned him?"

Apparently she hadn't heard about the holy water incident. "A little."

Her blue eyes widened. "Do you think he had something to do with what happened to Leyna?"

"I'm not sure," I said honestly.

She leaned an elbow on the counter. "Have you always done investigations through your business? I thought a concierge company would be less . . . dangerous."

Sometimes I forgot she hadn't lived in the village all that long—she hadn't been here the first time I'd snooped into a murder. Sylar had been a suspect in that crime. Sometimes, I reflected, life came full circle.

"It's a long story." One I couldn't fully explain, because she wasn't a Crafter. "But most of my work is fairly tame. After I get back from my honeymoon, my tasks will include helping a high school senior with college applications, tracking down a rare book, and buying a birthday gift for a client's picky aunt. Hopefully there won't be any more *investigations* for a good, long while."

Tucking a loose strand of hair behind her ear, she said, "Do you do interior design, by any chance?"

I sat up straight and smiled as I quoted my business motto. "At As You Wish, no job is too big or too small. Why?"

"My condo is so blah, and I'm hopeless when it comes to making decisions. I'd love some help. Do you have time soon?"

"Probably not for another couple of weeks. Do you want to make an appointment?"

"Definitely," she said.

I made a note on my phone with a day and time. I'd transfer it over to my planner when I went home.

"Are you ready to order, Darcy?" Ula asked as she approached.

She slid a mug of coffee in front of Stef, who thanked her, took a long sip, and let out a deep breath.

I tried not to be jealous over a cup of coffee.

I placed the lunch order, choosing only those garlic fries and my usual banana milk shake—what Godfrey didn't know wouldn't hurt him—for myself and two sandwiches, fries, and a soda for Nick.

"Would you like the shake to sip on while you wait for the rest of the order?" Ula asked.

I bobbed my head and rubbed my hands together. "Please. And thank you."

Stef laughed. "I need to talk management into putting that drink on the menu."

"Well, you know you have at least one steady customer." I looked over at Sylar. He dabbed at his forehead with a napkin and kept glancing at the door. "Do you know if Sylar is waiting for someone?"

"I'm not sure," she said. "But *I* am. A catering appointment." She glanced at her watch. "Who's now five minutes late."

As the scent of coffee rose enticingly, my gaze lingered on her mug. It took all my effort not to lean over to breathe in the steam.

"Would you like a cup of coffee, Darcy? I can get you one."

"No—no thanks," I said, shaking my head. "It's just . . ."

Her eyebrows dipped low. "What?"

"I'm trying to cut back on coffee is all. Loving coffee makes that really difficult."

She laughed. "I can't even imagine. I drink five or six cups a day."

"No need to rub it in," I joked.

She slid her mug away from me. "I'll just remove temptation."

"I take it Feif hasn't shown up here again today?"

She shook her head. "Not that I've seen. You haven't found him yet?"

As the blender whirred in the background, I said, "He seems to have vanished this morning."

"On the run? That doesn't seem like the behavior of an innocent man, does it? Oh, there's my appointment." She set her mug behind the counter and signaled to Ula that she was heading to her office. "I'll see you later, Darcy. I'll let you know if I see Feif."

As she rushed off, I looked down the bar top at Sylar, who was still dabbing his face with a napkin. Sweating profusely at the sight of me didn't seem like the behavior of an innocent man, either.

I headed his way, and the closer I got, the more he perspired. I sat on the empty barstool next to his. "Hi, Sylar."

"Darcy." He nodded, fidgeting on the stool.

Ula slid my shake in front of me, and I thanked her. I took a sip, nearly moaned at how good it tasted, and then said to him, "How're you doing?"

"As long as Dorothy's locked away, I'm fine." He kept dabbing his forehead and cheeks, his actions belying his words. "She's not getting out early, is she?"

Not unless she *broke* out. It was a thought that almost caused me to start sweating as badly as Sylar. I wrapped my hands around the cold drink, and suddenly realized Ula had put it in a glass and not a to-go cup. She was busy with another customer, so I let it go for now. "No," I said to him. "She's not getting out early."

Hopefully I sounded more confident than I felt.

"Good, good," he said, more to himself than me. "That gives me some time."

"Time for what?"

"To get out of town."

"I knew you wanted to leave, but so soon?" I asked.

"As quickly as I can." He looked toward the door. "I'm waiting for Noelle Quinlan. She's meeting me about selling my house. She assures me it'll sell quickly."

No doubt about that—unless Dorothy burned it to the ground first.

As troubling as that thought was, I couldn't shake what Vince had said about the possibility of Dorothy being poisoned. Then something Sylar had said the other day came back to me.

I should have seen it coming, with the way she was talking crazy on Friday night. I found her up in the damn tree again.

What if she had gone there not only to spy on him—but to confront him? Had *she* suspected he'd been the one poisoning her? It was an easy leap to make—I'd done it myself a few moments ago.

I pushed the glass back and forth between my palms. "You said you spoke to Dorothy Friday night . . ."

Dab, dab. "Yes?"

"Behind your shop, right?"

"Yes? What's this about, Darcy?"

"You said she was talking crazy. Did she happen to say anything to you about poison?"

His eyes flew open, his cheeks reddened, and he started dabbing at his forehead more vigorously.

"Sylar?" I pressed. "Did she say anything about someone poisoning her?"

He opened his mouth, but before he could say anything, a loud voice filled with irritation came from behind us. "You've wasted my time. You need to leave. Now."

Sylar and I swiveled on our stools. Stef was pointing a woman toward the front door.

I almost fell off my seat. "Carolyn?"

Carolyn Honeycutt looked my way and frowned deeply.

I looked at Stef's angry face and knew I had to find out what their meeting had been about. "What's going on?"

Stef said, "You know her, Darcy?"

"She works with the festival." I held Carolyn's gaze. "And I have a few more questions for you."

"More? How is that possible?" she asked.

"Darcy?" someone called out. "Your order's up."

I glanced at the other end of the bar and saw Joelle, the hostess, with a paper bag in her hand.

"Hold that thought. I'll be right back," I said to Carolyn.

I wanted to ask her what she knew of Kindred Tours. It seemed an important part of the puzzle, and I was grateful to Pepe and Mrs. P for tracking down that particular clue. And I wanted to know why Carolyn had made an appointment to talk with Stef.

Trying to keep an eye on Carolyn, I quickly paid for the order. She was digging in her purse while holding what looked to be a deep conversation with Sylar. A fuming Stef watched them both from behind the bar.

As I signed the credit card receipt, I glanced back at the trio.

Carolyn was gone.

Of course she was.

"Where'd she go?" I called out.

"Just left," Stef said, pointing over my shoulder.

I turned in time to see Carolyn barreling out the front door. I abandoned the lunch sack on the bar top and quickly went after her, nearly knocking over a busboy in the process. The sunshine practically blinded me as I ran outside. Shading my eyes with my hand, I scanned all directions, but didn't see any hint of her, and suspected she'd made a run for the Enchanted Trail, behind the restaurant. She had too much of a head start on me for me to track her easily, and I was forced to give in to the fact that she had slipped away.

For now.

Pivoting, I marched back inside, gathered the to-go bag and the shreds of my patience where this case was concerned, and sat myself down next to Sylar again.

"Who was she?" he asked, eyebrows raised.

"Carolyn Honeycutt," I said at the same time Stef answered, "A phony."

He raised a glass. "To the phony Carolyn, who just very generously paid my tab."

I frowned at him. "Why would she do that?"

"Said she knew what it was like to be on the receiving end of your questions and told me to drink up for fortification."

"Well, isn't she just the sweetest," I said sarcastically.

Sylar waved at someone over my shoulder, and I turned and saw Noelle Quinlan speaking with Joelle at the hostess station.

"Darcy, Stef," he said with a stiff salute and hurried away. He said something to Noelle, she nodded, and they strode out of the restaurant without looking back.

"Is that Carolyn woman involved with Feif?" Stef asked, her arms crossed over her chest. "She made a phony catering appointment just to grill me about him."

How had Carolyn even connected Stef to Feif? "It's complicated," I said. My phone buzzed. It was a text from Nick—he was waiting for me on the village green. "Could I please get a to-go cup for this shake, Stef? I need to get going." I handed her my glass.

She turned for a paper cup, and over her shoulder, she said, "It's *strange* is what it is. The sooner all these psychics get out of the village, the better."

As I said my goodbyes and headed for the green to meet up with Nick, I realized two things. One, I never had gotten that answer from Sylar about Dorothy regarding the mention of poison.

And, two, I was in full agreement with Stef.

In fact, I wished the psychics had never come in the first place.

Chapter Twenty

"Sorry I'm late," I said as I hurried up to the picnic table. I gave Nick a kiss and handed him the bag. "If you don't have anything pressing after lunch, you might want to track down Sylar to ask a few questions."

"Like?"

"Like, did he poison Dorothy?"

Nick's eyes flew open wide, and the dappled sunlight brightened his dark-brown irises. "Poison?"

I quickly filled him in as he unpacked the bag from the Stove, placing all the goods onto the scarred wooden table.

He frowned at the contents he'd laid out. "Are fries and a shake really the only things you're going to have for lunch?"

"You know my stomach's been a mess," I said. "They're the only things that sounded good." I didn't mention how the combo of garlic fries and chocolate torte had also sounded amazing for a brief moment, because I'd come to my senses where that pairing was concerned.

The sea breeze picked up as he pulled me into a hug, held me close. He didn't say anything. He didn't have to.

I wrapped my arms around him and rested my head on his chest. "Longest week ever."

"It's only Monday," he said, and I could feel his lips curve against my temple as he smiled.

"Exactly. But after tomorrow . . ."

He gave me a kiss. "After tomorrow . . . ," he echoed with a nod.

We sat down, and I said, "In addition to Sylar, Carolyn Honeycutt was also at the Stove. She wanted to talk to Stef about Feif. I can't quite figure out how she knows about Stef's connection to this case."

"Your guess is as good as mine. If she's looking for Feif as well, she's probably following the same bread crumbs we are."

It was yet another question to ask Carolyn when I saw her next.

The canopy of an oak tree cast the picnic table in shadows, and I was grateful festival scents were blowing downwind. "Any signs of Feif on your end?"

Nick unwrapped a chicken sandwich and said, "No, he's still MIA."

I jabbed a straw against the picnic table, freeing it from its wrapping. I stuck it into the tall paper cup and took a sip of the shake. I winced, the sweetness overwhelming.

"Something wrong?" Nick asked.

"My taste buds are apparently in full revolt. This tasted just fine ten minutes ago, but now it's too sweet."

He pulled it over and took a sip. "It's sweet, but not overly so."

"That's because *your* taste buds aren't in cahoots with your topsy-turvy stomach. I'll trade my shake for a bite of your sandwich."

With a smile, he handed me the whole sandwich and unwrapped his second one. As we ate, I explained the conversations I'd had with Carolyn, Stef, and Vince today.

"I've been thinking about what you said about Dorothy being poisoned," Nick said. "We might not need to test the hair Amanda has. I'll make some calls to have labs drawn on Dorothy. If she'd been systemically poisoned, it's bound to show up in her blood, one way or another."

Talking about poison must have made him lose his appetite, because he didn't finish his sandwich or fries. He dumped the remnants back into the sack and balled it up.

"Can Dorothy refuse testing?" I asked, thinking about her hands-off approach with Dennis Goodwin.

"Unfortunately, yes, but why would she? If she's been poisoned, it only helps her case. Her lawyer will support consent, I'm sure. If not, we get a court order."

He dumped the trash, including the half-full shake, which was apparently too sweet even for him. We crossed the street, headed for home to wash up and check on Higgins before getting back to work.

"Will positive labs get her released sooner?" I asked as we walked up the driveway.

"No," he said. "That's not going to change, one way or another. She'll just start receiving any necessary medical treatments while she's on hold."

That was good news, and while I didn't want to think about her escaping the psych ward, I thought it best to warn Nick.

As he unlocked the mudroom door, he said, "Unfortunately, I don't have the authority to allocate security at the hospital. We'll just have to hope

Dorothy doesn't have the kind of powers she needs to escape."

Hoping, I feared, wasn't going to cut it in this case. *Rage and hatred.*

She'd been kicked off the Coven, reprimanded, her powers suspended. She had everything riding on her agenda to take over the Eldership, which would be considered only if Harper declined the role.

Dorothy had a lot at stake tomorrow night, and my gut instinct told me she wasn't going to miss that ceremony. And if the Elder *was* renewed, I had the feeling Dorothy wasn't going to take that news well, either. In fact, all hell was probably going to break loose.

I took a deep breath before I freaked out. *Precautions*, my mother had said. No one knew what she was up against more than the Elder. I needed to keep faith that any trouble Dorothy might cause would be squelched quickly.

Nick went upstairs, and as I let Higgins out I wished with all my might that my mother would show up just so I could give her another hug, but I didn't see any sign of a mourning dove outside. There was only Higgins, who was licking the patio door. Drool slid down the pane.

My phone buzzed, pulling me away from the door. It was Glinda, ready to start the search for Feif once again. I told her I'd meet her in front of Spellbound in ten minutes. Hopefully we'd come across Carolyn as well.

I let Higgins inside, gave him a cookie, washed up in the downstairs powder room, and then went to the foot of the stairs. "Nick?"

Annie came slinking down the steps, stretching her paws out with each step. I picked her up and scratched under her chin.

A moment later, Nick slowly came down the steps, holding his stomach. I set Annie down. "What's wrong?"

"My stomach . . . I'm a little queasy."

I knew queasy. This wasn't it. His face had lost all color, his hair was damp with sweat, and he was breathing rapidly. I shook my head. "It's probably food poisoning. Honestly, I don't know why we eat at the Stove with their history of food gone wrong."

Even as I said it, my stomach started acting up more than usual. Sympathy nausea, I told myself.

He abruptly bolted for the powder room. I paced the hallway, wincing every time he was sick. When he finally opened the door, I said, "We need to get you to a doctor."

"No," Nick said, leaning against the wall. "I'll be okay."

But his actions defied his words. He spun, ran back into the bathroom, and slammed the door.

I was going to get sick myself if I kept listening, so I opened the front door and stepped outside for fresh air, gulping it in like I'd been oxygen deprived.

"Darcy?" Cherise leaned over the fence, a sun hat shading her face. "Is something wrong?"

I took one look at the kindness in her eyes and burst into tears.

Next thing I knew, she was hugging me, and I was babbling every last secret I had.

"Come, come," she said, leading me back into the house. "Let's have a look at Nick and then we'll deal with the rest."

Nick stumbled out of the bathroom as we walked back inside. Higgins was going round in circles, crying.

"I don't—" Nick took a look at us, then fell to his knees.

"Nick!" I cried, running to catch him before he fell forward onto his face.

Higgins laid down next to Nick and put his head on his foot. He kept whimpering.

Cherise was already rubbing her hands together. "Darcy, Dennis is next door. Go get him. Now."

I wanted to argue that I needed to stay with Nick, but when I saw her grim expression I took off running. Terry must have seen me coming, because he already had the door open as I raced up the steps. "Dennis," I gasped.

Dennis, who stood behind his father, took one look at my face and followed without argument.

It couldn't have taken more than a minute before we were back in my foyer. Cherise had her hands on Nick's chest, just below his collarbone.

Cherise said, "I've called an ambulance."

Dennis dropped down next to her. "Heart attack?"

"Food poisoning," I said, kneeling down and taking hold of Nick's hand. It was cold and clammy. "It came on so fast."

Cherise shook her head. "No, dear. Not food poisoning. Just *poison*. Antifreeze, if my abilities to detect what's in his system are correct, and they always are. What has he ingested lately?"

Oh, god. I'd worked another case once where antifreeze had killed a woman. My heart pounded. "Lunch. A chicken sandwich. Some fries. What he didn't finish is in the trash can right across the street, near the picnic table under the oak tree."

Dennis ran out the front door.

I met Cherise's gaze. "Is Nick going to be okay?"

She said, "I've counteracted most of the toxin. He'll need fluids, though, so it's best he take a trip to the hospital. He'll be fine soon enough."

I exhaled. "You're sure?"

She nodded. "It's good you saw me when you did, or this would have been a vastly different outcome. I'll clean up and meet you at the emergency room."

My eyes blurred with tears as Nick squeezed my hand.

Not a minute later, Dennis came running back up the steps with the empty paper cup that had once held the banana shake. "The poison was in here. I can smell it. Most of the contents leaked into the trash, but there's still enough remaining to test for evidence. And the squad's on the way down the street," Dennis added, right as the ambulance pulled up in front of the house.

The EMS team rushed inside, and I spotted a police car pull up behind the ambulance.

"You'll come with us?" I asked Dennis as the emergency team worked on Nick.

Dennis nodded. "I'll be right behind you."

I watched with tears in my eyes as Nick was loaded into the ambulance, and I was shaking as I got in behind him.

It wasn't until we were out of the village and well on our way to the hospital that reality truly hit me. Someone had poisoned the milk shake.

My milk shake.

Chapter
Twenty-One

"You shouldn't have done this," Harper said. "Not tonight, not after what happened with Nick."

I'd spent nearly all afternoon with Nick in the emergency department as he received treatment—from the doctors at the hospital and from Dennis. It was a miracle that Nick had suffered no permanent damage. After receiving two bags of IV fluids, he'd been released. I'd been checked, too, but had sipped so little of the drink that I hadn't been affected aside from a little extra nausea.

Mimi hadn't left Nick's side from the moment he'd walked in the door at home until we'd arrived here tonight, and even then it had taken some doing to separate the pair. It was understandable. Mimi had already lost one parent—I couldn't imagine her pain if she'd lost Nick, too.

A sudden vision of him laid out on the foyer floor made me break into a cold sweat. I couldn't imagine *my* pain if I'd lost him, either.

There'd been such a small window of time for someone to have tampered with the shake. It had tasted fine when Ula had first given it to me, but then it'd been sickly sweet at the picnic table. I had left it unattended only while I paid for lunch and chased after Carolyn.

Who, though? Who had done it?

I tried to keep my voice light as I said, "It's because of what happened this afternoon, Harper, that it's important to celebrate life. What's a better way to do that than with a birthday party?"

The police had conducted a field test on the contents of the cup. There had, in fact, been antifreeze in the drink, as Cherise had declared. Enough to have been lethal if all of it had been ingested. I knew without a doubt I'd never order the drink again. Just the thought of bananas made me queasy.

Police detectives had questioned everyone who'd been at the Stove, including all the staff, Sylar, and Carolyn Honeycutt. Everyone had denied seeing anything. It was beyond frustrating.

Sylar, however, had admitted during his questioning that last Friday night a drunken Dorothy had accused him of poisoning her. He thought she'd just been lashing out at him. Acting crazy. Talking crazier.

Verbal vomit.

He claimed he'd taken her home, left her on the doorstep, and that was the last time he'd seen her. The police had released him because there hadn't been enough evidence to prove he'd done anything wrong.

Yet.

My mind, however, couldn't stop thinking about Carolyn digging in her purse while I paid my lunch bill. According to Sylar, she'd been paying his bar tab. But what if she'd had a flask of antifreeze in her purse that she'd somehow poured into my drink?

I couldn't imagine that Sylar, Stef, or Ula wouldn't have noticed it happening, though. And, unfortunately, the Stove didn't have indoor security cameras.

"Are you sure *you're* okay?" Harper asked, giving me a nudge with her elbow.

"I will be," I said with a wan smile.

There was no point in thinking of the could-have-beens. Everything was okay. We were all fine.

I looked across Ve's kitchen at Nick, and he smiled. I'd begged him to stay home to rest, but he wasn't having it. He'd insisted on attending Harper's surprise party, and I didn't doubt he'd go to work tomorrow. I'd already made plans to meet up with Glinda bright and early tomorrow morning.

Someone had taken this case to a whole new level by trying to kill me, and it was more imperative than ever to figure out who—before they tried to do it again.

Harper put her arm around me. "While celebrating life is all well and good, I'm sure I mentioned no big to-dos. Remember?"

I pushed cake around my plate and watched Nick and Pepe playing chess at the counter, with Mrs. P and Andreus standing by to give pointers to both. I said, "This is just a wee little to-do. Tiny. Miniscule."

"Don't make me take your thesaurus away."

"It's actually *your* thesaurus. I borrowed it and never gave it back."

She laughed, and it was like music to my ears. I didn't know what tomorrow would bring to her world, but for right now, she was happy.

"Thanks for doing this," she said. "It's a lovely *miniscule* family party."

I heard Starla's laughter echo from the family room, closely followed by Ve's, Evan's, and Mimi's. Missy barked, as though joining in on the joke.

Family. I'd never been so certain that it was love that created a family, plain and simple.

I felt a surge of emotion and blinked back sudden tears. I nodded. "It is lovely."

Harper glanced across the room. "I should probably go rescue Marcus. I think Archie is practicing soliloquies on him. I blame this on the Chadwicks, by the way."

The Chadwick family ran the local Shakespearian society and had asked Archie to be part of their big fan festival this coming August. "I wouldn't be surprised if Terry and Cherise put the Chadwicks up to it."

"I don't blame them if they did. If anyone needs a break from his chattering, it's them." She suddenly flinched. "Is Archie reciting lines from Macbeth? He couldn't have picked a more cheerful play?"

"I'd say he's actually bellowing more than reciting."

Archie's wings were flying out this way and that. Marcus sent a pleading gaze our way, his light-green eyes pained. Tilda sat on the third step of the stairs, looking like she'd had more than enough of Archie's theatrics as well. Her tail swished menacingly as her blue eyes sized him up.

I said, "You best hurry. You know how Archie gets when he's acting the 'Out, damned spot' scene. Marcus might become collateral damage."

"Oh geez." She flew across the kitchen, her belly leading the way. "Archie! Don't you think it's time for some karaoke?"

I groaned, thinking I'd rather listen to his soliloquies than his singing.

Heaven help us.

"Splendid idea!" Archie cried. "Pepe, my good man, fire up the karaoke machine."

Tilda climbed back up the steps, resuming her favorite spot at the top of the stairs.

"One moment, my feathered friend," Pepe said. "I'm about to trounce Nick but good. For the third time. Ha-ha!"

"Now you're just bragging," Mrs. P said, wagging a finger.

Pepe laughed. "*Oui!* I never win—let me revel for a moment."

Nick caught my gaze and winked. I had the feeling he'd thrown at least one of those games. Maybe two. Or all three.

Smiling, I gave up all pretense of eating and set my plate on the counter.

Cherise sidled up beside me. "Not hungry?"

I shook my head.

Her blue eyes shined and she patted my hand. "It'll pass."

I bit my lip. "Thanks for staying with us at the hospital, and for being such a good listener." She'd let me cry on her shoulder all afternoon. Sharing the weight of my burdens had been just the therapy I'd needed.

"I'm glad I was there for you." She winked. "Always remember, Darcy, the fates are in control."

I knew, deep down, that she was speaking of more than Nick's poisoning.

Secrets.

Speaking of secrets . . . "Where'd you say Terry was tonight?"

Both he and Godfrey were suspiciously absent.

"Oh, you know Terry," she said vaguely. I arched an eyebrow, but before I could question her, she quickly added, "Has Dorothy's blood test for antifreeze come back yet?"

As I mentally added Terry Goodwin to my list of Coven members, I said, "There's no rapid blood test for ethylene glycol—the main component of antifreeze—so it had to be sent away. Results take twenty-four hours. Other tests, however, showed that her kidneys are failing, so she's being given dialysis."

We were all working on the assumption that Dorothy had been poisoned. All her symptoms fit with long-term exposure to antifreeze. I considered it a miracle that she'd consented to the blood workup at all. Leyna's reading must have been weighing on her mind.

"That makes sense," Cherise said. "If we find that Dorothy's been systematically poisoned—a little at a time, over a period of months—organ failure was only a matter of time. It would also explain her increasingly bizarre behavior, especially if it was antifreeze used. It can cause severe neurological damage."

"She looked so frail and weak the last time I saw her. I can't imagine that she would have survived it much longer." Which explained the dark energy Leyna had seen. No wonder she had felt compelled to intervene. I said, "What I don't understand is, why not give her one big dose and be done with it? I know if I was intent on killing her, I'd want it to be done as quickly as possible."

Cherise said, "But that would raise questions, would it not? A person in failing health who passes away isn't nearly as suspicious as a perfectly healthy woman dying suddenly. The bigger question to me is, who is doing the poisoning?" She narrowed her gaze. "Sylar has to be at the top of the list, since he was also at the Stove today and had access to your drink. Perhaps he doesn't want to give Dorothy half of his money."

I knew he didn't—Glinda had said so the other day.

"And," Andreus said, joining the conversation, "Sylar did say he wanted to move out of town as soon as possible."

Nick stepped up beside me, his arm resting against mine. His warmth was reassuring, and I leaned into him as I glanced at the counter—the chess game had been cleared away. I'd been so wrapped up in thoughts of Dorothy that I hadn't noticed what was going on around me.

"Yet, how does all this poisoning relate to Leyna's death?" Andreus asked. "There must be a link, if Darcy's questions have someone rattled enough to make an attempt on her life with the same method used on Dorothy."

Nick's arm went around me protectively. "All we know is that there's a link between the poisonings. Darcy's been asking a lot of questions about Dorothy during her investigation into Leyna's death, but the cases might not be connected in any way *except* through Dorothy."

Still, I couldn't help feeling they *were* connected. Despite that notion, I couldn't for the life of me figure out how.

For Leyna's murder, my suspects were Dorothy, Feif, and Carolyn.

For Dorothy's poisoning, my main suspect was Sylar.

Sylar had no tie to Leyna.

Feif and Carolyn had no ties to Dorothy.

Obviously, I was missing something big. I had to look harder, because I was never going to give up on finding the truth. Not after what happened today.

"There's still been no sign of this Feif fellow?" Andreus asked. "People rarely vanish without a trace."

"There's been no sightings anywhere after his visit to the Stove this morning," Nick said. "His credit cards haven't been used, and his bank accounts are untouched. His cell phone locater has been deactivated. We've checked all the bus and train stations. Checked with all the private car companies. If he left the village, he did it on foot."

What I couldn't understand was, if Feif was innocent—and it was looking like he was—why had he run?

Cherise suddenly perked up when the music changed. "Oh! Is that a Neil Diamond song they're singing? You all will have to speculate without me for a few minutes."

Strains of "I Am . . . I Said" floated into the kitchen. It sounded as though Evan and Archie were singing it as a duet. Who'd known Cherise was such a big Neil Diamond fan? I hoped she had just as much adoration for Elvis, for Terry's sake.

"I'm in need of more wine," Ve said as she came rushing into the kitchen, stepping aside to let Cherise pass.

"But seriously," Harper said, hot on Ve's heels. "You have to know at least one of the past Elders. Surely they're not bound by the same secrecy laws. I need names, Aunt Ve." Her voice dropped to a whisper. "The Renewal is tomorrow, lest you forget."

"Lest?" I echoed.

"Don't judge me," Harper said.

"Oh, there's no forgetting," Ve said. "Trust me on that, dear."

"What's that mean?" Harper asked. "Do you know something?"

"I know I need more wine. Lots more wine." Ve mouthed "help me" to Nick, Andreus, and me as she ducked low to pull a bottle from the wine fridge.

I searched my brain for anything to change the topic of conversation, and suddenly remembered that I wanted to ask Andreus about the stone that had flown out of my tote bag. It was the perfect thing to distract Harper. I clapped my hands twice, and the blue rock appeared in my palm. "Andreus, did you give this to me when I wasn't looking?"

Andreus glanced at my hand and picked up the stone. "This didn't come from me."

"What is that? What have you got there?" Harper asked, edging closer.

Behind her back, Ve mouthed "thank you" and scurried back into the family room, her wine glass so full it was almost overflowing. She left the bottle open on the counter—for easy refills, I assumed.

"*Not even the chair!*" Evan warbled in the background.

I winced. I'd known karaoke was a bad idea.

Andreus turned the stone round and round with his fingers. "Where did you get this, Darcy?"

I said, "I don't know. It fell out of my bag this morning. It didn't seem like any old rock."

"It's not," he said, concern in his tone. "I believe this is the Tilsam Stone."

"What's that?" Nick asked.

"It's rare, quite rare. It's a black-magic rune."

"A real rune?" Harper asked, holding out her hand. "Did you know *rune* literally means holding secrets?"

Andreus smiled as he set the stone in her palm. "Its secret is that this stone is a powerful *white* magic talisman. It *protects* from black magic. It's highly valuable, Darcy."

In my head, I could suddenly hear Vince's voice.

There's one talisman in particular that will protect a single person.

The moment I associated the stone with Vince, I knew why the stone had seemed familiar to me. I'd seen it while at his apartment the other day. It had been one of the rocks in the candle holder. He must have slipped it into my bag on my way out the door.

And I'd have bet my last frozen peppermint patty that he hadn't just *heard* of that stone in a little hole-in-the-wall shop in New Orleans, but had bought it there. "I think it was Vince who gave it to me," I said, and explained why.

"A valuable gift," Andreus said.

It was just like Vince not to just tell me he was doing something nice. Darkness and light.

I wished with all my might that he'd find his light soon.

Harper handed the stone back to me. "He must think you need protection from black magic." She took a big step back, away from me.

Nick said, "Why wouldn't Vince just give it to you instead of sneaking it into your bag?"

I was about to say something about Vince's wild-card personality when Andreus spoke up.

"I can answer that," he said. "The power the stone holds is nullified if its secret is exposed to the recipient by its giver. If Vince told you why he was giving you the stone, the stone wouldn't protect you."

Secrets.

I wasn't the only one who was keeping them.

"Is it invalidated now?" Harper asked. "Since we all know what it is?"

"No," Andreus said. "Because it wasn't Vince who revealed its secret. Its powers remain intact. Take great care with it, Darcy. There must be a good reason he gave it to you."

Rage and hatred.

I closed my hand over the stone. "I know he gave it to me, but can I give it to Harper?" In my mind, Harper needed it more than I did. If I could have wrapped her in a bubble for the rest of her days, I would.

She pressed her hands to her chest. "Me? Why?"

"A birthday gift?" I gave her a cheesy smile.

"No thanks. I don't want it," she said. "If Vince wanted me to have it, then he would have slipped it into *my* bag. Since he gave it to you, Darcy, he must think you're in danger. And you are, obviously, since someone tried to poison you today."

Harper probably wanted a bubble for me, too.

"Okay, then, I'll keep it. For now." Not wanting to think too hard about any danger I was in, I tossed the stone into the air, and it disappeared.

"Maybe you should sleep with that thing under your pillow, Darcy," Harper suggested. She glanced behind her. "Hey, where'd Ve go?"

"Let's go find her, shall we?" Andreus asked as he put an arm around her shoulders. "Do you think I can convince her to sing 'Islands in the Stream' with me?"

Harper led the way down the hallway. "Definitely, especially since she's had so much wine. But I still want to ask her about the Elders . . ."

Nick cupped my face with his hands. His warm gaze nearly undid me. "It'll be okay, Darcy."

I fought tears. "I'm protected, but what about everyone else? Harper and Mimi and you. *Everyone.*" My breath hitched.

I didn't know what was going on with the poisonings or with Leyna's death, but I knew Dorothy's stance on the Renewal quite well. Sick or not, she wasn't going down without a fight. A bitter one.

"We need to have faith that we'll figure it out."

I rested my head on his shoulder and tried to relax. It was futile. I was tight with tension from head to toe. I wanted to have faith, but I was struggling.

Behind me, I heard Ve say, "There's not enough wine in the world."

"Come on. One name of a past Elder. One," Harper said, dogging her every move.

Ve grabbed the wine bottle and took a deep breath as she poured. "I don't know. There might have been a Mathildie at one point."

"Ooh, that's good. Last name?" Harper said, practically bouncing with excitement.

"Wait. Did you say *Mathildie?*" I asked.

"Don't you start on me, too," Ve said, grabbing the bottle and striding back to the family room.

Harper grinned at me. "If I can keep her drinking, I might have the names of all previous Elders by midnight." She raced after Ve. "It would really help if I could get a last name, Aunt Ve. Did you know it's my birthday tomorrow?"

"What are you thinking about?" Nick asked. "You have the strangest look on your face."

"Hildie, with an *ie*," I said absently.

No wonder she had known so much about me. She was a *relative*.

I should have known she was—her eyes were a dead giveaway. That blue-gold color was the same shade as Aunt Ve's eyes. And mine.

In weakness, there is strength. Out of darkness, there comes light. From the ashes, there is rebirth. I rubbed away sudden goosebumps.

"Maybe we should think about leaving early," Nick said. "Tomorrow's a big day."

"The biggest."

Maybe Nick was right—and everything would be okay.

Because now that I knew I had a former Elder on my side, I found I had a little faith stashed away after all.

Chapter
Twenty-Two

"**D**oes it feel like we're running in circles?" Glinda asked me as we went inside the Pixie Cottage early the next morning.

We'd already met for a cup of coffee at the Gingerbread Shack—now the only place in the village where I trusted the drinks—and hashed out everything that had happened yesterday afternoon.

"It's starting to," I said.

Harmony Atchison stood at the front desk and grinned as she greeted us. "I had a feeling I'd be seeing the two of you."

"Are you psychic too?" Glinda asked.

She laughed. "Not hardly. Colleen gave me a heads-up that you might be back."

Harmony was one of the first friends I'd made in the village, and as far as I knew, she was a mortal. In her late forties or early fifties, she was a little too young to be an original flower child, but she was making up for lost time. With her long, unruly silver-streaked strawberry blonde hair, flowy tunics, and Birkenstocks, she preferred a nature-based way of life. A lifestyle she tried to incorporate into the Pixie as much as possible.

Harmony came around the desk. "Darcy, I was so upset to hear what happened yesterday. Thank goodness you and Nick are all right."

Her sincerity brought tears to my eyes. "I'm grateful it turned out the way it did. It was terrifying."

She looked between Glinda and me and said, "I can imagine this investigation is taking an emotional toll on both of you. If either of you need goat therapy, you're always welcome here to play with Cookie."

"Thanks, Harmony." Playing with Cookie all day sounded like a wonderful way to pass the time. Unfortunately, there were people to interview, clues to find, a poisoner to track down, and a murderer to locate. Not to mention that conference call I had on my schedule for later this afternoon, and the Renewal tonight. The outcome of that phone call would determine my evening plans.

I might be at the Renewal ceremony.

Or I might be home, waiting for news of what had happened.

I had already called Harper and sung her an off-key rendition of the happy birthday song, so at least the day had started off with happiness and not just an over-abundance of nervous energy.

Glinda said, "If you're ever looking to find a new home for Cookie or Scal, I have a big backyard. I could truly use all the therapy I can get."

Harmony laughed and patted her shoulder. "You're welcome here anytime. Now, am I right to assume you're here about the case?"

"We are," I said. "We really need to speak to Feif. Did he ever return to his room yesterday?"

Through village gossip, we already knew he'd never shown up for work at the festival yesterday.

"Not to my knowledge," Harmony said. "I haven't seen him, and he's had his DO NOT DISTURB sign on the door since his arrival, so I don't know if he's inside or not. Is he missing?"

"Maybe?" I said. "We don't know. He seems to have vanished."

"Perhaps," Glinda suggested, "a welfare check is in order?"

Harmony lifted a thick eyebrow, then smiled as she opened a drawer and grabbed a key. "The welfare of my guests *is* of utmost importance." She put a sign on the desk saying she'd be right back and walked us down the hallway. "The last time any staff saw Feif was yesterday morning, a little after seven. He came in with items from the Witch's Brew but left again within minutes."

That would have been just after Starla and I had seen him while we'd been out running.

After that encounter, he'd gone to the Stove to look for Stef, but where he'd gone from there was a mystery.

The hallway we walked was a familiar one, as it housed Mrs. P's old room. She'd once owned the inn. It was amazing to me how much life could change in just two short years.

We slowed to a stop in front of an arched wooden door with a wrought-iron number eight secured to it. A DO NOT DISTURB sign hung from the doorknob. Harmony gave a quick knock and said, "Management!" She listened, then knocked again. "Mr. Highbridge?"

Silence.

She stuck the key in the door. The lock tumbled with a loud click and the door creaked softly as she pushed it open.

The room was empty.

Harmony said, "I'll keep watch."

"We appreciate your help, Harmony." She was doing us a huge favor letting us take a look around. "Thank you."

"You're more than welcome. If he had anything to do with poor Leyna's death, then I don't want him staying under my roof."

Glinda came out of the bathroom. "Nothing in there but your standard toiletries. Toothbrush, shaver. Feif is very tidy. I'll give him points for that."

I looked under the bed. Nothing.

As I stood up, my gaze swept the room, looking for the smallest details. A halfheartedly made king-size bed with a handcrafted wooden headboard took up most of the space, but there was a small seating area in front of a stone-faced gas fireplace that consisted of a sofa and a coffee table. A small desk sat under the window.

The pastry bag from the Witch's Brew Feif had been holding when Starla and I saw him was in the trash can along with a napkin and a used tea bag with a red label. I didn't see the leather portfolio and paperwork Pepe and Mrs. P had looked through, which was odd. Had Feif come back for it at some point?

A suitcase was propped open on a stand near the bed, and Glinda poked through it. "I should get hazard pay for this."

"If only anyone was paying you," I said.

She laughed as she unzipped compartments and peeked in. "All empty."

We checked under the mattresses and couch cushions and behind the drawers of the nightstand and desk.

I looked in the closet and found several pairs of black pants hanging along with some black shirts and one blazer. Two pairs of shoes were on the floor. A phone charger was plugged into the wall, but there was no sign of a phone. No wallet, either. A laptop sat on the nightstand, but it was password-protected.

Feif's screen saver was a headshot of himself.

Harmony said, "I have to say, it's pretty exciting watching you two. I rarely get to participate in catching a potential murderer. Have you found anything useful?"

Glinda put her hands on her hips. "A whole lot of nothing."

Definitely no contracts. What had happened to them?

Harmony pushed away from the doorframe. "I'm not sure whether to be disappointed or relieved."

Personally, I was disappointed. "We didn't find much, but we know he didn't cut and run. He wouldn't have left the village without his laptop, would he?"

"Stranger things have happened," Glinda said.

Taking one last look around, I turned toward the doorway. "Harmony, could you call us if he shows up?"

"Sure thing," she said.

Glinda flashed her a bright, cheesy smile. "I don't suppose you'd let us into Carolyn's room?"

She said, "I can if you want, but I have the feeling it'd do you no good. It's already been cleaned. Carolyn checked out an hour ago."

"Checked out?" I looked at Glinda. "That doesn't make sense with what she told me yesterday, about how she was staying on until the festival finished its run here." I glanced at Harmony as we went out into the hallway. "Apparently, she tendered her resignation with the festival."

"She said that?" Harmony asked. "Yesterday?"

Her confused expression gave me pause. "Yesterday morning," I confirmed. "She told me she'd quit. Why?"

Harmony said, "I hate to tell you this, but Carolyn lied to you."

I sighed. "Sadly, it wouldn't be the first time. What did she lie about now?"

"Early yesterday, I heard arguing, round about six thirty out on the patio. It was Feif and Carolyn. They went their separate ways before I could ask them to keep their voices down, but not before I very clearly heard Feif tell Carolyn that she was fired."

*   *   *

"What now?" Glinda asked as we stepped outside. "Feif's missing. Carolyn's gone. I can't see any way to prove Dorothy *didn't* kill Leyna."

A gusty breeze shook the branches above our heads as we headed back toward the main village. We were in investigative limbo. We had suspicions but no answers and few facts. We were out of leads to explore.

I said, "Vince's reasoning for believing Dorothy's innocence regarding Leyna's death is persuasive. I'm willing to cross her off as a suspect."

"Crossing her off and clearing her name are two different things."

"For now, it's all we have. It closes a door and allows us to narrow our focus."

"Okay," she said, "then the question becomes, where do we go from here with Leyna's murder? With our two lead suspects unavailable . . ."

"We start at the beginning," I said with determination. "We're obviously missing something. For all intents and purposes, this nightmare began with the fire at Divinitea." From where I stood, I could just see the tarp covering the tea shop's blackened roofline. "Let's talk with Amanda again. She was there the whole day. Maybe she saw something she doesn't know is important."

I quickly called Amanda, who agreed to meet us at the Gingerbread Shack in an hour. While we waited, Glinda and I made another loop through the festival, checking Feif's tent again and finding nothing but disappointed clients. We asked around about Carolyn, but no one knew where she was, either. It had taken all of ten minutes.

We'd just walked past Spellbound when I heard, "Darcy!"

Harper stood just outside the front door of the bookshop, waving us toward her. There was a gleam in her eyes when she said, "Angela told me that you'd been by the Pixie this morning—she'd received a text from Harmony."

"We were there, but we didn't find anything helpful," I said. "There's been no sign of Feif."

Glinda added, "And Carolyn checked out and is probably long gone."

Harper waved us inside and said, "I have a present for both of you."

"But it's *your* birthday," I said, confused.

"I know, but I have a giving nature." She grinned.

"What's going on?" I asked. "You're acting suspiciously."

Harper said, "For goodness' sake, stop dilly-dallying. Carolyn's here in the bookshop, parked in the cookbook section with her carry-on suitcase, eyeball deep in casserole recipes."

My jaw dropped. "You're serious?"

"I don't joke about casseroles." Suddenly, she laughed. "Okay, I do joke about casseroles. But she is in here. Angela recognized her—I had no idea who she was." Harper held open the door. "Hurry up, before she does decide to leave."

Glinda and I rushed through the door. I certainly wasn't going to chance Carolyn slipping away again.

And hopefully this time when we questioned her, we'd learn something that would lead us straight to Leyna's killer.

Chapter
Twenty-Three

"Oh my god, not you two again," Carolyn Honeycutt said from her spot on the floor in the cookbook section. "What now? This isn't about the poisoning thing, is it? Because I already talked to the police. I didn't have anything to do with it."

She was, in fact, eyeball deep in a casserole cookbook. She set it back on the shelf and stood up, dusting herself off.

Glinda said, "If you didn't lie to us so much, we might believe you." She eyed the suitcase. "Are you going somewhere?"

"I may not be psychic," Carolyn said, "but I know when there's bad energy, and this little town is loaded with it. I'm bailing before I get sucked into the deep, dark beyond."

She was going to be sorely disappointed that she was going to have to stay just a little bit longer. I'd texted Nick—he was on his way here. We couldn't let Carolyn leave the village before we figured out if she had anything to do with Leyna's murder . . . or tampering with my shake. She'd told so many falsehoods that a thorough interrogation was in order.

"Did you see anyone go near my shake at the Stove yesterday?" I asked.

"I didn't even know there was a drink unattended. I was talking to the sweaty guy. I paid his tab—have the police talked to him? He seems the shady sort— and didn't seem to like you," she added, glancing at me. "Can't imagine why."

The police *had* talked to Sylar. He'd claimed not to know anything about the shake, either, other than that I'd been sipping it while chatting with him. But I wanted to talk to him myself and see if my witchy instincts could tell if he was lying. At some point today, I knew I'd also find myself back at the Stove to talk with Stef and Ula. Someone had to have seen *something*.

"Besides, who carries around antifreeze? Something like that has to be premeditated, and I didn't know you were going to be at that restaurant. Do you want to check my purse? Feel free." She handed it to Glinda.

Glinda shrugged and went through the leather bag. "Clear," she finally said.

Carolyn smiled smugly. "I told you."

The search was silly at this point, as she could've already dumped the evidence. But she had made a good point—whoever had tampered with my shake had to have had the antifreeze on their person, in a container small enough to avoid detection, as no one had witnessed the drink being spiked. The action *had* to have been premeditated.

"Seems to me," Glinda said as she handed the purse back to Carolyn, "that you'd know the shady sort when you saw it. Are you sure the reason you're leaving town early isn't because Feif fired you yesterday?" Glinda asked, her eyebrow arched.

Carolyn lifted an eyebrow and seemed oddly amused as she said, "Did Feif tell you that? Because you must know by now that you can't trust that man. He lies as easily as he breathes. I *quit*. Do you want to see my letter of resignation?" She gestured toward the suitcase. A brown leather portfolio stuck out of one of the front pockets.

It couldn't be a coincidence that it matched the description Pepe and Mrs. P had given me of Feif's portfolio.

Which meant that Carolyn wasn't only a liar but a thief as well. But why would she want it? Pepe and Mrs. P had said it contained only business contracts regarding Leyna rejoining the festival.

I said, "Harmony at the Pixie told us you were fired. She overheard you and Feif fighting yesterday."

"Eavesdropping, was she? I'll be sure to put that on my review of the place. It doesn't matter what she heard. Feif doesn't have a say concerning my employment," she said, dripping arrogance.

The haughtiness in her tone instantly triggered suspicion. Why was she so confident that Feif had no say in her employment?

Suddenly, Pepe's voice went through my head.

Feif Highbridge was not the sole owner of the festival. There's an unnamed majority owner, which was listed as an LLC.

My jaw dropped. "Oh my gosh. *You* own the festival, don't you? You're Kindred Tours?"

I had wanted to ask her what she knew about the LLC, but I had never dreamed she *was* the LLC.

Her mouth fell open in shock. "How did you know that?"

No wonder Carolyn had stolen that portfolio—if anyone found those contracts in Feif's room, they might be able to trace the LLC back to . . . her.

"*What?*" someone gasped.

I peeked around the birch bookshelf and found Harper on the other side, crouching low.

"Harper, you must know by now that we can't trust this woman." I motioned her around to join us, since I knew she'd only continue to eavesdrop. "She lies as easily as she breathes."

Glinda looked my way, surprise in her eyes. "Carolyn is Kindred Tours? I didn't see that one coming."

"I didn't either," I admitted. "Not until I saw Feif's missing portfolio sticking out of Carolyn's bag."

Carolyn glanced over her shoulder, then back at us, her eyebrows pulled low. "You two are annoying."

Glinda said, "*We're* annoying? That's rich, coming from you."

I said, "We have our moments, I admit. But at least we don't concoct elaborate lies about being a lowly festival employee when we actually own the company."

"Touché," Carolyn said, shrugging. "So what, I own the majority of the festival. Big deal."

I asked, "If Feif tried to fire you, he couldn't have known you were *his* boss. How is that possible?"

She lifted a shoulder in a smug shrug. "All our correspondence was done via email or through my lawyer."

Glinda glanced at me, then back at Carolyn. I could practically see her mind spinning with questions. "We know he had the approval to present Leyna with that new contract," Glinda said. "*Your* approval."

"So?" she asked. "I wanted Leyna back as well. That's never been a secret."

"The motive behind the action, however, is now in question," I said. "You said you wanted her back out of friendship, but you owning the festival just revealed a financial link."

"Ooooh," Harper murmured. "Good point."

Glinda picked up my thread. "The business was failing without Leyna. You needed her back to keep the festival out of the red. But she said no. Were you angry enough to kill her over it?"

"She does seem the type to fly off the handle," Harper pointed out.

"Are you all out of your minds?" Carolyn asked.

"That remains to be seen," Harper mumbled.

I swatted at her. "Don't make me send you back behind the shelves."

"*Hmph*," Harper grunted.

Carolyn said, "Feif wanted Leyna back for the money. I have enough money, thank you. I wanted Leyna back because I missed her. It's that simple. I would have found a way to join her and Feif on tour one way or another—assistant, tour manager, *something*. I was disappointed when Leyna said no to the contract, but I wouldn't have killed her over it. I eventually would have moved here to this village, maybe bought a shop or two."

"That's not creepy at all," Glinda said dryly.

"I know it's a little creepy," Carolyn said. "But I don't care. I didn't care. Leyna was the only friend I had."

It was more than a little creepy, I thought, thinking about how Feif had called her a stalker. I sighed. If Carolyn was a true sociopath, she'd just keep on lying to us.

But even as I thought so, I recalled the first time I'd seen Carolyn, in front of Divinitea after the fire. I could easily picture her reaction when Leyna's body had been brought out. That raw grief. There was no faking that level of emotion.

Which didn't match at all with the sociopath theory. A true sociopath wouldn't have had that kind of response. Sociopaths lacked empathy.

I held Carolyn's gaze. "All we want is the same thing as you, Carolyn. We want to know who killed Leyna. We know it wasn't you."

"We do?" Glinda and Harper said at the same time.

"*I* do," I said, keeping my gaze on Carolyn. "I saw you that day in front of Divinitea when Leyna was carried out. I saw your pain. You might have lied to us about many things, but you didn't kill Leyna."

"Of course I didn't!" she said. "Haven't you been listening to me? I loved her."

"Then help us figure out who killed her. We need all the facts to do that," I said. "You and Feif have lied about so much, we don't know what's true."

"Pretty much everything I've told you is the truth. I just left out a few details, like me owning the majority share of the festival. I grew up in an extremely wealthy family. I had no siblings. Friendships were hard because I never knew if I was being used for my money. I kept to myself, which made me socially awkward. When my family first acquired the festival, I visited one of the fairs undercover to check on it, to see how it was run, see where changes could be made."

"Like *Undercover Boss*?" I asked.

"Exactly like that. No one knew who I was, because the festival was purchased under an LLC. And no one with the festival cared one bit who I was as a customer—to them I was just money in their pockets. Until I met Leyna. I sat with her as she read me, and she truly seemed to care. She saw the loneliness, the distrust, my cynicism. She offered to have coffee with me that day, just to chat."

It was entirely likely Leyna had also known Carolyn was hiding her true identity, but I suspected the need to connect with someone as lonely as she was outweighed the secrets Carolyn was keeping.

"We became friends. It was hard to see her go when the festival left town, so I became a groupie. Leyna eventually got me a job," Carolyn said, using air quotes around *job*.

I was definitely never using air quotes ever again.

"You see, my lies are harmless," she went on. "However, Feif's lies tend to destroy people's lives."

"And we're supposed to believe you now?" Glinda asked. "Why?"

"I don't really care if you believe me or not," Carolyn snapped. "Nothing's going to bring Leyna back at this point."

"Do you truly think Feif would have killed her?" I asked. "He doesn't really seem the violent sort."

Carolyn said, "Even the most docile people might get pushed to their limits if their deepest, darkest secrets were going to be exposed."

"What do you mean by that?" Glinda asked. "Had Leyna threatened to expose a secret of Feif's?"

"Yes," Carolyn said. "I heard them fighting in the office at Divinitea on Saturday. I had arrived for my reading appointment early, so I was waiting for her in the reading room. Their voices carried easily. I eavesdropped. Sue me."

"What did she threaten him with?" I asked.

"She told him that she never wanted to see him again, and that if he ever came back she was going to tell the world he was a phony. She accused him of having no psychic abilities at all. He tried to deny it, but she said she could read him perfectly, and always could. She read him in that moment, too. His panic, his fear. He argued that it would always be his word against hers, and that he wasn't one to back down. Then she had him thrown out."

"Feif *is* a fraud. I knew it!" Harper said excitedly.

A fraud, maybe.

But we still didn't know if he was a killer.

"Did you see him go back to the office?" I asked. "After he snuck back in?"

"As much as I want to say yes, I can't. Someone came down the hallway to use the restroom, and I had to stop eavesdropping and go back into the reading room. Every time I poked my head back out, someone else was in line. Next thing I knew, the alarms were going off."

"But you weren't wet," I said, frowning at the discrepancy.

"I climbed out the window before the sprinklers went off. There was already so much smoke . . ." A tear slid down her face. "I never would have thought Leyna wouldn't make it out. And I can't say for certain that Feif is the person who killed her, but he's the only one with motive. That's why I went to see Stef Millet yesterday at the Sorcerer's Stove. I wanted to make sure she knew Feif's game. He'd been bragging yesterday morning that she could clear his name. I wanted to warn her of his charms, because I could see him manipulating her into going along with any lie he fed her. He's that persuasive."

Motive always led to the killer, and Carolyn was right—Feif had a great motive if he'd silenced Leyna to keep his big secret. I also recalled that Ve had said she'd seen Carolyn lurking in the doorway of the reading room, which gave Carolyn's story credence.

"However, Feif's witness—Stef—wasn't open to hearing what I had to say, and that tells me one thing."

"What's that?" I asked.

Carolyn's eyes narrowed. "Feif already got to her."

But I knew he hadn't, so I didn't know where that left us. Except back at square one.

"You're going to need to talk to the police," I said. "They need all this information on record, especially since you're leaving town soon."

"I will," Carolyn said. "I'll go over there right after I leave here."

I didn't quite believe she would do as she said, so I was glad when I saw Nick pass in front of the shop's window. The front bell jangled as he came inside.

"Perfect timing," Glinda said. "Carolyn, meet your police escort, Nick Sawyer."

Carolyn's mouth dropped open, then she snapped it closed again.

"He's Darcy's fiancé and the chief of police. Hi Nick," Harper said. "Just another quiet day in the village, eh?"

I smiled at how Harper had listed Nick as my fiancé first. The order of importance said a lot about Harper's family values.

He smirked. "Is it ever quiet when Darcy and Glinda are together?"

"Isn't that the truth?" Harper nodded.

I said, "Carolyn called us annoying."

Nick's brown eyes flared with amusement. "Was she wrong?"

"Not the point," Glinda said, cracking a smile.

"Can we go?" Carolyn asked. "I have a driver arriving soon to pick me up."

"By all means." Nick swept an arm in front of him, inviting her to lead the way.

Despite her hurry to leave town, I knew Nick wouldn't let Carolyn go without getting every last detail from her.

If, that is, she was telling the truth. I thought she was, this time around.

But I'd been wrong about her before.

I put my hand on Nick's arm as he started walking away. "Before you go, have you had any luck finding Feif? We haven't been able to."

"No," Nick said, shaking his head.

Carolyn stopped in her tracks. "Feif cut and run? That little weasel. He's probably halfway to Tulsa by now. How much more proof do you need that he's guilty? Only guilty people run."

Glinda pointed at the suitcase. "Aren't *you* cutting and running?"

"Touché, again. But I'm not guilty."

"So you say," Glinda said.

She shot her a dour look.

"Besides," I said, "if Feif skipped town, why did he leave his suitcase and laptop back at the Pixie?"

Harper said, "If I was skipping town, I'd leave some important stuff behind to make it seem like I was coming back soon. It would give me more of a head start."

She said it with such authority that it sounded as though she'd put some serious thought into the subject at some point. Which should have worried me, but my mind was too busy processing everything Carolyn had told us.

We chatted with Nick for a few moments before he and a reluctant Carolyn left for the police station.

The story Carolyn had told about what she'd heard and seen at Divinitea rang true, and it did seem as though Feif was the only one with motive, but . . .

"What's wrong?" Harper asked me. "You have a strange look on your face."

"There you go calling me strange again," I said.

She sighed. "*Darcy.*"

"You don't believe Carolyn's chain of events?" Glinda asked. "Because I don't. I'm not sure we can trust her at all. Talk about a weasel."

"I honestly don't know what to believe at this point," I said. "But I'm suddenly having trouble with the idea of Feif being guilty."

"Really?" Glinda asked. "Why? Because I can easily see him killing Leyna to keep his dirty secret of being a fraud. His livelihood depended on that information never getting out."

"Oh, I can see him killing her if she threatened him," I said. "Everyone has a breaking point. And I can even see him lighting a fire to cover his crime. That's not what I'm having trouble with."

"Then what?" Harper asked.

I looked between the two of them. "How did he know to plant Leyna's hairpin on Dorothy? He doesn't know Dorothy from a hole in the wall. How would he know to frame *her* for the murder?"

Glinda opened her mouth, closed it again.

Harper said, "Village gossip? I'm sure it made the rounds to all the psychics."

"Maybe," I said, not really believing it.

I was certain there was more to this case than we'd discovered, and I was glad we were going to be meeting with Amanda.

With any luck, she'd be able to help us break the case wide open.

Because right now, it felt as though we were not only running in circles, but also running out of time.

Chapter Twenty-Four

After seeing Nick take Carolyn away for questioning, Glinda and I decided to run home to our respective houses to check on our dogs, then meet up again at the Gingerbread Shack to talk to Amanda Goodwin.

At home, I let Higgins out, checked voice mail, ate a frozen peppermint patty, worried about the phone call coming later in the day, and tried not to stress about the Renewal.

It wasn't long at all before I was back outside, my face turned toward the sun. I was due at the bakery in fifteen minutes, which gave me plenty of time to swing by Third Eye to talk to Sylar.

But as I approached the shop, I was dismayed to see it was closed, even though it was business hours. There was a sign on the door that explained that the shop was closed for a few days due to a family emergency.

I wondered if he considered trying to pack up his life, sell his house, and settle his business affairs in the three days Dorothy was locked away an emergency. If so, then yeah, he was in full crisis mode.

I glanced across the square to the neighborhood where he was renting an apartment. Unfortunately, I didn't have time now to drop in on him at home. It was too far for me to get there and back before I was due at the Gingerbread Shack.

I did, however, have time to stop at the Stove.

Walking quickly, I tried not to think too hard about where I was going and why. I just wanted to get in and out as quickly as possible. It wouldn't take but a few minutes to speak with Ula and Stef, to find out what they'd told the police. And also try to see if I could ferret out any further details about what had happened yesterday afternoon.

When someone had tried to poison me.

My stomach hurt as I pushed the thoughts away and pulled open the door of the restaurant.

It took only a matter of seconds, however, to learn that my trip here had proven fruitless as well. It was Stef's day off, and Ula wasn't working until later on.

With that information, I headed back out feeling increasingly frustrated.

I crossed the green, heading for the bakery for the second time today. I pulled open the door, sucked in a lungful of decadent scents, and waved to Evan, who was helping a customer. Neither Glinda nor Amanda had arrived yet, but I was happily surprised to see Starla sitting at one of the high-top tables, poring over photographs.

"What's all this?" I asked as I sat next to her.

Her blonde hair was pulled up in a tight topknot that accented her beautiful bone structure. A set of three bracelets clinked harmoniously on her arm as she pushed photographs into a pile to clear a space on the table. "Glinda asked for my help in copying these old photographs for Vince. I thought I'd take some time to sort them before taking them to my studio."

"She did?" It seemed a little insensitive to me, given Starla's history with him . . . and Glinda. Starla's friendship with her had come a long way—light years—but I didn't think they were close enough quite yet for such a favor.

"Well, I kind of forced her to let me do it. Glinda only asked me for a recommendation on where to get it done, and when I told her I'd be happy to do it, she balked."

Now that made more sense. "Because the albums are for Vince?"

Starla nodded. "She didn't want to put me in an awkward spot, but I'm happy to help. Truly."

"That's because you're the nicest person in the entire world."

Laughing, she said, "I wouldn't say that, but Vince and I are still friends, and I think it's sweet that he wants to learn as much as he can about his sisters when they were younger. It's probably a little hard on him that he missed out on that time with them. He's come a long way."

He had. There was a time, out of anger, he had cut himself off from everyone and everything. These days he was becoming more active in the community and was a prominent and charitable entrepreneur, a loving brother, a great boyfriend to Noelle, and a good friend.

A long way was an understatement.

I picked up a photo of Zoey riding a bike. She looked to be about seven or so and was missing a front tooth as she smiled for the camera. I also noticed the bruises on her arm that looked a lot like finger imprints. It made my heart hurt.

Starla leaned against the stool's backrest and adjusted the spaghetti straps of her sundress. "By the way, I haven't found a single bad picture of Glinda yet."

"I'm not sure she can take a bad picture."

Starla grinned. "I might start trying to photograph her in awkward moments. Chewing. Coughing. *Something*. Just to see if it is possible."

I laughed. "I dare you."

"Oh, it's on." She grimaced as she picked up a picture. "Do you think we were ever this gangly?"

I glanced at the photo of Zoey as a teenager at some sort of school dance. Her reddish hair was pulled back, which made her braces and austere nose stand out even more. She was smiling, though, and it looked like she was truly happy in that moment. "There are many times I'm glad we don't have photographic evidence of our awkward teenage years."

Starla, who was a hybrid Wish-BakeCrafter, had grown up being unable to be seen on film as well. I said, "I cringe when I think about some of my fashion choices."

"You should have seen my hair the time I decided I really needed a perm."

"Oh no."

I laughed. "Oh yes."

"I kind of wish I could see that, actually."

"And I'm kind of glad I can't grant that wish." By Craft law, Wishcrafters couldn't grant the wishes of other Wishcrafters.

Evan came over with a plate of cupcakes and a cup of coffee and set them in front of me. His ginger hair was slicked back in a mini pompadour, and there was a smudge of flour on his chin as he smiled. "I heard you've been running around the village like a madwoman. I thought you could use a little sustenance."

Starla snagged the plate. "Maybe these should be withheld as an incentive to tell us about your wedding dress. Pepe and Mrs. P were in here earlier and wouldn't say a word—for a change. C'mon, one little detail, Darcy."

"One detail? Okay. It's white," I said.

They both groaned.

I smiled. "I want it to be a surprise. Pepe and Godfrey worked so hard on it."

"They're magical," Evan said in a whisper. "How hard could it have been?"

"How hard was it for you to make Harper's birthday cake?" I asked. "Thank you, by the way. It was beautiful."

He made a sour face. "Point taken, and you're welcome."

"For all your running around, did you ever catch up with Feif or Carolyn?" Starla asked. "Pepe and Mrs. P left us on a cliffhanger."

"With Carolyn," I said, explaining the big bombshell that she owned the majority of the festival. "But it looks like Feif skipped town. No one's seen him since yesterday morning around eight."

"I saw him after that," Evan said. "Around eight fifteen, eight thirty."

"You did?" I asked. "Where?"

He stuck his hands in his apron pockets and rocked on his heels. "Here. He came in, lured by the scent of my brownie bites in the oven, and we got to talking. He eventually asked if I knew where Stef Millet lived."

"Don't tell me you told him," I said, thinking that Feif hadn't come in for brownies at all, but for information. Joelle hadn't told him where Stef lived, and the Gingerbread Shack was the closest shop open at that time of the morning.

Evan's cheeks colored. "I might have told him—"

I groaned.

"—*if*," he added loudly, "I hadn't just seen Stef pull into the gym parking lot a half hour before that. So I told him he wouldn't find her at home, and he mumbled something about catching her at the Stove later on."

I wondered if Feif had abandoned the idea of speaking to Stef altogether when he realized it was possible he wouldn't get to her before she was warned against him—and instead cut his losses and skipped town. Maybe he *had* left some belongings behind on purpose, as Harper had suspected.

"Can you use the Lost and Found spell to find him?" Starla asked, referring to a spell that found lost objects—and sometimes people.

"I'm not sure," I said. "That spell can only find people who're truly lost. If Feif is on the run, he doesn't want to be found."

"No man has a right to be that pretty," Evan said on a sigh. "I probably would have given him all my passwords if he'd asked."

That was most likely how Feif made such a good living as a psychic—he had an innate ability to get people to tell him things.

I patted Evan's cheek. "You're far prettier."

He grinned. "I was hoping you would say that. And just because you did, those cupcakes are on the house."

I stared longingly at the coffee but didn't pick it up. I was nervous enough today without adding caffeinated jitters to the mix. "The cupcakes look amazing," I said, "but my appetite is iffy. Can I get a to-go box?"

"Are you feeling okay?" Starla asked. "Don't tell me you're coming down with something a week before your wedding."

"It's just a case of the Dorothys," I said. I wanted to tell them both what was going on with the Renewal, but I couldn't. Elder's orders.

"Understandable," Evan said. "Black magic. What is she thinking?"

I wasn't sure she was thinking. More likely, she was *reacting*. "I don't know, but even though we now know she's sick, when she gets released, we need to keep in mind that she's extremely dangerous."

An influx of customers came into the shop, and Evan excused himself to go take orders.

"Are Dorothy's lab results back yet?" Starla asked.

"Not yet. A few more hours," I said.

We talked a little bit about the poisonings and how there weren't many leads, except for Sylar.

"But why would he want to poison you?" Starla asked.

"All we can think of is that he is the one who's also poisoning Dorothy. Maybe he believed I was close to figuring out his secret? He knows what a snoop I am." After all, I'd once helped clear his name when he'd been falsely accused of murder.

My phone buzzed, and I checked the text message that had come in.

"What's wrong?" Starla asked. "All the color just drained out of your face."

"It's from Glinda." I glanced up, held Starla's gaze. "Dorothy just tried to escape from the psych ward."

* * *

Fortunately, Dorothy's escape attempt had failed.

She'd set a fire in a trash can and tried to sneak out in the chaos. She'd been caught—but I couldn't help but wonder how soon it would be until she tried again. An hour? Two?

After all, the Renewal began a little after sundown. Dorothy was running out of time, too.

I was doing my best to ignore a stomachache as I walked side by side with Amanda Goodwin along the Enchanted Trail, the paved path that looped around the village.

Glinda and Vince were on the way to the hospital, hoping they'd be able to talk to Dorothy, get her to calm down, and to see reason. It was a long shot they'd be able to talk to her, but they felt they had to try.

The news of the escape attempt had pushed me from being nervous to being a nervous wreck. I'd thought about canceling with Amanda but ultimately had decided to keep the meeting. I couldn't sit still, however, and had been grateful when she agreed to take a walk with me.

"I feel like I'm living in an alternate reality," Amanda said. The breeze blew blonde hairs across her face. "It's surreal. Between Leyna's death, Dorothy, and the poisonings—it's like a bad dream."

I could easily picture Nick passed out on the hallway floor.

This was no dream. It was a nightmare.

"We're so appreciative of your help, Darcy," she said, her eyes filling with tears. "I know you didn't know Leyna well."

"I know your family well. I'm losing track of how many times Dennis and Cherise have come to my rescue or Nick's or Harper's . . ."

She took my hand and squeezed it. "Family."

I nodded. "Family."

Wild roses bloomed along the path, surrounding us in their sweet scent as we walked. I said, "I wish I had more leads on Leyna's death. I don't think Dorothy is guilty of killing her, and I can't find a link between her death and the poisonings, so I don't think they're related."

"What about Sylar?" she asked.

"Nick questioned Sylar at length about the poisonings, but he has no connection to Leyna."

She stopped walking and faced me. "But he does, Darcy." She set her hand on my arm. "He was at Divinitea on Saturday."

My jaw dropped. "He was? He wasn't on the list you gave Nick."

Her cheeks infused with redness. "I am *so* sorry. I wasn't thinking of him as a guest, because he didn't stay. He stopped in, trying to get an appointment for a reading with Leyna."

"Did he get one?" I asked.

"She agreed to squeeze him in, but he was with her for maybe five minutes, tops. That's barely enough time to pour the tea, so I'm not sure what he was after."

It didn't make sense that he'd want a reading. Not after the way he'd doused Glinda and me with holy water. I would have thought he'd avoid any kind of metaphysical happenings.

"How did he seem when he was there?" I asked.

She took a deep breath and closed her eyes as though trying to remember every detail. A moment later, she blinked. "He was . . . uncomfortable. Fidgety." Her eyes widened. "When he arrived, he asked me if I really believed Leyna could read people's health. He was troubled when I said she absolutely could. I remember worrying about him being ill. That's when Leyna called him back. Like I said, he couldn't have been with her for more than five minutes. And this was early in the day—she was alive after he left."

I didn't doubt the surety of her characterizations. As a Vitacrafter, she could easily read his demeanor.

Amanda went on, saying, "I've never had issue with Sylar and knew he'd filed for divorce from Dorothy, so I didn't connect him to what happened. Is it possible he had something to do with Leyna's death?"

My mind spun with what she'd told me, trying to find the connections I'd been missing. "We know Leyna read Dorothy on Thursday. We know Dorothy saw Sylar on Friday and that she accused him of poisoning her—and that she knew so because of Leyna. Now imagine if you're Sylar—and he *had* been the one who'd been poisoning her?"

Amanda's hand flew up to cover her mouth.

I said, "If all that is true, I don't think it's out of the question to assume that Sylar went to Divinitea on Saturday trying to find out *exactly* what Leyna knew about the poisoning. Do you know, when she saw him, if she would've been able to tell if he was guilty of the poisoning?"

"Since Leyna could read thoughts and feelings, she'd know if he had murder on his mind. And since she'd read Dorothy so recently, she might have been able to link the two, especially if he'd been thinking about poisons . . ." Tears filled her eyes. "Could he really be responsible? He just seems so . . . tame. He can be a loudmouth, sure, but violent? I don't usually misread people."

Carolyn Honeycutt's voice went through my head.

Even the most docile people might get pushed to their limits if their deepest, darkest secrets were going to be exposed.

"Did you see Sylar leave that day?" I asked.

"No," Amanda said. "I saw Leyna walk him out of the reading room, but I didn't see him leave the shop."

He could have easily hidden somewhere in the building, waiting . . .

I let that thought sink in, and with it came a deep sense of sadness. Sylar had once been a decent man. Flawed but decent. If he had done this, what had happened?

Then I realized Dorothy had happened. She'd declared war on him.

If he was guilty, I was convinced it was because he'd been fighting back.

Unfortunately for Leyna—and all who loved her—it looked like she had been caught in their crossfire.

Chapter
Twenty-Five

"Let me go with you," Nick said as I came down the hallway into the family room, my Craft cloak draped over my arm.

It was a little after eight PM, and pink streaked the sky as the sun sank on the horizon. "Mimi," I said, reminding him why he needed to stay. Right now she was upstairs working on homework, not completely oblivious to the danger in the air, but unaware exactly what was at stake if Dorothy proved successful in another escape attempt.

To everyone's relief, Glinda and Vince had been able to speak to her, but to everyone's dismay, Dorothy had sent them away almost immediately. Glinda had reported back that she'd seen nothing but hatred in her mother's eyes the whole time, even after explaining that Sylar had become the prime suspect in Leyna's death.

Rage and hatred.

There hadn't, however, been another escape attempt since they left the hospital.

I had the feeling Dorothy was biding her time.

Higgins was hogging most of the couch, giving Nick about one square foot of cushion space. Annie was upstairs with Mimi. Missy, too—the little dog seemed extra protective of Mimi this afternoon. It was possible she sensed the danger in the air, too.

I raised my arm, showed him the chill bumps. "Do you feel it? In the air? There's evil blowing around." It had come in earlier on the sea breeze, salty sea air mixed with doom and gloom. I took hold of his hands. "I want you to stay home with Mimi. Protect her."

The pink sky faded to purple. I needed to get to the Elder's meadow.

"I don't want you to go to the meadow alone," he said.

Nick was still in his uniform, having arrived home only fifteen minutes ago. He'd been questioning Sylar most of the afternoon, pressing him for answers. Sylar hadn't had anything to say for himself other than to proclaim his innocence. He'd claimed that he'd spoken to Leyna only briefly on Saturday—that being around her energy had freaked him out enough that he had chickened out of asking her if she really thought Dorothy was being poisoned.

According to *him*, he'd sought Leyna out in concern for Dorothy's well-being. Nothing less, nothing more, and he certainly hadn't harmed the woman.

Nick had been forced to let him go, as he hadn't had enough evidence yet to arrest him.

I sat on the edge of the coffee table and petted Higgins's head. "My mother will be there. Harper, too. The Coven of Seven. I have the magic stone Vince gave me and about eighteen other protection charms. I'll be fine."

I didn't particularly want to go alone, either, but I had to be there. I had the power to put an end to Dorothy's coup attempt, once and for all.

Nick rested his forehead against mine and squeezed my hands.

I said, "I'm not sure how long I'll be. An hour. Two at—" I was cut off by the sound of rapid-fire knocking on the front door.

I looked down the hallway and saw an anxious-looking Vince peering in the sidelight. Higgins started barking, and Nick shushed him. Remarkably, the dog quieted as he galloped down the hallway beside me as I hurried to open the door.

Before I could get a word out, Vince's voice shook as he blurted, "Archie's nowhere to be found, Darcy. You need to show me how to get to the Elder." There was no disguising the naked terror on his face. "I need to talk to her right away."

"What's wrong?" Nick asked, coming up behind me.

"It's Dorothy," he said, breathing hard. "I just got word that she's escaped the psych ward."

"When?" I asked, throwing my cape over my shoulders.

"No one's quite sure. There was another fire. It was chaos. Maybe a half hour, maybe an hour."

Nick's phone rang. He quickly answered, then covered the mouthpiece and said to us, "Sylar and Dorothy's house is on fire. Sylar's injured. Glinda's going with him to the hospital."

Vince said, "We need to go, Darcy. We have to warn the Elder."

I faced Nick, and almost crumpled at the look on his face. The naked terror for all he could lose. All *we* could lose.

"Be very careful," he said, his voice thick. "Please."

With tears in my eyes, I gave him a quick kiss. I took a look up the stairs and fought the overwhelming urge to go tell Mimi how much I loved her.

I didn't have the time.

Because as chill bumps rose all over my body, I knew without a doubt that Dorothy was already at the Elder's meadow.

*   *   *

Vince and I ran through the woods, along a trail I knew by heart. Dusk turned into full darkness. We didn't talk as we ran, but I had the feeling we were thinking the same thought.

We had to stop Dorothy before she hurt someone else.

As we approached a large cake-shaped rock, I held out my hand and slowed to a walk as I heard Harper say, "This is ridiculous. Of course I'll take the oath. I'm ready to take the oath. *Someone* give me the oath already."

"Do not take us for fools," a woman said. "We all know you do not want to be Elder."

Vince sucked in a breath. "That's Dorothy. She's already here."

I'd suspected she would be, so I had braced myself for this moment. But Dorothy's calm, even, controlled voice scared me more than if she'd been screaming.

"What should we do?" Vince asked.

"I think we should lay low for a minute or two before we barge in there. Get a feel for the situation."

"I'm telling you right now," he said, "this situation is going to go to hell real fast. Dorothy isn't here to make nice."

I knew—I just didn't know what to do about it quite yet.

My gaze swept over the meadow, noting immediately that it wasn't bright and sunny as usual. Instead, floating lanterns glowed like fireflies, circling a group of nine people, all dressed in Crafting cloaks, except my mother, who wore a gauzy golden gown, and Dorothy, who was wearing the same white dress I'd seen her in on Saturday. They were all gathered around what looked like a small floating campfire. The cunning fire. The Elder's tree, with its weeping branches, loomed large in the shadows.

I tried to make out the identities of those in the Coven, but they had their hoods pulled low, shading their faces. I noted with interest that there were only six of them. Apparently Dorothy's replacement hadn't been appointed yet.

My mother said, "You should not be here, Dorothy. None of this concerns you any longer."

I easily recognized Godfrey's voice as he said, "Harper has stated she'll take the oath, and that is that."

"Let's sneak as close as we can," I said, duck-walking along the edge of the forest.

"This doesn't concern me?" Dorothy said, her tone flat. "I believe it does. *This* should all be mine."

I winced as a twig cracked under my foot, but no one but me seemed to notice. I took cover behind a tree stump. Vince hid behind an oak tree.

"Don't you mean *Glinda*'s?" Andreus said—I recognized his voice, too. "Be careful, Dorothy; your true motives are showing."

I shivered, thinking about how he must look right now in this lighting—and because it seemed to me like he was provoking Dorothy.

Harper slid off her hood. "I'm not sure what's going on here, but I'm ready to take the oath."

My heart swelled at her insistence. I knew she preferred a position on the Coven to being the Elder, but she must have sensed the importance of this moment and made the decision with her heart instead of her brain.

Dorothy said, "You will not be taking the oath tonight. Or any night."

My mother floated in front of Harper, shielding her. "You do not make the decisions, Dorothy. It is time for you to leave."

I heard Vince utter a curse under his breath.

My pulse was pounding in my ears as I clapped my hands twice, softly. The Tilsam Stone appeared in my palm, and I closed my fist around it.

Dorothy laughed, a sound that chilled me to my soul.

"We can't just stay here," Vince whispered, side-stepping over to me.

"I know," I said, "but we can't rush in there, either. We need a plan."

Dorothy swung her arm out, and with a flick of her finger, the Elder tree went up in flames. "It is not my time to leave. It's yours, Deryn. Your reign is over, effective immediately."

"*Now!*" my mother shouted.

Before I could even reconcile what was happening, the Coven members encircled Harper, and my mother, leaning down, touched the earth with her fingers, then arced her arm over her head.

A clear, glittery dome formed over them all. Inside the bubble, my mother joined hands with the others.

Harper, too. I could see their mouths moving, speaking among each other, but no sound was coming through their protective sheath.

Dorothy fired lightning bolts at the bubble, which bounced off and ignited fires when they hit the ground.

"You cannot protect them forever, Deryn. As soon as your precious tree turns to ash, so will you."

I gasped—my gaze flying to the tree. Flames had traveled up the bark, onto the branches. Leaves shriveled in the heat as smoke billowed.

"With you gone, your precious bubble will pop, and then you'll all be exposed. I can wait you out. I'm a patient woman." She sent another ball of flames toward the Elder tree. Branches cracked, fell.

She sent more bolts at the bubble. The smaller fires were growing quickly, spreading in the field of wildflowers. The strangest thing was, I couldn't smell the smoke. Couldn't feel the heat.

I opened my palm and looked at the stone in my hand. The gold flecks were glowing in the darkness.

"I wish it would rain," Vince said.

I looked at him, saw flames reflected in his glasses. "Wish I may, wish I might . . ." I cast the spell.

Inside the bubble, my mother's head snapped upward, and she looked all around.

A moment later, it began to rain.

Dorothy looked upward, then laughed. "Surely you're joking." She waved a hand, and the raindrops turned into sparks. "Your magic is no match for mine!"

Vince said, "Okay, I wish it would stop raining." He lurched forward into the meadow as I was casting the wish, before I could stop him.

The falling sparks stopped as he hurdled flames. "Mother, stop!" He planted himself between Dorothy and the bubble. "Stop it."

"Well, well, well. Look who's here."

More branches fell from the Elder tree, breaking apart as soon as they hit the ground.

"You want me to stop? Whose side are you on, son?" Dorothy asked him, her eyes glowing. "You need to decide right now."

"There doesn't need to be sides," he said, his voice firm. "Don't you see? We can all work together. It doesn't have to be this way."

"No," she said, using that calm, terrifying tone. "You're either with me or against me."

Hildie's voice floated through my head.

In weakness, there is strength. From the ashes, there is rebirth.

There was no give in Dorothy's voice, no weakness. Only strength.

Hildie had warned me of this moment. Of Dorothy going from weak to strong, of the ashes of the Elder tree being Dorothy's rebirth as the new Elder. A dark Elder.

Dear lord, I didn't know how to stop her. She was too powerful.

"Are you with me?" Dorothy asked, stepping closer to Vince. "Or against me?"

When he didn't answer right away, she lifted a hand and sent a bolt his way. It hit him in the shoulder, knocking him to the ground. He let out a scream as he sat up, clutching a blackened wound.

The bubble, I noticed, was inching forward, creeping up on Vince.

"Are you with me, *son*?" she asked. "Or are you against me?"

He tried to stand up but groaned in pain. "I am not with you. I'll never be with you."

She raised her hand and said, "You disappoint me, Vince."

The bubble movement picked up its pace, but it was still too far away.

Do you have enough faith in yourself and your abilities to keep on leaping?

I hopped out of the shadows and raced toward him just as she fired off another lightning bolt. I leapt in front of Vince. "No!"

The bolt bounced harmlessly off me and dissipated into a cloud of glitter. I grabbed hold of Vince's hand, wishing with all my might that the stone's power would protect us both if we were connected by touch.

Weakly, he said, "Darcy, no."

His hand went limp and he collapsed backward, his eyes rolling upward. I put my free hand to his neck and felt a faint pulse. His shoulder was bleeding profusely. I fought a wave of nausea and dizziness at the sight of the blood and wiggled out of my cape. I balled it up as best I could with one hand and pushed it against his wound.

Out of the corner of my eye, I noticed the bubble coming closer and closer.

"Don't waste your time trying to save him, Darcy. You'll all be gone soon." Dorothy sent a barrage of bolts toward Vince and me. They all burst into glitter.

Fury and confusion contorted Dorothy's face, twisting her features into that of a monster as she threw bolt after bolt at us. She glanced at her hands as though wondering what was going wrong, and then her eyes flared wide when she suddenly noticed the bubble's approach. She threw her hands downward, palms open, and the earth began to rumble and split.

The ground cracked, opening behind me. I scrabbled forward, tugging on Vince, but I realized the crack was going away from us, around the bubble. I glanced downward at the flickering flames at the bottom of a deep chasm.

The bubble was now isolated, an island in the middle of a ring of hell.

Dorothy shot her hands toward Vince and me, and the earth all around us peeled back and fell into the abyss. I kept tight hold on Vince's hand, and we didn't budge.

Dorothy tried again to shove us over the edge, failed, and let out a cry of frustration. "You will not win!" she shouted, sending more flames at the Elder tree.

The tree split in half, part of it falling behind her, the other half remaining standing, listing toward us.

Dorothy was growing wilder with each passing moment, losing the control she'd once had. The entire meadow was engulfed in flames, except for the bubble and the area around Vince, me, and Dorothy.

Dorothy approached slowly, that glow in her eyes evil and menacing. She tried to open the earth beneath Vince and me, but it held firm.

I looked up at her and said, "You will *not* win. Evil never wins."

She threw a look at the Elder tree. "But I will win, Darcy. I will. Deryn won't be here much longer to protect all of you."

I glanced back at my mother and gasped. She still held Harper's and Ve's hands, but she was growing transparent. Fading away. It suddenly seemed like the brighter the Elder tree burned, the less I was able to see of her. I didn't understand what was going on—if anything, she should be turning into a mourning dove. Not . . . vanishing altogether.

A loud cracking sound split the air as the rest of the Elder tree fell forward as if in slow motion. Dorothy's mouth dropped open and she dove out of its way, landing next to me on the scraped earth.

The tree landed with a crash, breaking apart. Sparks flew.

"Darcy?" Vince said, blinking.

"You're okay," I said. "You're going to be fine."

Vince and I were untouched by the shower of sparks, but the hem of Dorothy's dress had caught fire. She slapped at the flames, extinguishing them, but as she went to stand up again, the broken earth gave way. Her eyes went wide as she started flailing, trying to catch her balance.

I let go of Vince's shoulder and reached a bloody hand toward her. "Quick! Grab hold!"

Rage burned in her eyes as she ignored my hand and said, "I win." The earth fell away beneath her feet, and she tumbled backward into the fiery chasm.

I screamed and reached for her, but Vince grabbed my hand and pulled me back. I burst into tears. Not for the loss of Dorothy, because she had truly only caused me pain. But for Vince and Glinda and Zoey. Because I had hoped that Dorothy would find her way to the light, that she would atone for her mistakes and realize what gifts she had in her children and treasure them as such. Above all, I had hoped that she would finally fix what she had broken and give them all a sense of peace.

"I'm so sorry," I said to Vince as the fires immediately died out. The earth closed. Wildflowers bloomed again, and lanterns floated. Everything was as it had been before Dorothy lashed out.

Everything except the Elder tree. Where it once stood, only a pile of gray ash remained.

"Me too," Vince said softly.

Cherise nudged me aside. "I'll take over caring for Vince, Darcy. Go to your mother."

I looked over my shoulder, saw my mother as barely a glimmer, half of her body already one with the earth. I stumbled to my feet and ran to her.

"Why is this happening? Mom!" I didn't understand. The worst outcome of tonight was supposed to have been that she turned into her familiar form. Not . . . this. A sob stuck in my throat.

Someone knelt next to me. "It's the tree, Darcy." It was Ve. Tears sparkled in her eyes. "The tree is the keeper of all the Elder's power. Deryn used what was left of her power to create the protection sphere. With no tree, she cannot renew her powers, and there's not enough magic remaining for her to morph into a familiar. Her spirit is being called back to the earth."

Harper was on her knees, sobbing. "Don't go! Please don't go!"

Mom reached her hands out to us. "I'll always be with you, my darlings. Always."

"No! No, no, no!" I yelled, reaching to take hold of her hand, but there was nothing to hold on to. The blue stone dropped from my palm and landed on the ground where my mother disappeared into the dirt.

My tears fell freely as I tried to understand how this had happened. How evil had taken her away.

Harper sat next to me, her small body shaking with silent sobs.

I could feel people standing around us, heard crying, but they let us be. To grieve our mother all over again. I could feel anger rising inside me, felt it starting to beat in tandem with my heart.

Rage and hatred.

I forced myself not to think of all Harper and I—and this whole village—had just lost and tried to focus on all we had gained by having known my mother.

I pictured my mother's smile. Heard her laughter. She'd brought me so much happiness. Had given me so much love. I had been grateful for each and every day I'd had with her. I hadn't taken any of that time for granted.

The budding anger within me died down, but sadness remained, making my chest hurt, my throat burn, and my eyes sting with unshed tears.

My palm ached where the stone had been pressed against it, sandwiched between my hand and Vince's, seeing us through Dorothy's fury. With blurry eyes, I looked at the skin, expecting to see a blister, but instead saw only the smallest red mark, barely even a mark at all, and yet it was warm to the touch.

It reminded me of another time recently when my palm had heated up. Could it be? Hildie had said I'd know when the time was right . . . I sat up, suddenly filled with hope. I clapped my hands twice, and the velvet pouch appeared.

I shook it, and the silvery-green seed Hildie had given me landed in my palm, matching the red mark on my skin perfectly.

Letting out a cry of joy, I tugged on Harper. "Come on! I know how we can get Mom back." I jumped to my feet and started running.

I sprinted to what remained of the Elder tree and dropped to my knees. I made a gulley in the ash, set the seed inside, and smiled as a seedling sprouted immediately. I said, "From the ashes, rebirth."

Harper knelt beside me and took hold of my hand, squeezing it tight. Tears shimmered in her eyes as we watched and waited.

Hildie's speech about ashes and rebirth hadn't been talking about Dorothy at all. She'd been talking about my mother, this tree, the *Craft*.

"Where did you get that seed?" Harper asked.

"Someone magical gave it to me."

"That's not vague at all."

I smiled at her as the seedling turned to a sapling, and we jumped backward as the tree continued to grow. Branches sprouted, silvery-green leaves unfurled. Soon enough, a mourning dove emerged from the treetop. The bird circled once, twice, before swooping low, where it morphed from mourning dove to woman.

Mom smiled wide and held open her arms, and Harper and I ran to her. As we clung to our mother, Harper glanced at me, her eyes shining. It might have been her birthday, but she gave me the best gift in the world when she said, "I believe in magic. I *believe*."

Mom held us for a long time before pulling back. "Girls, tonight has been a nightmare, but we must set aside our emotions for a few moments to tend to Craft business. We don't have much time left until Midsummer. We must act quickly. Harper, my darling, are you sure you want to take the Elder's oath?"

I spoke before she could, saying, "Harper won't be taking the oath after all."

"I won't?" she said. "Why not?"

"You don't want the Eldership. You want to be one of the Coven, and since there's an open position at the moment, I think this is a good time to lobby for the job. Someone else is going to take the Elder's oath instead."

"Who?" Mom asked, her voice high.

I smiled at her. "You are."

And then I told them both why.

Chapter Twenty-Six

It could have been my imagination, but the air smelled fresher, clearer the next day. Pure. The sea breeze whirled around the village green, bringing with it a sense of summertime and fresh starts.

"I don't know how to feel," Glinda said, her gaze on Clarence, her golden retriever, as he sniffed a boxwood hedge. "I'm sad. I'm mad. I'm relieved. I'm upset that I'm relieved. I'm sad. Yes, she was my mother, and I loved her, but I also know she was a deeply troubled person who hurt a lot of people."

It was a little past noon, and the reality of what had happened last night was still setting in. Higgins pulled at his lead, wanting to sniff the same bushes as Clarence. "I don't think there's any right way to feel. Especially now, when the emotions are so raw."

Sometime during the night, Glinda and Vince had received news from the psych ward that the previously missing Dorothy had been found dead in her bed by a night nurse. There had been no signs of foul play, and heart failure was noted as the preliminary cause of death.

It was—and would forever be—the mortal version of events.

The truth of what had happened to Dorothy would be known only within the witch world, shared openly among witches in the name of transparency, which the Coven—at the urging of its brand-new seventh member—had agreed was best.

How Mom and the Coven had unearthed, transformed, and transferred Dorothy's remains, I didn't want to know, but I was glad it had been done. A proper burial and a sense of closure could only be beneficial to all who'd ever cared for her.

And selfishly, I didn't want Dorothy interred beneath the Elder's meadow, tainting it somehow with her hatred. It was time to start healing.

"You know what Liam said after I finally got home from Vince's last night and told him what happened?" Glinda asked, and then said sharply, "Clarence, do not eat the dandelions. No!"

He looked up at her, his big brown eyes not showing the least bit of guilt as he wagged his tail.

"What did Liam say?" I asked, picking up the conversation. She had gone to Vince's after her trip to the hospital with Sylar. He'd been admitted for second-degree burns but would be okay in time.

"He said he couldn't believe that after all you went through with Dorothy, not only last night but always, you'd still try to save her."

I flashed back to the rage in Dorothy's eyes as I had reached out my hand to her. If she could have killed me, she would have. And yet, I still wished she had taken my hand. "What did you say to that?"

"I told him that obviously he didn't know you well enough yet. We need to fix that."

We walked among the Firelight mystics who were dismantling their tents and booths. They'd be gone by the end of the day. "There's time. Oh, I know of this big shindig going on next weekend. You two should totally be there."

She laughed. "I already RSVP'd for the wedding and reception. Liam will unfortunately miss the ceremony due to a conflict with work, but he'll be at the reception."

"I'm sorry he'll miss the wedding, but I'm glad you RSVP'd, because otherwise Harper would be tracking you down soon, pen in hand."

She laughed. "No one wants to be on Harper's bad side."

I threw a look at the bookshop and recalled the look on her face last night as we hugged our mother.

I believe. She'd finally embraced her heritage and the magic in her life. The Craft would only be better for it.

"How are *you* doing?" Glinda asked.

"Physically, I'm fine, thanks to that stone Vince gave me. Mentally, I'm mostly sad. Sad for everyone who cared for her. Sad she couldn't be saved. And extremely grateful the village didn't burn to the ground."

"Dorothy was her own worst enemy," Glinda said on a sigh. "For what it's worth, I'm sorry for everything she put you through."

I faced her. "Look behind you, Glinda."

Her cool blue eyes sparkled in the sunshine as she glanced over her shoulder. "What am I looking at? Did Clarence eat something he wasn't supposed to?"

I laughed. "No. I mean, well maybe. He does eat the strangest things. What do you *see*?"

Clarence wagged his tail like he knew we had been talking about him. I rubbed his head. Higgins was busy eyeing a squirrel, and I tightened his leash so he wouldn't try to go up the tree after it.

Glinda said, "This is all very *Lion King*. Why do I expect Archie to pop out of nowhere to start singing 'Circle of Life'?"

"Don't say that too loudly, or you might give him ideas." I couldn't help smiling. "I guess I've been watching too many Disney movies—it's your shadow I wanted you to see."

"My shadow?" she asked. "Why?

"Because I wanted you to really understand that you walk in *your* light. You don't have to live in Dorothy's shadow. Not ever. But especially not now, because she's gone. You don't need to make her apologies."

"I know. I *know*." Her flip-flops flapped against the pavement as we walked. "It's just that I feel this weight on my chest from all the horrible things she's done. I don't know how to make it go away. It will go away eventually, right?"

I mulled over what she'd said. As much as I could say she didn't have to atone for Dorothy's sins, I recognized it was easier said than done. Glinda would find her way. It was going to take time, however. "It will," I assured her. "And I'll do whatever I can to help you figure out how."

Nodding, she said, "Thanks, Darcy."

I put my arm around her for a quick side hug.

She took a deep breath. "Does it feel like the air is cleaner today? It just seems like I'm breathing a little easier."

"I was thinking the same thing earlier."

Higgins's tail was thrashing the air as if he agreed as well, but I realized he was leading me toward a hot dog vendor packing up his stand. I tugged hard to the left to get the big dog back on track.

Last night my mother had insisted I tell her where I had procured the Elder tree seed, and I'd explained all about the mysterious Hildie, who'd turned out to be my great-great aunt. She'd been the Elder before my grandmother. Mom had also told me why I'd been sworn to secrecy about the seed—because if Mom had known of its existence, she would have been obligated to ask for its return. Only Elders were supposed to be entrusted with the magical seed, and until this point no one had known the power it held. Except Hildie, apparently.

In another few steps, we came upon the area where Feif Highbridge's tent had stood. It had been taken apart and was lying in pieces on the ground, waiting to be packed onto trucks and moved to the next city. Where it would undoubtedly remain on the truck.

Feif hadn't surfaced yet, and his absence bothered me a great deal. If Sylar was guilty, as we suspected, why would Feif run?

"Have you checked on Sylar this morning?" I asked.

"I called this morning, but he was asleep. He's stable for now." She took a deep breath. "Last night, to see him injured on that stretcher, begging me to stay with him. I couldn't say no. I hope you understand."

"I understand compassion," I said. Neither of us knew for certain that he was behind the poisonings, but he was still the prime suspect. Nick was seeking a warrant to check Sylar's house—what was left of it, at least—his business, and his car for anything related to antifreeze, and he'd be questioned further once he was well enough.

Then she said, "I hate thinking Sylar could be a killer. I always liked him. He was a bit pompous sometimes, but I felt like he had a good, well-meaning heart at his core."

"I thought so, too," I said. "I hate that I might have been wrong."

Could be. Might have. Sylar was innocent until proven guilty, but if not him . . . I was out of suspects. At the thought, my mind immediately went back to Feif and his sudden disappearance. It didn't *feel* right. My instincts told me there was more to it than him skipping town. I just couldn't explain why I thought so.

"It's such a rare occurrence when you're wrong, that's why," she said, a hint of humor in her voice.

I said, "Come on. I'm wrong all the time."

"Like when?" she asked. "Name one time in the past week."

"Like when I thought Carolyn might be guilty. Or Feif. Or Dorothy. Or that Andreus gave me that stone. Or—"

She smiled. "Point taken. I won't tell your boss what a lousy guesser you are. Speaking of . . . tell me what happened with the Renewal. All I've heard about is Dorothy. How did it go with Harper?"

I spent some time telling her everything that had happened, including why my mother, my *boss*, was still the Elder when Harper hadn't taken an oath. There were tears from both of us by the time I finished.

We walked in silence for a few moments before Glinda said, "I keep thinking it shouldn't have come to what it did with my mother." She sighed. "Do you think the poison made Dorothy behave more irrationally than she would have otherwise? Made her make the bad decisions and choices? Or did it just accentuate what was always there?"

Dorothy's lab results had come back and were conclusive. She'd been subjected to long-term antifreeze poisoning. "Hard to say."

"Part of me hopes it was the poison. She was always a cruel woman, but she wasn't a monster. Not until all this happened."

Rage and hatred.

Whether it had been the poison that triggered the dark shift in Dorothy or whether she had simply reached her own breaking point, we might never know.

But for Glinda's peace of mind, and for the sake of trying to lighten that heavy weight on her chest, I said, "Poison can definitely cause personality changes."

"I just wish . . ."

I looked over at her and she met my gaze, her eyes glassy with tears.

"Never mind," she said. "There's no point in looking back. It's time to move forward."

"You know, one of the many things that stands out to me from last night was Vince telling Dorothy that we should all be working together. I think the Coven will take that to heart, moving forward. It's time Craft laws change—without eliminating our meaningful traditions. There's a balance there if we all take the time to find it without the backdrop of hurt and anger."

"If the Coven wants to create some sort of committee or council to collect and oversee ideas for amendments and additions to the laws, I'll be happy to lead it."

A fresh start. For a lot of us.

Maybe a job such as that would help erase Dorothy's shadow from darkening Glinda's life. "That's a great idea. I'll pass it along." I let Higgins stop for a moment to sniff a water fountain. When we started off again, I said, "Have you seen Vince today? I stopped by his place earlier, but he wasn't home, and the shop had a CLOSED sign on it."

"After he filled me in on what happened at the meadow, he went to Noelle's house. He spent the night there."

Cherise had healed his shoulder, good as new. It wasn't the outward wounds I was worried about, however.

I recalled Dorothy's parting shot to him.

You disappoint me.

Words like that from a parent left lasting emotional scars. And it was all because he hadn't followed her evil ways.

"Noelle's probably the best medicine for him right now," I said.

"Is there a medicine for when your mother tries to kill you?"

"No, but Noelle loves him, and I think he loves her, and love is what he needs right now."

Love was what he'd always needed. Not from anyone else, but from himself. He'd stood up to Dorothy last night, for what he knew was right even when it came at great risk to himself. I hoped that meant he'd finally buried the last of his self-hatred.

The breeze blew Glinda's hair into her face. "I'm hoping I can talk him into a vacation. Me and Liam, him and Noelle. Somewhere far away from this village, just for a little while. A cruise, possibly. What's that smile?" she asked.

"I'm just trying to imagine Vince lounging on a cruise deck, fruity drink in hand. If you go, I want pictures."

"The better to bribe him with?"

"You know me too well," I said.

We walked the length of the green, the dogs sniffing the whole way. I spotted a construction truck in front of Divinitea. Contractor extraordinaire Hank Leduc, Terry Goodwin's nephew, looked to be studying the building. I was happier to see that Starla stood by his side, chatting away. The two of them had flirted for months before Starla took a step back from the budding relationship. I'd always thought they'd be good together, so I was hopeful she was about to dip her toes back into those particular waters.

"Do you want a cup of coffee at the Gingerbread Shack?" Glinda asked. "I think it'd be a safe haven from the gossip going around the village this morning."

I laughed. "Clearly, you don't know Evan well enough yet."

She smiled. "There's time."

I glanced at the bakery. "I already had my one cup of coffee for the day, but I could always go for a therapeutic cupcake."

"There's always herbal tea . . ."

I made a face. "I'm not really a fan of herbal tea. Only black. Because, well, caffeine."

She said, "I actually don't like tea at all, so you don't have to explain it to me. There's always hot chocolate . . ."

She actually doesn't like tea.

Vince's voice suddenly buzzed around my head. I put my hand on Glinda's arm.

"What is it? Are you okay, Darcy?"

"In Stef's kitchen the other day, there was a Witch's Brew cup on the counter that she emptied into the sink. It had tea leaves in it. I watched her rinse them away."

"Okay," she said, drawing the word out. "Why is that bothering you?"

Higgins licked my hand, probably wondering why we had stopped. I said, "Stef doesn't like tea. Vince told us so himself, remember?"

Our gazes went to the Sorcerer's Stove. "So why did she have a cup of tea?"

My thoughts raced. "What if it wasn't *her* cup of tea?" I asked.

"If not hers, whose? Where are you going with this, Darcy?"

In my head, I saw images of Feif that Monday morning, a tea cup in his hand, the red tag fluttering in the breeze. The tea bag had been in his trash can at the Pixie.

The cup had not been.

He'd been looking for Stef that morning. What if he had lied to Evan about finding Stef at the Stove later that day and had found her elsewhere? "I think it was Feif's cup."

That's what had been bothering me about Feif. He wouldn't have given up on finding Stef until he spoke to her. He knew his charms and had full confidence in himself. Even when Leyna had threatened to expose his phoniness to the world, he'd stood his ground. It was against his character to run.

"Feif?" Glinda's voice resonated with shock. "What? How? *Why?*"

I told her what I'd been thinking. "I don't know the why yet. We need to talk to Stef. If nothing else, she lied to us about seeing Feif that day."

"If nothing else . . . You don't think she had something to do with his disappearance, do you?"

I started for the Stove. "I don't know. My mind is spinning. Don't you see, Glinda? Stef was at Divinitea the day Leyna died. She was down that hallway during the time frame Leyna went missing. I didn't even think of her as a suspect, because, well, she's Stef. And by all accounts she didn't know Leyna at all."

"Stef wasn't even supposed to be at Divinitea that day—Vince talked her into going. Why would she just randomly kill a stranger and light the place on fire? It doesn't make sense."

The dogs kept the rushed pace as we hurried toward the restaurant. "It doesn't make any sense, but yet . . ." I raised my arm to show her the chill bumps. "I'm feeling evil in the air all of a sudden."

"Damn," she said. "Okay, let's talk to her. See if we can trip her up with the tea cup or find inconsistencies with her timeline for Leyna's death. Look, there's Stef right there, coming out of the Stove."

Stef held a cardboard box as she walked quickly toward the closest public parking area near the playhouse. I could see her car parked in one of the spots near the street.

"Stef!" I called out. I picked up my pace, which Higgins thought was an invitation to run. "Whoa!" I yelled. "Higgins! Slow down!"

He didn't listen to a word I said as he raced along the sidewalk. I had to let go of his leash or risk my arm being pulled from its socket.

Clarence strained to go after him, but Glinda managed to keep him in check.

He had much better doggy manners than Higgins.

Higgins galloped ahead, his nose in the air. It was then that I saw Stef had a to-go bag on top of the box. "Higgins!" I took off running. "Stef! Look out!"

I wanted to question her, not knock her unconscious.

She paused at hearing my voice, looked over her shoulder, and let out a scream. She dropped the box and jumped sideways out of the way, just as Higgins leaped. He bit the takeout bag, shaking it side to side until a burger and fries fell out. He happily slurped up the mess he'd made.

"I am so sorry," I said to Stef. "Are you okay?"

She had her hands to her heart. "I thought I was a goner."

Glinda bent to pick up the box while Clarence joined Higgins in the doggy buffet.

Maybe Clarence didn't have better manners after all.

"We were hoping to run into you," I said, "but not like this."

"Why did you want to run into me?" she asked, suspicion bright in her eyes.

"We had a few more questions about what happened to Leyna." Glinda held out the box to Stef, and the flaps on the bottom suddenly gave way. The box's contents crashed at our feet. A small glass bottle shattered when it hit the sidewalk, as did a picture frame. I cringed when I saw it was the picture of her husband that had been in her office since she'd first started working at the Stove.

"Watch the glass. I'll tie the dogs up," Glinda said. She tugged Higgins and Clarence over to the playhouse's fence, loped their leashes around the iron spindles, and gave them a stern, "Stay."

Glinda returned, crouched down, and said, "Stef, this box looks like you packed up your desk. You weren't fired because of what happened to Darcy's milk shake, were you?"

"No," she said quickly. "I quit. All the crime in this village is too much for me. It's time to move on."

I tried to pick the photo out of the glass before it was torn during the cleanup. When I lifted the corner, I realized there was a photo behind it as well. Two, actually.

"I can get those," Stef said, reaching for the pictures.

But if she was trying to hide them, it was too late. I'd seen both. One was of Stef and her husband, quite young, in a hospital room. Stef held a small baby in her arms. The other was of the baby alone. A perfect round face with a head of fluffy blonde hair.

I handed the photos to Stef, a question in my eyes and a motive taking shape in my head.

Motive always led to the killer.

I'd been so close when I'd guessed Sylar's motives. Hating Dorothy, wanting to silence Leyna before she could reveal his truths.

I'd just had the wrong killer.

Stef grabbed the pictures and held them close to her body, the blank side facing out. "I'm sorry," she said, stooping low to place the photos back into the box. "I don't have time to chat. Some other time?"

She quickly threw a journal, pens, and a calendar into the box.

"I think you should make time," I said, pulling my phone from my pocket and texting a 911 to Nick, along with our location.

Because I recognized the baby in that picture. It was a newborn Zoey Wilkins. Glinda's little sister. Her adopted sister.

Stef's biological daughter.

Why hadn't I seen it? She and Zoey had the same nose, the same high forehead and hairline. The same color eyes. It had all been right there before my eyes this whole time.

"Nick's on his way," I said. "I told him to meet us here with police backup."

Stef froze, her gaze going to the ground.

That's when I noticed the liquid pooled under the broken bottle. It had a greenish tint and an oily sheen. It looked a lot like antifreeze to me.

I thought back to the day at the bar when I'd asked Stef to hand me a to-go cup. If she'd had that bottle in her pocket, it would have been easy enough to pour some into the cup when she transferred my shake from one container to the other.

It now made perfect sense why no one had seen anyone messing with the drink—the tampering had been done behind the bar.

I said, "I can't believe you tried to poison me! And don't even try to deny it. I know it was you. All it's going to take is one lab test on that antifreeze from that broken bottle to match what was in my cup that day . . ."

Stef had to have known antifreeze would be easily masked in a drink—it was probably why she'd chosen that particular poison in the first place. It would have been easy to hide in a cocktail, especially. Like the ones Dorothy loved to drink at the Stove, where Stef had access to her every time she drank there.

Stef eyed the liquid on the ground. "I knew you had seen Feif's tea at my house, and I didn't like the loose end. When I saw you eyeing my coffee at the bar, I truly thought you'd put it together, and I knew I had to do something drastic."

Why had I not seen how absolutely crazy she was? I tried not to blame myself too much. She'd masked it so well behind a friendly smile and a sad story of widowhood.

She went on. "Since you told me you'd been questioning Sylar, I thought I'd push the investigation in his direction that afternoon. I really never intended to hurt anyone but Dorothy, but sometimes there's collateral damage."

Loose end? Collateral damage? Dear god.

And now it made sense why she'd had the poison at hand. Undoubtedly, she kept it in her office for Dorothy's frequent visits to the bar.

Stef's gaze darted left, then right. She looked like she was going to make a break for it.

"Don't even think about running," I said. "You won't get far. Not between Glinda and me, and Higgins. And here comes Nick, too." I nodded down the sidewalk—he was sprinting toward us.

Clenching her jaw, Stef said, "It doesn't matter now. I got what I wanted. Dorothy is dead."

Glinda looked at me, confusion clouding her eyes. "What am I missing?"

I reached into the box and pulled out the pictures.

Glinda's eyes widened. "You're Zoey's mom?"

"I gave birth to Zoey. I got pregnant at sixteen, and Adam and I were not prepared at all to raise a baby. We decided the best thing for all of us was to give her up for adoption."

"Hers was a closed adoption," Glinda said. "How do you even know who she is?"

"I saw her once. And you, actually. At the beach, years and years ago. Zoey was around one at the time, and still so recognizable by that hair. I knew who she was the minute I saw her. You two were there with your dad."

"Zoey's dad," Glinda corrected. "My stepdad."

Stef went on, not seeming to care. "You were all having a blast, laughing and playing in the waves. I followed you home, just out of curiosity. From the address, I learned your names. And I left the village that day feeling like I made the right decision. Zoey had seemed happy. She had a family who loved her. Obviously, I hadn't seen Dorothy that day, or I would have known immediately I'd made a huge mistake letting that woman anywhere near my child. I didn't know how bad of a mother she truly was until I came back looking for Zoey a year and a half ago . . ."

Her words came back to me.

The doctors tried just about everything. God, I'd have done anything to save him.

"Were you looking for Zoey to heal your husband, somehow?"

Stef nodded. "Bone marrow. But Zoey couldn't donate from prison, could she? Adam died not long after, and all I could think about was how a sweet, beautiful baby could end up in prison for attempted murder. I snooped around a little and quickly found out how: Dorothy. The evil, narcissistic Dorothy. That's how."

Nick breathed heavily as he approached, his hand on his gun. "Ladies," he said, throwing me a look.

Faint sirens sounded in the distance.

I said, "Stef was just telling us why she poisoned Dorothy."

Stef's voice hardened. "She needed to know how it felt to have her life slip away with no way to stop it until death finally came. I only regret that I wasn't there to see her die, but I know one thing for certain. She didn't suffer nearly enough for what she did to Adam, or for what she had taken from me."

"And Leyna?" I asked.

Her eyes hardened. "What about her?"

"Did you kill her?" I asked.

She lifted her eyebrows. Coldly, she said, "I don't know what you're talking about."

"What happened?" I asked. "Did you bump into her in the hallway of Divinitea?" I looked at Glinda. "If Stef killed her, it's because Leyna read her energy somehow. She had just read Dorothy two days before and warned her she was being poisoned. It makes sense that she would have sensed that Stef was the one responsible and said something."

"I can see it," Glinda said. "And Stef probably freaked out and panicked about her plan to poison Dorothy being uncovered. She knew Dorothy had been having issues with Divinitea, so framing her for the crime was a breeze. We know that she likes to frame people—she just told us she was trying to pin your poisoning on Sylar."

Stef's face had turned to stone, but she didn't deny any of our theory.

"Speaking of pins," I said. "She probably stole the hairpin out of Leyna's hair at that point to plant on Dorothy."

Glinda nodded. "She then started the fire in the closet, which also gave her time to get back to the table before it truly took hold."

"You two think you're so smart," Stef said.

"Are we wrong?" I asked. "I don't hear any denials."

She said, "I'm done talking to you."

Glinda, I noticed, was standing in cop mode, as I called it. One leg planted in front of the other, knees slightly bent, her hands resting lightly on her hips.

"What I can't quite figure out," Glinda said, "is how did you know where to find Dorothy to plant the pin?"

Stef's eyes had gone cold as ice, and I nearly shivered.

I said, "I bet she looked around for Dorothy for a while and couldn't find her. But then she probably remembered the stories about Dorothy's penchant for climbing trees behind Third Eye."

Though Glinda and I were just speculating, I felt the hairs on my neck rise. My witchy instincts were rarely wrong. If we hadn't known Dorothy was unable to slip past the protection spell, she might well have been arrested and convicted. It made me queasy thinking that Stef could very easily have gotten away with this crime.

And I couldn't help but wish to turn back time. Because Stef wouldn't have been in the tearoom that day if not for a favor to Vince. If she hadn't been there, she wouldn't have crossed paths with Leyna, and Leyna might still be alive today.

If.

But Leyna hadn't been the only one to fall across Stef's murderous path. "And Feif?" I asked her. "I have the feeling you know where we can find him."

Psychics give me the willies—I don't want anyone reading my mind.

She gave an exaggerated shrug. "I don't know what you're talking about."

"We know he was at your house. You said it yourself—I saw his tea cup there."

"Slip of the tongue," she said stiffly.

Nick said to me. "I'll get a warrant. We'll find him. For now, I can take her in on the poisonings."

I closed my eyes against the knowledge that Feif had probably been in Stef's house when I'd been there on Monday.

Stef had acted so cool, so calm when talking to me, while he'd likely lain dead somewhere nearby.

Her words were echoing in my head. *She didn't suffer nearly enough for what she did to Adam, or for what she had taken from me.*

It struck me suddenly that Stef hadn't cared about how Zoey had been raised or the physical and mental abuse she'd endured at Dorothy's hands. Stef had only cared that Zoey hadn't been available to save Adam's life. Zoey had been nothing to her but a means to an end.

And as Nick read Stef her rights, I wondered if she had any idea that she was more like Dorothy than she could ever possibly imagine.

Chapter Twenty-Seven

Evan wore a simple black tux, tailored to an inch of its life, as he stood under a pink rose-covered arbor on a beautiful June afternoon. His blue eyes glistened as he said, "And do you, Nick, take Darcy to be your lawfully wedded wife? To have and to hold, to provide copious amounts of peppermint patties, coffee, and devil's food cupcakes, to love and to cherish, in sickness and in health, for as long as you both shall live?"

"I do."

Nick's warm gaze held mine, promising without words so much more than what had been spoken aloud. I couldn't have wiped the smile off my face if I tried.

Evan grinned. "It is my utmost honor to now declare you husband and wife. Nick, you may kiss your bride."

Archie let out a catcall, and everyone in attendance hooted as Nick lifted my veil and kissed me.

I wrapped my arms around him as he dipped me low. When we finally broke apart, I reached for Mimi's hand. Her eyes were bright with tears as she joined us in a group hug. I didn't think I could be any happier at this moment, surrounded by those who loved us most.

Mimi, Mom, Harper. Ve, Starla. Cherise, Terry, Archie, Evan. Godfrey, Pepe, and Mrs. P. Glinda, Vince, Marcus, Andreus.

Family.

Champagne flowed as Nick and I hugged and laughed and cried, sharing our joy. Our reception would start in an hour, but until then, we were going to enjoy every moment with the people who meant the most to us in this world.

"You look beautiful," Vince said, giving me a peck on the cheek. "Nick's a lucky guy."

"I'm a lucky girl," I said, watching Nick being sandwiched by Ve and my mother's bear hug.

My mother glowed with happiness, floating around in a gauzy cream-colored satin sheath. I was beyond grateful she was here this afternoon, sharing this day with us.

"I'm glad you could make it," I said to him.

"I wouldn't have missed it." He glanced around. "I heard this was where all the cool kids were hanging out today."

"I don't know about that." I laughed, smiling as Higgins and Missy ran around the yard, the lace bows on their collars bouncing with each step. "We're just one big family here. After all, it's love that creates a family, not blood," I said, echoing the thought I'd had at Harper's birthday party. I held his gaze, making sure he understood what I was telling him.

He rocked on his heels. "Family, you say?"

My heart nearly broke at his hopeful smile. Finally, after all this time, he had found a loving, giving family. If not for what had happened to Dorothy, I wasn't sure this day would've come.

Or maybe, just maybe, he'd found his way to us on his own.

I blinked back tears and couldn't help wishing that Zoey had been able to escape the damage done by her mother.

Both mothers.

I let myself think of Stef for only a moment, locked away, just like her daughter. Feif's body had been found in the trunk of Stef's car, and with the discovery, she'd finally confessed to his—and Leyna's—murders.

It turned out that Feif had approached Stef when she'd come out of the gym that fateful Monday morning, saying he wanted to talk about what had happened at Divinitea. She'd panicked, thinking he knew what she'd done to Leyna, that he'd read her mind, too. She'd invited him home, where they could talk privately . . . and she'd made him a fresh cup of coffee, because his tea had gone cold. The coffee had been laced with antifreeze.

"Darcy?" Vince put his hand on my arm. "You okay?"

Stef was locked away—and would be for life. She couldn't hurt anyone anymore. Dorothy, either. "Yeah, I am."

Archie started singing "Cell Block Tango" from *Chicago*. That crazy bird was lucky I loved him.

"Did I mention we're one very loud, happy, albeit a tad strange family?" I asked.

He glanced at Archie. "The strange part is easy to spot."

I laughed and gave Vince a hug. In his ear, I whispered, "Just so you know, I'm throwing the bouquet to Noelle tonight at the reception."

"Joke's on you," he said. "Ve's already told everyone not to stand in her way of that bouquet."

I laughed. "No way."

"Way," he said, his eyes glinting with humor.

"Hey, Darcy?" Glinda asked, walking toward me with a concerned look on her face.

I asked, "Is something wrong?"

"You tell me. Is there a reason Starla is stalking me with her camera?"

I looked over Glinda's shoulder and saw Starla giving me a big thumbs-up. I couldn't help smiling. Apparently, Glinda *could* take a bad photo.

"What?" Glinda asked. "What's going on?"

"Excuse me," Nick said, stepping up beside me. "I need to borrow my lovely wife for a moment."

"What's this about?" I asked as Nick tugged my arm.

"You'll see," he said.

"Intrigue," I said to Vince and Glinda.

Behind me, I heard Glinda saying, "Starla, come back here."

"Seriously, though," I said to Nick. "Where are we going?"

He didn't say another word as he led me to his woodshop in the garage. He opened the door and flipped on a light. A sheet-draped object with a bow on its top sat in the middle of the cement floor.

"I made you a wedding gift. It's more for us, really. Well, not for us, exactly . . ." He laughed. "You'll see."

"I thought you were working on cornhole boards?"

"I lied."

"Nick Sawyer, lying is not the way to start a marriage."

He laughed. "What was one more secret? You ready?"

"Since the minute I walked through the door."

Smiling, he pulled the sheet free, revealing a beautiful maple cradle.

"Oh!" My hand shook as I reached out to touch the satiny wood, ran a finger over the Elder tree carved into its headboard. "It's the most beautiful thing I've ever seen."

Nick put his hand on the small of my back. "It's not as beautiful as you are. Or Mimi is. Or our daughter is going to be."

I tried to imagine what our little girl was going to look like. Would she have my golden-blue eyes? Or Nick's brown? I'd loved her from the moment I'd learned she existed, as shocking as that discovery had been. Nick and I had wanted children, but had long decided we'd wait until after the wedding to start trying. The fates had other plans.

I was pregnant.

I'd never been happier or more terrified in my whole life.

Because as soon as we'd found out, we'd also known that we couldn't let anyone in on the secret. Not with the Renewal coming up and the danger involved with Dorothy's quest to take over the Craft. If she had discovered I was pregnant, I hadn't known what she would do to ensure that I wouldn't have a little girl. I'd been determined that Dorothy would not harm my baby. No way, no how. And if that meant not talking about the pregnancy—not even allowing myself to *think* about the baby—until it was safe to do so, then that was a small price to pay. There were going to be no hints, no clues from Nick or me.

But we also couldn't ignore the timing of the pregnancy and how the existence of my child, if the baby was a little girl, would change the course of Craft history. With how early along I was, an ultrasound wouldn't have been able to determine the sex of the baby. So I'd found a doctor in Boston and had a genetic test done at ten weeks along. It was during that fateful

Tuesday afternoon phone call a week and a half ago that I'd received the results of that blood work.

Nick and I were having a perfectly healthy baby girl.

"I'm so happy we don't have to keep the news a secret anymore." I set my hand on my stomach. I was twelve weeks along now, and not yet showing. I couldn't wait for the day I was able to hold the baby in my arms.

Or drink as much coffee as I wanted.

I set the cradle to rocking, and something sparkled from a corner of the mattress. "What's that?"

"What's what?" Nick asked.

I reached into the cradle and lifted the glass object, holding it aloft in the palm of my hand. "A crystal cat," I said, smiling as I picked up the scent of roses in the air.

"I don't know where that came from," he said, eyeing it suspiciously.

"It's a baby gift from someone pretty special."

"Who?"

"An old relative of mine." I kept hold of the crystal cat and took his hand. "What do you think about naming the baby Hildie, with an *ie*?"

He wrinkled his nose.

I laughed. "I suppose we have some time to decide."

"A little time," he said. "But for now, I think it's high time we celebrated."

He twirled me, and the bottom of my dress swung out. I said, "I think I know a big party we could crash. Are you ready to dance all night long?"

Twirling me back toward him, he kissed me. "Maybe not *all* night, Mrs. Sawyer . . ."

* * *

Two hours later, music pulsated along the street from the goings-on over on the green. Melina "Missy" Sawyer stood at the gate, trying to see as much as she could from her vantage point. It was the first time in a long time that she'd thought about escaping the yard. She wanted to be closer to the action.

Mrs. P sat on the fence's lower crossbar, her tail wrapped around a spindle. She sniffed loudly. "It's all just so wonderful."

"*Oui*," Pepe said from his spot next to her. "A truly lovely day."

"It almost makes me believe in love again," Archie said with a dramatic sigh from his perch on the upper crossbar.

The cat sitting next to Missy abruptly turned and started back toward the house.

"Where are you going? They haven't yet cut the cake," Archie said. "You're going to miss everything."

The cat kept walking.

"Tilda," he said.

Missy rolled her eyes. Tilda's favorite pastime was to annoy Archie.

"Tilda," he said again. "*Mathildie*, I'm speaking to you."

The cat stopped walking and looked back at the group of them. "I don't need to watch. I know how it all ends."

"And how's that, Miss Smarty-pants?" Archie asked.

Her whiskers twitched. "Have you had your beak so buried in Shakespeare that you've forgotten to read fairy tales? Happily ever after is how this ends, of course." She flicked her tail and went up the steps.

Archie blew a raspberry at her back.

"I heard that," she said, walking inside.

Pepe folded his small hands on his rounded belly. "Do any of you feel something stirring in the air? Another adventure for our crime-solvers, perhaps?"

It seemed to Missy there was no lack of crime in this little village, so something was bound to happen sooner or later. If she weren't immortal, she'd have thought twice about living around here.

Mrs. P wiped her eyes with a tiny handkerchief. "I do so love their adventures."

"That's not adventure stirring the air. It's Higgins's tail," Archie said with disgust.

Higgins put his massive paws on the top of the fence and licked Archie's face.

"Not the saliva! Oh! Stop. For the love of mankind! I just cleaned my feathers. Who invited this furry beast, anyway? I thought this was a private, familiar-only party. Does no one have a handy wipe?"

Missy walked down the fence line, keeping her eyes on the dance floor across the street, watching Nick and Mimi swirl around and around. Her eyes misted over, and her heart was full as Nick handed Mimi off to . . . Darcy—and they started laughing as the music changed over to an upbeat piece that had Godfrey moonwalking past them.

This was all she had ever wanted for Mimi. To have a happy, loving family.

To be happy. To be loved.

It was all she had ever wanted for Nick as well.

Darcy had made that happen.

With her help of course, though it hadn't always been easy.

But mostly . . . it had been Darcy.

Missy's stubby tail wagged as she watched them dancing and laughing. This happily-ever-after had been a long time coming.

It had been worth the wait.

Acknowledgments

My heartfelt thanks to my agent, Jessica Faust, and everyone at BookEnds who has championed this series from its very beginning and continue to do so.

Thank you to editor Jenny Chen for her steady and sure guidance, and to the whole team at Crooked Lane who help bring Darcy's adventures to bookshelves and e-readers everywhere.

A big thank you to keen-eyed beta reader Jan Lancaster for giving this book a good once-over, and to Jeff Marks for his assistance with a pesky wedding detail.

And finally, thank you to all the readers who adore Darcy and the Enchanted Village as much as I do.